Elena's murmur of arousal was his undoing

"Holding you, kissing you like this is driving me crazy," Stephen groaned. "Very soon I won't be able to stop."

"I'm—I'm not asking you to stop." The words were bold, yet her voice quavered. His touch had reduced her to jelly.

Oh, how he wanted to strip that filmy nightgown off her and bury himself in her softness. But his legs refused to cooperate. What if she were on top...? His fists clenched at the thought of her moving above him, her body fluid with passion....

No. The first time had to be perfect—for him and for her.

"Elena, I can't get up and walk out of here. You have to be the one to leave...please."

Her eyes filled with tears. "Don't ask me that, *querida*. Not now. Not this night of all nights...."

ABOUT THE AUTHOR

Though romance is Ruth Glick's first love, she has been widely published in the juvenile, young adult and nonfiction markets. A former teacher, Ruth has written or cowritten more than forty books under various pseudonyms including Amanda Lee, Rebecca York and Samantha Chase. This talented and prolific author lives in Maryland with her husband.

The Closer We Get

RUTH GLICK

Harlequin Books

TORONTO • NEW YORK • LONDON
AMSTERDAM • PARIS • SYDNEY • HAMBURG
STOCKHOLM • ATHENS • TOKYO • MILAN

Published December 1989

First printing October 1989

ISBN 0-373-70382-1

**To Norman
with love**

CHAPTER ONE

NO OTHER MAN had ever dared look at her with such frank sexual interest. But she had known from the beginning that Stephen Gallagher was different.

Would he be waiting for her plane? Elena wondered, glancing at the narrow silver watch on her slender wrist. It was one in the afternoon; she had been traveling since early the day before.

Wearily she brushed a lock of raven hair away from her forehead, then leaned back once more in her seat and closed her dark eyes. Her blue suit was wrinkled. She longed to wriggle out of her panty hose. But her anticipation was not dulled.

It had been almost five years since she'd seen Stephen. Yet his face surfaced in her mind like a reflection in a pool of rippleless, crystal water. An artist of remarkable ability, she had painted those features from memory more than once, striving to get just the right hint of reddish highlights in the dark hair, the maddening twinkle in his clear blue eyes, the look of authority that firmed his not quite full lips. She had never met anyone more alive, more in command of life.

Capturing the uniqueness of the man had demanded all her artistic talent. But she had enjoyed the challenge. Words to express her feelings sometimes failed her, but the sure strokes of her brush never did.

Tucked among her luggage was a wedding present that she hoped would tell Stephen just how she felt about him. It was a small portrait of him, astride her father's most prized black stallion. The horse was galloping, the rider leaning forward, one square hand on the animal's neck, the other firmly on the reins. She had sketched the likeness many times before finally executing it in oil. The bold application of color was her special talent. Vermilion, cerise, midnight blue—she knew how to use them to bring almost any subject to vibrant life.

Elena found herself smiling slightly as she thought about seeing Stephen again. She had painted him as he'd looked at twenty-seven, already a formidable force in the world of international mining and manufacturing. In the five years since they'd parted, he had consolidated his position. His power and prestige were two of the reasons her father had finally accepted the *norteamericano*'s request for the hand of his daughter in marriage. The other reasons were more complicated. The warmth she'd felt disappeared as she thought about them, and a little frisson of fear shot through her body. She was doing the right thing, she assured herself yet again.

For a moment her slender fingers gripped the padded armrest of her seat. There had been so many new experiences over the past thirty hours. Not that she was a stranger to travel. She knew all about delayed flights and jet lag and airplane food. Over the years she'd visited the great cities of Europe and their famous art collections—the Louvre in Paris, the Prado in Madrid, the Tate Gallery in London, the splendors of Rome and Florence. But she had never been alone. Always before her father had smoothed the way.

But there had been one country to which he had refused to take her. When she had asked to visit the United States, his eyes had hardened and his mouth had flattened into a grim line. She had learned long ago that it was dangerous to persist in the face of that look. So she had given up the dream of seeing her mother's country—until now.

Thank God, her mother had insisted that she learn English. At least she spoke the language, although not as idiomatically as she would have liked. Though she had been born and raised on a ranch in Venezuela, Elena Castile held dual citizenship. That was one of her mother's few legacies.

But she was not without her own resources. She was not fragile. From earliest childhood she had begun to develop an inner strength. And as she had matured, her artist's vision had endowed her with a perception far beyond her years.

A bell chimed. "The captain has activated the seat belt sign in preparation for our landing at Los Angeles International Airport," a flight attendant announced.

Elena was getting off here, rather than continuing to Santa Barbara, because of the long wait for a connecting flight. Now she peered out the window, anxious for a glimpse of land. At first there was only a cottony blanket of clouds. As the plane descended, she spied a blue-green expanse of water that suddenly gave way to miles of roadways and large buildings. There was no sense of open countryside. Yet it couldn't all be like this.

As Elena exited the plane into a busy lounge area, she looked around, expecting to see her fiancé. Instead she saw a short, stocky man with wrinkled, sun-browned features approaching her. He glanced down at a photograph in his hand. Then his gaze returned to her, obviously taking in her dark, wide-set eyes, oval face, smooth skin with pale pink undertones, and dark hair that fell gracefully around her shoulders.

"Señorita Castile?" he inquired.

"Yes."

"My name's Hal Burnside. I'm Steve's ranch manager."
He looked at her more closely. "I expected something different."

She straightened her shoulders and raised her chin
slightly. "That picture was taken when I was nineteen. I've
changed a lot since then." It was no lie. Her father's problems over the past few years had accelerated the transition
from girl to woman. Sometimes she felt a thousand years
older than when Stephen had snapped that picture on the
veranda of the hacienda.

"Didn't mean to ruffle your feathers."

"I beg your pardon?"

He grinned. "An American expression. You know, ruffled feathers—like a hen that's tried to steal another one's
piece of corn and gotten a good sharp peck for her trouble."

Despite herself Elena smiled. Ruffled feathers. She could
picture it exactly and filed the idiom away for future use.

"Is *Esteban*—Stephen—waiting in the car for me?" she
asked, struggling to keep the excitement out of her voice.

"No, ma'am. He hasn't left the ranch much since—" The
man broke off in midsentence, an odd catch in his voice. In
response to the look of disappointment that flickered across
Elena's delicate features, he continued quickly, "We'd best
get started. It's over a two-and-a-half-hour drive."

Elena nodded, remembering that though Stephen Gallagher chose to live on a ranch just north of Santa Barbara,
he was a busy man, running a multimillion-dollar business
empire. He couldn't be expected to drop everything on a
Wednesday morning and make a five-hour round trip to Los
Angeles. Hal took her down to the luggage area and secured the services of a porter. Then he left for the parking
lot.

When the luxury car, a large black sedan, arrived, Elena sank into the plush upholstery of the back seat. She was glad of the air-conditioned coolness. Now that she was no longer in public, she couldn't resist the temptation to kick off her shoes and swing up her legs onto the broad seat.

"There's a bar in back with soft drinks and orange juice, if you want anything," Hal informed her as he pulled out into the flow of traffic.

"*¡Gracias, no!*"

Hal laughed. "Yeah. I forgot about that attentive first-class airlines service. You've probably been offered fifty soft drinks and cartons of juice since you left Caracas." She saw him studying her in the rearview mirror. "You look done in. Did you get any sleep last night?"

She wasn't used to the easy familiarity. Only Anna among her father's servants would have dared ask such a personal question. The thought of her old duenna made her chest tighten painfully. Anna had been with her ever since she could remember. She'd spent more time with the woman than with either her mother or her father. It had been a close relationship—marred only by Anna's strict adherence to the old ways and an answering show of teenage rebellion from Elena. But the old woman had held firmly to her allegiance to a social system that had been functioning almost undisturbed for hundreds of years. Elena realized with a sudden start that this ride with Hal was one of the few times she had been alone with a man other than her father. That Esteban's employee took the situation completely for granted told her a lot about the new environment into which she had just plunged.

"Why don't you stretch out and take a nap?" he asked now.

"Thank you. Maybe I will." She didn't want to explain that she was too tense to sleep. But the pretense could forestall further conversation.

Closing her eyes, Elena leaned into the thick upholstery and let her mind drift back over her first meeting with Stephen Gallagher at her father's hacienda. She had been coming down the stairs after an art lesson with Señor Santiago. Her father had been standing in the hall talking to the *norteamericano* who wanted to discuss an iron ore leasing arrangement.

She would always remember the way Stephen had looked up at her with frank male interest and undisguised admiration in his blue eyes. Her reaction had been a completely unfamiliar shiver of awareness.

Her father had seen the look, too; he hadn't liked it. But deference to an important and powerful guest had won out over Latin protectiveness, and he had introduced the visitor to his daughter.

She could still remember his look of delight when she had answered his *"Buenas tardes, señorita,"* in perfect English. That, of course, had led to an explanation of how Señor Castile had married the daughter of an American diplomat, and how Elena's mother had insisted that her daughter be bilingual. Somehow, during the course of the introductions, Stephen had also made it impossible for Señor Castile to exclude Elena from the dinner table that evening. So, under Anna's disapproving eye, she had dressed in her best silk gown and joined the men in the dining room.

The conversation, she remembered, had been quite literary. Stephen had been surprised that she had read all of James Fenimore Cooper's Leatherstocking tales as they were some of his own boyhood favorites. She had been impressed that he had read *Don Quixote* although in an English translation. Her father had wavered between pride in his daughter's unusually broad education and wariness. For, although Elena was well acquainted with the local codes of conduct that kept apart the young and unmarried, Stephen was from a different culture.

He'd asked if Elena could show him the estate on horseback. The wish was granted, although they were accompanied by her father's *caporal*, Juan. Later, with Anna trailing behind, Stephen came up to the art studio to see Elena's paintings, standing so that his body was almost touching hers as she described the scenes and people she had depicted. His nearness made her heartbeat accelerate and her breath catch in her throat. And when he turned to her with a look in his eyes that was reserved only for her, the color rose in her cheeks.

After that there were many meetings. Stephen knew exactly how to flatter Anna so that the older woman invited him to sit with them on the patio after siesta.

Beside the old stone fountain with the sound of the splashing water in the background, they chatted about literature, the mining business, the great Spanish and Venezuelan painters. She caught his enthusiasm when he talked of his love for the outdoors—riding, sailing, wilderness camping. But more than that, her awareness of him as a man grew with every word they exchanged. She was enchanted by the stroking of his finger along the side of his chin when he was thinking, fascinated by the way he cut the skin off a peach, captivated by the look of his lean, yet muscular body under his casual slacks and shirts.

For years art had been the consuming passion of Elena's life. When she thought about her father arranging a marriage or even her falling in love, it had always been in terms of something that would happen in the future. But with the arrival of Stephen Gallagher at the ranch, all her feminine instincts had suddenly blossomed. And she knew that he was just as attracted to her as she was to him.

She wanted to see him alone—away from the sharp eyes of her duenna. She knew he felt the same way. But they managed it only once. She had played the memory of that meeting over and over in her mind like a cherished strip of movie film. But unlike celluloid, it had not faded with age. It had only grown sharper and more vivid.

Stephen had remained at the hacienda for almost two weeks, ostensibly trying to persuade Señor Castile to embark upon a joint venture to open up a promising new iron mine. Long before the discussions were over, both men knew that the answer would be no. But Stephen had stayed on for the sake of the moments he could spend with Elena.

On his last night, as they were getting up from the dinner table, Stephen's hand had brushed hers, and he had slipped a folded piece of paper into her fingers. "Meet me at eleven near the old well in the garden," it said.

She knew how her father felt about Stephen. The thought of disobeying him made her stomach knot. His anger could be terrible. Yet there was no way she could deny herself the chance to be alone with Stephen. Barefoot, with a thin robe thrown over her cotton gown, she had tiptoed down the steps and across the lawn to the stone well.

Though the darkness of the garden was moon-silvered, she didn't see him at first. He was hidden in the shadows of the rose bower.

She found herself smiling at the memory. She had been so young then. And so naive.

"¿Esteban?" she had whispered into the blackness.

"Here *querida*." He called her sweetheart. The very endearment was a forbidden intimacy. As he spoke, he pulled her gently into the bower and folded her into his arms.

All her training told her it was wrong to be with him like this. But it felt so right. The warmth of his body seemed to seep into her soul as he pressed her tightly against his hard length.

"Querida," he whispered again, his lips brushing her cheek. His hands roamed over her dark hair and down her back, making her shiver again as she had the first time his eyes had caressed her.

"You've never come to a man like this before." It was a statement, not a question. "You don't really understand what kind of trouble this could lead to."

"I'm going to be in trouble with Anna if she finds I'm missing."

He laughed, his voice rich and deep. "Is that the worst thing you can imagine?"

"It would be much worse if my father caught me here." The words made her tremble. He hugged her tightly.

"Why did you risk so much for me?"

"I wanted..." She tipped up her face toward his, studying the dark intensity of his features, sensing that she was far too inexperienced to know what she wanted. She only knew that standing here with him made her feel alternately hot and cold, giddy and supremely clearheaded.

His fingers reached out to trace the line of her brow, the slope of her nose, the soft curve of her cheek. Though he held himself very still, his eyes were alive with seething emotions reined in only by the force of his will. For a timeless moment his gaze caressed her face. Then, with deliberate gentleness, his head descended and his lips tasted hers, moving with unhurried persuasion. Not until she was quivering with the need for something more substantial did his tongue begin to investigate the corners of her mouth. As he pressed inside to stroke the satiny interior of her lips, the serrated line of her teeth and then the warm cavity beyond, her little gasp of surprise ended on a sigh of pleasure.

"Elena, you're so sweet," he murmured, lifting his head and looking down into her dark eyes.

His hands skimmed up and down her ribs, brushing lightly against the sides of her breasts.

Yes, touch me there. The silent plea remained unspoken.

"And innocent."

She wanted to protest. Instead she clung to him, her soft form molding itself to the hard contours of his. She felt a tremor shake him, sensed some change she didn't fully understand.

"Ah, *querida*, we're playing with fire now." Hands on her shoulders, he put a few inches of space between them.

She could hear the ragged edge of his breathing. It matched her own.

The night air was still and sweet with the fragrance of the roses and yet heavy with tension. It was like the moment of anticipation just before a storm, when the wind begins to blow. But Elena knew that the disquiet was not something external. It came from the two of them, and suddenly she understood that all her previous encounters with Stephen had only been a prelude to this meeting.

"We have to go back inside," he told her firmly. "I was crazy to think I could meet you out here."

Was it to be over before it had really begun? "Kiss me again like that. *Por favor.*"

Almost roughly he pulled her to himself. As his lips sought hers, his hands slid urgently down her back to mold her buttocks and pull her upward against the rigid shaft of muscle in his groin.

"It was meant to be like this between us," he muttered.

The feminine core of her being seemed to ignite as though flint had been struck to steel. With a little cry, she began to move against him.

"Yes, *querida*, like that, exactly like that," he groaned.

For a moment longer he held her body tightly against his, as if to let her go would be to die. Then with hands that trembled he thrust her away. "Go back in the house before it's too late."

She was confused, disoriented. But the commanding tone of his voice had made her obey. Once, long ago, Anna had warned her sternly of the needs of men. Now Elena sensed that Stephen Gallagher was fighting a force that threatened to overwhelm him.

Trembling, she had turned and fled back to the hacienda. She hadn't seen Stephen again. For almost five years she had struggled with the crushing knowledge that she would never see him again. Before he'd left the ranch, he'd asked her father for her hand in marriage—and had been turned down—with no appeal. Even her own pleas had been cruelly ignored.

Then what had been forbidden had suddenly become possible. There had been many letters and phone calls back and forth between the *norteamericano* and her father. A bargain had been struck. Now, at last, Stephen Gallagher was less than an hour away.

The scenery outside the car window had been an almost unbroken line of housing developments, followed by shopping centers, followed by apartment complexes. So many people, Elena thought. Six lanes of traffic. She could not have imagined such congestion, such bustle.

Many of the buildings were Latin in style. And some of the signs were in Spanish. That was a small comfort—a reminder of home. They were just passing a turnoff to somewhere called Las Virgenes. Which virgins? she wondered.

The car crested a hill; now she could see the ocean spread out before her on the left. It was a clear, penetrating blue. Like Esteban's eyes. She had never seen such eyes before.

"Where do the Gallaghers come from?" she asked Hal.

"So you're awake." The older man smiled at her in the rearview mirror. "The Gallaghers come from Ireland, the west of Ireland. County Galway. Steve's great-grandfather came over during the potato famine. He was a blacksmith who started a machine tool business in Boston. Defense contracts put them on the map during World War I. And then Steve's father saw the possibilities in combining manufacturing with mining the raw materials. Did pretty well for himself, I'd say. And Steve has done even better."

"Yes." She was well aware of Esteban's wealth. It was her father's reason for the marriage, but not hers.

Now that she had asked a question, Hal kept up a mostly one-sided conversation for the rest of the ride. By the time they reached Santa Barbara, she knew quite a bit more about the Gallagher family and about Southern California. But she noticed that Hal said very little about Stephen.

She was so anxious to see him. Had he changed? Almost certainly. The thought brought an unexpected pang of worry. It had been so long. Was she wrong in coming here? But then she silenced the doubts as she had ever since her father had negotiated the terms of the marriage contract. Stephen Gallagher wanted her. He had sent for her. And she wanted to be his wife. Those were the important things. True, they came from different cultures. That had caused insurmountable problems for her parents. They had divorced when Elena was twelve. But she and Stephen were different. They would work things out.

The powerful car seemed to eat up the miles. Elena craned her neck as they skirted Santa Barbara. She'd wanted to know about the place where Stephen lived. So she'd read everything she could about the area. Now it was taking on reality.

As they left the city behind and headed into the brown hills dotted with live oaks and California sycamore, Hal seemed to run out of conversation. Finally the large sedan swung off a secondary road and across a cattle guard. The unobtrusive sign on the gatepost said Rancho Palo Colorado. "That's the name of the street—Calle Palo Colorado—where Steve's father lived when he first came to town. He took it for his property," Hal remarked.

The first sight of the sprawling hacienda brought a tightness to Elena's chest. The style was traditional Spanish. White stucco, red tile, and iron grillwork on the balconies. Brilliant magenta-flowering bougainvillea and blue plumbago vines twined up the arbor near the front door. It wasn't so different from the home she had left.

The circular driveway was paved in large red bricks. As Elena alighted from the car, she looked expectantly as one of the heavy carved oak doors opened. Esteban didn't emerge. Instead, a plump, round-faced woman with short, curly salt-and-pepper hair came bustling down the steps.

"Elena, child. You must be exhausted."

She found herself folded into fleshy arms and soundly hugged.

"I'm Maggie Donaldson, Stephen's housekeeper." A warm, motherly smile accompanied the greeting.

"I'm very glad to meet you, Señora Donaldson."

"Not *señora*. I was too busy taking care of Stephen and his father to get married. Call me Maggie. Stephen asked me to show you to your room. You can freshen up, or even take a nap if you'd like."

Again Elena struggled to mask her disappointment. "Isn't Stephen here?"

"He's in his study working. There was some business that wouldn't wait."

The long front hall was wide and cool. The house seemed empty, and Elena's shoes echoed on the terra-cotta floor as she allowed herself to be led toward the stairs. Was her fiancé simply too overwhelmed with work to greet her? Maggie's explanation was plausible. But she sensed it was more than that.

"Is Esteban all right?" she questioned.

Maggie turned slightly. "Oh, he's much better. And now that you're here, that's all the medicine he needs."

Elena struggled to control her expression, glad that the housekeeper's back was toward her. She felt disoriented—as though she had somehow stepped into the middle of a conversation. Medicine? Was Stephen sick? She wanted to ask what had happened. Somehow she had the feeling that she was expected to know.

Maggie reached the end of the hall and opened a carved oak door. Stepping aside, she waited while Elena entered. The room beyond was large and airy. The walls had been painted an oyster white; the quilted spread on the canopy bed matched the blue flower pattern of the curtains. Bright Mexican throw rugs covered the tile floor.

The housekeeper seemed to be waiting for Elena's approval of the decor.

"It's charming."

Maggie fairly glowed. "I picked out the curtains and spread myself."

Just then Hal appeared with some of the luggage.

"I can unpack while you take a nice warm bath," the housekeeper suggested.

Elena nodded gratefully. She felt grimy, tired—and bewildered. Despite the obvious solicitude of these two people, this was not the welcome she had been imagining. While

Elena found a change of clothing and her toilet articles in one of her cases, Maggie drew a bath in the square, jade-colored tub. The bathroom was large and had apparently been modernized recently. The fixtures were all of the same jade color, including the double sinks in the long counter.

After closing the door, Elena stripped off her wrinkled travel clothes and pinned up her hair. Sinking into the tub, she closed her eyes and sighed. The warm, scented water was a balm to her weary body.

A half hour later, when she stood up and reached for a fluffy white towel, it was with a new sense of resolve. Pausing in front of the mirror, she brushed out the dark shining waves of her hair and applied a bit of lipstick and blusher. Giving her oval face a critical inspection, she decided that she still looked too pale. But she had never worn much makeup and feared using too heavy a hand.

She wished she could look as carefree as she had five years ago when she and Stephen had first met. But that was no longer possible. Then her wide-set brown eyes had viewed the world with innocence. Circumstances had changed that, but perhaps her fiancé would appreciate the fact that she had grown up.

When she returned to the bedroom, she was dressed in a crisp white linen skirt and a short-sleeved turquoise knit top.

Maggie, who was still unpacking, glanced up approvingly. "It's wonderful what a hot bath can do. You look positively radiant. Now, how about a nice glass of fresh orange juice out on the balcony? The oranges are from our own trees."

"*¡Gracias, no!* I would like to see Esteban *ahora*—now." Despite her outward calm, Elena's emotions made it difficult to keep speaking in English.

The housekeeper's face took on an almost pleading look. "Perhaps you should wait until he's ready to—"

"I have waited long enough. Where is his office?"

Maggie sighed with obvious resignation. "Go back downstairs and turn right. It's the second door on the left."

"Thank you."

Despite her show of determination, Elena hesitated outside the door Maggie had indicated. She found herself digging her teeth into her bottom lip as she raised her hand and knocked.

A muffled answer might have been, "Come in."

Elena turned the knob and pushed the door open. The curtains were closed and the light was dim. A lamp illuminated the surface of a large desk, where papers were scattered across a blotter. To one side stood a computer, the screen glowing in the gloom. Dominating the far wall of the office was a large painting lighted by a narrow brass lamp. Elena's eyes widened in surprise. It was one of hers—a picture of the grasslands and mountains that she had painted a year and a half ago, a combination of realism and romanticism. She had done it on commission for a collector who had heard about her work and written to her father. What was it doing here?

But the question had barely formed in her mind when a sudden movement to her right drew her attention. Her eyes swung back toward the desk. Now she could make out the figure of a man behind the wide expanse of polished wood.

His form was in shadow. But she could see that his shoulders were rigid, his face turned in her direction.

"¿Esteban?"

"Elena, you should have waited until I sent for you."

At the sound of his voice, a flood of emotion washed over her. She had longed to hear him speak her name once more. Yet there was a harshness in his tone that she was not prepared for.

"Stephen. What's wrong?"

He laughed bitterly. "Stop pretending. You know what's wrong!"

"No, I—"

He reached out and tipped the shade of the desk lamp so that the light illuminated his face.

Elena was unable to suppress a gasp. The skin was as pale as a prison inmate's, the blue eyes were filled with pain and anger. But what drew her instant attention were the vivid scars slashing the left side from temple to jaw.

"I was wondering if they'd be more than you could take," he grunted. "Well, that isn't the worst of it." As she watched, he moved away from the desk. For a moment she was confused, for he had not stood up. Then she realized why. He was sitting in a wheelchair. Her mind reeled as she remembered the vital, assured Stephen Gallagher who had galloped with undisguised joy across her father's land and later held her with infinite tenderness in the moonlit garden. Desperately she struggled to reconcile her memories with the man who confronted her now.

He studied the look of astonishment on her face. "It's not just the shock. You really didn't know."

Mutely she shook her head.

"Then your father told you nothing about the accident—or my present debilities—before you agreed to come here," he clarified carefully.

"Accident? Esteban, I don't understand. Please, tell me now."

The man in the wheelchair ignored the question. "Your father assured me that he had informed you. That was one of my stipulations for going ahead with the marriage." Stephen's mouth hardened. "But that bastard lied to me. Well, I won't have you here. Do you understand?"

Elena shook her head.

"Let me be more clear then," he went on. "We will not be getting married, after all. I hope you haven't unpacked your bags, because you're going to be on the next plane home."

CHAPTER TWO

ELENA STOOD HER GROUND. "Then why did you send for me?"

"I told you I thought certain conditions had been met. I was wrong."

"But that is not my fault. And I will not return home. I came here in good faith to marry you. If you no longer want me, then I will go elsewhere." The impassioned words sprang automatically to her lips.

For the briefest moment admiration flickered in the cobalt depths of his eyes. Then the anguish returned. "It's not a case of wanting."

"No comprendo."

His jaw muscles tensed; the scar on the left side of his face grew more vivid as his skin flushed. "Then let me be very explicit. This is my house. You are here on my invitation. I withdraw that hospitality."

If he had slapped her, the sting could not have been more painful. Yet through the hurt, she knew what part of him spoke the words. He was a wounded animal trapped in a corner—striking out at whoever dared come close.

Elena squared her shoulders. "I will go elsewhere," she repeated, knowing that in English her words must sound stiff and formal. Yet she was not comfortable enough with the language to speak easily—or even to remember to speak it at all—when she was under stress like this.

"You're crazy. You can't. My God, you're a stranger with very few resources. What will you do? How will you live?"

She returned his gaze with defiance. "There is *nada*—nothing—left for me at home. *Pero no es importante.* I am an American citizen. I have as much right to live in this country—in California—as you do. If you don't want me here, I will earn my way with my painting."

He looked at her with undisguised incredulity. When he opened his mouth to speak, she hurried on.

"It is not conceit that tells me my work is very good. I am a well-trained critic as well as an artist. And I trust the judgment of my teachers. I have a little money to live on and to buy art supplies. I have read about Santa Barbara. There are many art dealers here. One of them will surely sponsor me. But if I have to prove my worth first, there is an art fair every Sunday. I will start there."

She heard him mutter something under his breath. "Art fair! You have no concept of what it means to be self-supporting, of how much money it takes to live. You have no idea of what it's like to be on your own—and certainly not in this country. I'm not going to be responsible for what could happen."

"Nevertheless, you can't stop me. I will go back to my room and pack. Hal can take me into town."

Stephen made a defeated gesture with his arm. "All right, you've boxed me into a corner. You can stay here for the time being. We'll talk about it later."

She didn't need to hear the tone of dismissal in his voice to make her leave. Turning, Elena strode from the room, pulling the heavy oak door shut behind her. Once in the hall, she stood trembling with reaction. Her defiance had been born of desperation. She had no idea what she would have done if Esteban had called her bluff and sent her away. He was right; she had no concept of how much money it would

take, or what it would be like to live on her own. Yet she
hadn't been lying to him. She wasn't going home. Certainly
not after what her father had done. She'd thought she
understood what Eduardo Castile was capable of. Now she
realized that she had only been dimly aware of his desperation.

Anger made her tighten her jaw painfully. Her father had
sent her thousands of miles away, with no more regard for
her feelings than if he had been selecting a stallion for one
of his prize mares in breeding season.

She remembered the day when he had called her into his
study and told her he had written to Stephen Gallagher. He
had asked if the *norteamericano* still wanted to marry his
daughter.

She had stared at him in shock, unable to believe that a
man with so much pride could have done such a thing. And
what about her own honor? She should have been humili-
ated. Yet her heart had started to pound as she waited to
hear the response.

Her father had gestured toward Stephen's answering let-
ter. "He still wants to marry you."

It was as if a great weight had been lifted off her chest.
Yet she could hardly believe the words. "After so many
years? He's not already married?"

"Fortunately not."

Her eyes were drawn to the lines of strain that furrowed
her father's face. They had deepened over the past three
years. She'd thought she understood what anguish had
carved them there. She had thought she knew why his black
eyes shifted away from her questioning gaze.

As he'd grown older, her father had become obsessed with
amassing more wealth. He had invested in too many risky
ventures and ended up losing huge sums of money. Not even
the sale of his horses and his art collection had been enough

to pay his debts. He'd been forced to liquidate part of the ranch—and the rest was going to be sold off as well, if he didn't find a way to come up with more cash.

The fabric of his life was in tatters. At first Elena had assumed that marrying her to Stephen was a way to remove one more agonizing burden from his shoulders. At least he wouldn't have to worry about his daughter anymore. Her husband would be responsible for her.

Then Elena found out about the money. Stephen had agreed to pay for her. If pride had been more important than love, she would have been furious at the way her father was using her. And at first it had been difficult to hold up her head. Then she reminded herself that she was getting what she most wanted in the world.

In the weeks before she'd left for Santa Barbara, the only real anger she had felt was for the fact that her father had kept her apart from the man she loved for so long, and then had decided to trade her to that same man when he needed money. Now that she knew the whole truth, she had to press her knuckles against her teeth to keep from screaming.

¡Madre de Dios! He should have told her. He should have trusted her. Instead he had thrown her like a sacrificial virgin into the dragon's lair.

Covering her face with her hands, she tried to regain her composure. Tears of mingled anger and pain closed her throat. She fought to hold them back and almost succeeded. What was she going to do now? In her wildest imaginings, she had not expected to find Esteban in a wheelchair. Not a man with his vitality. And the face. He had been so handsome before. What must it be like to confront those scars in the mirror every morning? A wave of pity swept over her. It was followed almost immediately by piercing insight. He didn't want that from her—or anyone else.

She pressed her fingers more firmly over her eyes. She had just been shocked to the core. Now her true emotions were breaking the surface like bubbles in a caldron of simmering liquid. Suddenly she realized that anger at her father was the least important of her emotions. If there was anything she had just learned about herself, it was that she still loved Stephen Gallagher—despite his stinging rejection.

When she'd seen the scars on his face, her reaction had been born of shock, not of revulsion. But what about the wounds she couldn't see? What mental injuries had he suffered? Did his rejection mean he was no longer capable of love? Or was he afraid to open himself to her?

Behind the oak door, she heard the reverberation of something hard being slammed against a rigid surface. Stephen's fist crashing against the desk? Well, he might be in a wheelchair, but he still had his strength.

His angry gesture was strangely comforting. Curiously it helped firm her own determination. She had strength, too. Perhaps she also had allies. Deliberately she took several deep, steadying breaths. When she felt more in control of herself, she turned and started down the hall toward the back of the house. In a small powder room, she stopped and splashed cold water onto her face and dried it with a towel. When her reflection told her her features were calm once again, she went in search of Maggie.

She found the gray-haired housekeeper in a large, well-appointed kitchen, her square hands covered with flour. She was kneading dough.

Elena regarded her for several seconds. She had been in such a hurry for answers that she hadn't stopped to think out what approach to take. She didn't know this woman, yet she sensed she had a deep affection for Stephen. On the other hand, perhaps she would feel disloyal talking about his problems. Well, there was only one way to find out. "I would appreciate it if you could tell me what's going on around here.''

Maggie turned around and wiped her hands on her apron. "You really don't know, then?"

Elena shook her head. "My father must have been afraid that I wouldn't agree to the marriage if he told me the truth. He was wrong."

Relief washed over Maggie's lined face. "You're so young and pretty. It's been so long since you and Stephen saw each other. I was terrified you wouldn't stay. And then when you didn't seem to know about the accident..." Her voice trailed off.

"Time hasn't changed my feelings for Esteban. And as for my age, a lot has happened over the past few years. I have had to grow up very quickly."

The housekeeper nodded. "I guess that's true, or we wouldn't be having this conversation."

"Yes."

The acknowledgement brought forth more words that must have been locked inside the older woman's heart. "Seeing Stephen like this tears me apart. When he was a little boy, he never let anyone comfort him when he hurt himself—or when he was troubled. It's the same now." She made a gesture to express her sense of futility. "I don't know what to do."

"Start by telling me everything you know. Please, everything."

"It's a long story. I think you'd better sit down."

Elena crossed to the wooden table beside the window and pulled out one of the captain's chairs.

"Can I get you a cup of coffee? Tea?"

"Tea would be very welcome."

For a few moments Maggie seemed glad to busy herself with filling the kettle and setting it on the stove. Elena guessed that she was gathering her thoughts. When the older woman joined her at the table, her lined face wore a thoughtful expression.

"I guess it started right after Stephen came back from visiting your family." She paused, as though searching for the right words. "He was different than I had ever seen him. One moment happy and talkative—the next moment withdrawn almost despairing. I decided that he must have fallen in love, but that there was some impediment to the relationship."

The ghost of a smile flickered on Elena's well-shaped lips. "Yes, we fell in love. It was like heaven and hell for me, as well. The worst was after I found out that he had asked to marry me the day he left the ranch. My father refused."

"You must understand that Stephen isn't the kind of man who talks about his problems. But he told me about your father's refusal. Did you know he wrote to Señor Castile after he got home, asking again?"

Elena shook her head.

"After your father turned him down that second time, he started drinking pretty heavily. He had never done anything like that before."

Maggie got up to finish preparing the tea. Although her back was turned, Elena could hear the pain in her voice. "He would sit in his office in the evenings with a bottle of bourbon. And sometimes, when I would come in to try to get him to go to bed, he would talk to me. He was in despair. He loved you. He used to dream up crazy schemes— like going back down there and kidnapping you. But when he was more rational, he'd realize there was no way he could have you."

Elena gripped the edge of the table. She had known that same overwhelming feeling of desperation. She hadn't turned to wild schemes or to drink—but to the comfort of her painting, as she had done when she had felt abandoned by her mother.

The housekeeper returned to the table with the teacups. "The drinking didn't help. Finally one day he poured the liquor down the sink. I thought he'd managed to pull himself together. But that wasn't really a change for the better. He just started looking for other ways to forget you." Maggie stared into her teacup. "You asked to hear the whole story."

"Yes. Tell me everything. I have to know."

"There were other women—a lot of other women," Maggie said in a low voice.

The words hurt, but they didn't surprise Elena. Stephen Gallagher had been a virile and attractive man—and a good catch.

"And he threw himself back into his work—with a vengeance. At first I was relieved, until I realized that he didn't have much regard for his safety anymore."

"What do you mean?"

"He started taking chances—like flying the company plane when weather conditions were hazardous, or personally inspecting mines that had safety problems. Things like that. It's a wonder something terrible didn't happen sooner."

"What happened to him?" Elena whispered.

"A mining accident. There were men trapped underground, and he went down to supervise rescue operations. There was a second cave-in." Maggie was silent a moment.

"Stephen was behind the rockfall. His light was smashed. He was feeling his way down a tunnel, still trying to get to the other men, when he went over the edge of a shaft. It was a fifty-foot drop. I still think it's a miracle that they got him out alive."

"*¡Madre de Dios!*"

For the first time, Maggie's expression became accusatory. "Tell me, why did your father wait so long to change his mind and allow you to marry Stephen?" she demanded.

Elena stared down at her hands still gripping the table. She couldn't look at Maggie now. But the woman had told her a great deal that was obviously very painful to her. Perhaps the truth would help matters.

"My father is not an easy man to understand, and his reasons were complicated. I think it goes back to the way he was raised. And then there was his own marriage to my mother. It was never a success. They were too different. In my culture, the parents pick a wife for their son—a husband for their daughter. Because my grandfather was dead, my father defied that convention. Unfortunately, it worked out badly. My mother couldn't live with him. They were divorced when I was twelve. So he had decided that the old ways were best, after all. He wasn't going to make the same mistake with his only daughter." She swallowed painfully. "I think he didn't really want me to marry at all. He wanted to keep me at home to make up for the loss of my mother."

"Then why—?"

"Everything changed. My father made too many bad investments, financed too many speculative mining ventures that didn't pay off. My family lost its—" Elena groped for the proper English word "—status. My father was ruined. Before all that happened, the son of a friend had asked to marry me. My father had said no but he changed his mind when . . . when he lost his fortune." She took a deep breath and plunged ahead. "They didn't want me anymore."

Maggie could not conceal her shock.

"So, through no fault of my own, I was disgraced, too," Elena continued. "But my father decided there was a way to salvage at least something for me and for himself. He knew how much Esteban wanted to marry me, and he knew Señor Gallagher was very wealthy. So he offered to make a deal. His daughter for enough money to start over again.''

''My God, your father must be an unfeeling monster.''

''He was a broken man, a desperate man.''

The housekeeper reached across the table and laid her hand over Elena's. ''You poor child. I didn't know.''

''But you will keep my confidence.''

''Of course.''

''The irony is that he gave me what I wanted most in the world,'' Elena said quietly.

Maggie nodded.

Elena looked down at her tea. When she took a sip, she found that it had cooled. ''Please, tell me about Esteban's injuries,'' she urged.

''He's so much better now. At first we didn't think he was going to live. After the accident, he was in the hospital for six weeks. Besides what you can see, the left leg was the worst. He shattered the kneecap, broke the other bones in several places. But he also damaged his right leg, his ribs, his left arm....'' Her voice faded.

''So many injuries! And for a man who loved to be active.''

''Yes. But he wouldn't give up. He started working with a private physical therapist before he got back home from the hospital, and he still works out with him every morning. He's pushed himself almost to the limit with his rehabilitation program. I know how much he wanted to be out of the wheelchair before you came.''

''Then he will be able to walk?''

''If a man can walk through sheer force of will, Stephen will be able to do it.''

''I can't imagine what it must have been like for him.''

"He didn't want you to see him like this, even. He was angry that your father wanted you to come so quickly."

"I guess my father was afraid that I might somehow find out—and refuse to go along with his plans."

Maggie nodded.

"And what about his face?" Elena finally asked.

"The plastic surgeon says the appearance of the scars can be improved. But they will always be there."

"It was a shock at first—mostly because I wasn't expecting them. But he acted as though he thought they would change the way I felt about him."

The two women regarded each other silently for a moment.

"Stephen's not the easiest person to live with now," Maggie finally murmured. "Lately he's been taking out his frustration and anger on others."

"When he found out my father hadn't told me about the accident, he threatened to send me home."

"He didn't!"

"Yes, he did."

The housekeeper sighed. "He's been through so much. But he's still a proud man. He didn't want—"

"My pity," Elena finished the sentence. "Well, I'm not staying because of that. I love him."

"I love him, too, Elena, as much as if he were my own son. His mother died when he was four, and after that I raised him. But I still want to strangle him sometimes. Maybe between the two of us we can put him right again."

"I'm willing to do whatever it takes."

They continued to talk for a few more minutes, but Elena found that the fatigue of the trip and the strain of the past hour were finally catching up with her.

Maggie gave her a considering look. "My girl, you need to get some sleep."

There was little point in protesting. "I think you're right," Elena agreed. "If I'm not up in time for dinner, please make my excuses to Stephen."

When she stood up, Maggie also pushed back her chair. As she had done earlier, she put her arms around Elena and pressed her close. "I'm glad you're here."

This time Elena returned the hug with heartfelt warmth. "I feel the same. I'm going to need your help."

"Well, you have it. And Hal's too, I trust. He's been here at the ranch even longer than I have. And he feels the same way about Stephen that I do."

"*Gracias.* You don't know how wonderful it is to be able to rely on you."

Maggie grinned. *"De nada, mi amiga. De nada."*

"You speak Spanish?"

"Only a little. I wish I spoke more, so I could make you feel as comfortable as possible here. I know how difficult it must be having to use a foreign language all the time."

"No. This is my home now, so I must improve my English. In fact, I am starting to think in your language. A good sign, no?"

"A very good sign." Maggie clasped her shoulder. "Do you need anything before you turn in?"

"Not a thing. You have provided for me superbly." Turning, Elena left the kitchen and made her way back upstairs to her room.

UNDER THE CIRCUMSTANCES, Elena had felt it might be difficult to stop the thoughts swirling through her mind. But she was so exhausted that she was asleep almost as soon as her head hit the pillow. When she awoke again, she knew for certain that she had missed dinner. Bright morning sunlight was streaming into her room. The clock on the bedside table told her it was a little past eight. She had slept for almost fifteen hours.

The sound of male voices drifted up from the open window. When she looked out, she could see only the empty patio and swimming pool. Quickly she took another casual skirt and top from the closet. Going into the adjoining bathroom, she spent a few minutes washing and dressing.

When she went downstairs to the kitchen it was empty. Instead of bothering Maggie, she found the makings for a simple breakfast in the refrigerator and cupboards. After eating quickly, she put her dishes into the sink and went in search of Stephen.

The voices she had heard seemed to be coming from a wing of the house on the other side of the patio. Walking around the rectangular swimming pool, Elena silently approached an open set of double doors. The large room on the other side was outfitted as a gym. There were mats, racks of weights, parallel bars set at railing height, and various formidable-looking machines that she didn't recognize. Stephen's wheelchair stood empty against one wall. She spotted the man himself with his hands folded across his chest, gripping a large, flat weight. Dressed in a T-shirt and shorts, he was doing sit-ups. His body was in profile to her, and she could see that his eyes were closed in concentration. A tall blond man with a professional athlete's physique was counting beside him.

Elena saw the sheen of perspiration on Stephen's skin and watched the muscles in his back and stomach bunch and stretch under the thin cotton T-shirt. Maggie had said Stephen was pushing himself to the limit. Now she could see that for herself. But the hard work seemed to be paying off. His upper body looked extremely fit. With his left side turned away from her, she could almost imagine that nothing had happened to him.

"Fifty-eight, fifty-nine, sixty. That's ten more today. Great progress. Let's work on the leg now. Any discomfort last night?"

"Some."

"Did you take anything for it?"

"Larry, how many times do I have to tell you, I don't want to be dependent on drugs!"

"Okay. Just asking. It's your pain."

"That's right."

Neither man had noticed her yet. Stephen set the weight down and reached to grasp Larry's outstretched hand. Using the leverage, he pulled himself to a standing position. Now the result of his terrible fall was much more apparent. Elena could see that the muscles of his right leg were far better developed than those of his left. From the angle at which he held it as he stood, it was obvious that there was only partial articulation in the injured knee. Even more noticeable was the network of fading pink scars that slashed the skin of his leg. A particularly angry one described a half circle at the bottom of his knee. Another seamed his calf like the zipper of a legging. As Stephen bore down on the limb, he winced. Elena had to bite her lip to keep from doing the same. Maggie had told her what he'd suffered. Seeing for herself was far more painful.

With their backs to her, the men slowly made their way across the room to the parallel bars. Stephen leaned on Larry and dragged the left leg slightly. When they reached the railings, the injured man transferred his weight to the supports and began to move along between them.

"Good," Larry approved. "You're getting better."

"Not good enough."

Stephen reached the end of the bars, and was about to start back when he caught sight of Elena standing in the doorway. "And just how long have you been watching the performance?" he demanded.

"Since sit-up fifty-eight."

Larry turned, his eyes widening in surprised appreciation as he took in her dark beauty. "Well, well. And where has Steve been hiding you?"

"I just arrived from Caracas yesterday. I'm Esteban's fiancée. Elena Castile."

"Larry Foster. Pleased to meet you. But I won't offer you a sweaty palm."

The man with the scarred face opened his mouth and then closed it again.

Larry looked at him and grinned. "You've been holding out on me, buddy." He turned back to Elena. "You've come a long way. Good flight?"

"Tiring."

"I'll bet."

"If you don't mind, I'd like to get back to work," Stephen interrupted.

"Sure thing. Give me another trip up the bars and back again." As he spoke, Larry moved back into position near his client.

"I don't like having an audience."

"I'm not here as a—a—" she groped for the English word "—voyeur. I was hoping I could help with your therapy."

"That's a great idea," Larry put in. "The left leg tends to cramp up. I could show you how to massage the kinks out." He laughed. "Steve would probably appreciate your hands on his bod a whole lot more than mine."

Elena felt her cheeks redden. She had never touched a man that intimately. What was more, she wasn't used to the physical therapist's brand of repartee. Yet she suspected it wasn't out of line in the free and easy Southern California society in which he probably moved. "Yes, you will have to instruct me," she managed to say.

Ignoring the conversation, Stephen had begun to make his way back up the bars. From the tight set of his jaw, Elena knew he wasn't really as oblivious to her as he pretended. Elena hesitated. She knew very well that Stephen wanted her to leave. Yet he wasn't going to make an issue of it in the presence of his physical therapist. Perhaps she could use the opportunity.

"How long have you been working with Stephen?" she asked.

"We started while he was still in the hospital—after the second operation on his knee. I guess you know his case was complicated by multiple injuries to the knee and the tibia. And then there were the torn ligaments."

Elena nodded as the physical therapist gave her more of the details. She didn't understand everything, partly because her English didn't extend to such technical language.

Larry was patient when she asked for additional clarification and seemed more than willing to continue the conversation—and the easy familiarity. After helping Stephen seat himself on the padded bench in front of the arm press, and checking the heavy stack of weights opposite the handlebars, he walked back to Elena. "So how did you two meet, anyway?"

"Stephen came down to my father's estate to discuss a business proposition several years ago."

"Years! If I'd met a looker like you, I wouldn't have waited."

"In my country, the family must give permission for marriage. My father had to be . . . persuaded."

"Well, I can see why Steve didn't give up." He glanced over at the man in question. "I'd say he's damn lucky to have someone like you."

Elena wasn't sure how Larry had meant the words. But she could imagine how Stephen might interpret them. In the next second, he let the heavy pile of weights drop with a resounding clank and turned to face the therapist. "Just what exactly is that crack supposed to mean?" he growled.

Larry held out his hands, palms up. "Just that your fiancée is definitely a class act."

Stephen continued to regard the other man, his face a mask of barely controlled anger, his knuckles white on the handle grips of the machine.

Instinctively Elena stepped between the two men and walked to Stephen's side. Reaching out, she covered one of his large, square hands with a small, delicate one. It had been such a long time since she had touched the man she loved. The physical contact unlocked a rush of feelings. She had meant to murmur something comforting, but her throat was too constricted for her to speak.

Instead she pressed her hand reassuringly over Stephen's, and then was unable to stop herself from running her trembling fingers across the tops of his. His skin was damp and slippery from exertion. She was surprised to find it somehow increased the pleasure of the contact. The masculine scent of his body enveloped her. It was strangely compelling.

His posture rigid, Stephen kept his face averted from hers. She looked down at the vibrant red highlights in his dark hair, and her chest tightened with emotion. With her free hand, she reached out and clasped his head, pulling it tightly against her midsection. Larry was forgotten. She had dreamed of being close to Stephen like this. Now the two of them might as well have been alone in the room—alone in the world.

For several heartbeats Stephen didn't move. Then, slowly, he turned his hand over and clasped her fingers in his powerful grasp, his thumb stroking across her knuckles. *"Querida."*

The whispered endearment was almost inaudible. But she heard, and her heart leaped with joy.

CHAPTER THREE

WANTING TO INCREASE the contact, Elena leaned over and rested her cheek against Stephen's hair. The hand that clasped his head moved to stroke the injured side of his face. When her fingers touched scar tissue, she felt him stiffen.

"Don't." The word was edged with pain.

"I—"

He drew back.

The world snapped into focus again. Elena looked around. They really were alone in the room. Outside the double doors she could see Larry standing on the patio with his hands clasped behind his back, staring out across the pool.

Stephen gazed up at her, the left side of his face averted. For a long moment he was silent. "You shouldn't have come in here," he finally muttered.

Elena hesitated. She had crossed the patio not knowing what to expect, but wanting to help in some way. Perhaps she was invading Stephen's privacy. Yet he had reached out to her however briefly. This might be the time to press that advantage. But her heart was pounding as she forced herself to speak. "Esteban, we have to talk about the future," she whispered.

He regarded her silently for several moments, then sighed. "You have a lot of determination."

"Yes."

"All right. We'll talk at lunch."

She felt as though a bargain were being reluctantly struck. "I'll see you later."

His tone became brisk. "Send Larry back in here on your way out. I've only got the mornings for working out. The rest of the day, I am still running a major corporation, you know."

Elena nodded and started for the door.

When she reached the main part of the house, she turned and looked back toward the gym. Through the window she could see Esteban raising and lowering the exercise bar again. She felt a mixture of elation and depression. For just a moment Stephen had let her glimpse his vulnerability. Then he had shut her out like a jailer slamming an iron door. Perhaps he was coming to terms with her presence here. At least it was something to build on.

She loved Stephen. But if she was honest with herself, she would have to admit that she didn't know a great deal about the man she had come so far to marry. Perhaps there was a way to get some more information before they talked at lunch. Seeing the way he had chosen to live might help her understand him better.

On the main floor was a large, comfortable sitting room decorated in burgundy and gray. Square modern couches flanked a fieldstone fireplace. But the tables and cabinet pieces were beautifully restored antiques. Elena admired the mix of styles, a satisfied smile playing around the corners of her lips. Only a man who was sure of his taste would have taken that approach.

The table and chairs in the dining room looked as though they might have been part of the original furnishings of the house. All were of solid mission oak, except for the leather chair backs and seats. They told her that Stephen was not a man who summarily swept away the past to make way for innovation. She liked that quality, too.

The library was cozier, with floor-to-ceiling bookcases and a small couch facing another fireplace. Elena ran a finger along the spines of the books, pausing to pull out several volumes. Apparently Stephen's taste was quite broad. She smiled again. Perhaps she would surprise him by reading some of the novels, so that they could continue their literary discussions.

Down the hall was the office she had already seen. Behind the solid oak door silence reigned. Stephen had told her a few minutes ago that he was personally running the Gallagher corporation. He must have an inviolable rule that no one call him in the mornings. That meant his staff was well trained—and that his authority was very much in force.

She passed by the office, not wanting to intrude on Esteban's privacy. When she opened the next door, however, she knew at once she had done just that.

The small chamber was Stephen's bedroom. Naturally she hadn't expected to find his sleeping quarters downstairs. Now she realized that for a man in a wheelchair, living entirely on the ground floor made sense. Unlike the other rooms she had just seen, this one had absolutely no warmth or charm. There was a bare minimum of furnishings, not even a rug on the tile floor to impede the rubber wheels of his chair. But what drew her eyes was the hospital bed against the wall by the window. Extralong and wide, it was the only concession to comfort in the room. But the covers were rumpled; the white wool blanket lay askew and almost dragging on the floor. Stephen must have spent a restless night. Were all his nights like that? And how much pain was he in? Elena questioned, her heart contracting as she pictured him tossing and turning.

Closing the door softly behind her again, she stood for several moments in the hall, wondering what she could do to help him through this ordeal. In the final analysis the answer was "nothing," unless he allowed her to.

Yet spending her days brooding about Esteban's problems would be one of the worst things she could do. She had to tend to her own emotional health. With a new sense of purpose, she went in search of Maggie. She found the housekeeper upstairs, making the bed. The older woman looked up as she entered the room. "You didn't have to fix your own breakfast," she said.

"I don't want to be any extra trouble to you. Besides, it gave me a chance to become a little more familiar with the kitchen." Elena paused. "Not that I want to take *your* place, of course."

Maggie laughed. "Don't worry. I'm not one of those old birds who has to rule the roost. Things have always been pretty informal around here. If you'd like to do some cooking, I'd be glad to show you where everything is—and teach you some of Stephen's favorite dishes."

"Oh, yes. That would be wonderful. I want to learn to cook what he likes. And I have some specialties of my own. Like *empañadas*. I fixed them when Stephen visited my father's estate."

"Well, then, it's a deal."

Maggie finished smoothing out the bedspread and then cleared her throat. "I saw you over in the gym. How did it go?"

Elena gave her a short—and slightly edited—report of the physical therapy session.

"He used to chase me out, too," the housekeeper observed. "So I never go over there anymore."

"I might have been too forward."

"Sometimes the only way to get through to that man is to hit him over the head."

Elena could imagine that an exasperated Maggie might be capable of exactly that. "But not in the morning, when he's busy with his physical therapy."

Maggie grinned. "You're probably right."

"I had planned to continue with my painting," Elena said, changing the subject. "Do you think Stephen would mind if I set up an art studio in one of the upstairs rooms?"

"Stephen said you'd probably want to paint. In fact, he took care of everything as soon as he'd heard from your father."

"What do you mean?"

"I'll show you. There's a tower room on the north side of the house that hasn't been used in years. Stephen had it fixed up as a studio. Said you'd want the northern exposure."

Maggie led the way to the second floor and then up another short flight of stairs. At the top, she paused and opened a wide door, then stepped aside and ushered Elena in.

When her eyes caught sight of the room's appointments, the young woman couldn't suppress a gasp of surprise and delight. A sturdy wooden easel had been set up by the window. Next to it was a small table holding a clean palette for mixing colors. Rectangles of blank canvas in various sizes were propped against one wall. Elena walked over to the new wooden shelves across from them. She had never seen so many art supplies. Tubes of oil paint in every imaginable color, solvent, brushes, palette knives, sketchbooks, charcoal, pencils.

Overwhelmed, she tried to take it all in. Stephen had even provided a drawing table and a comfortable chair. It was hard to keep her composure. "He didn't have to do this."

"Believe me, it gave him a great deal of pleasure. He made phone calls, bought books. He was like a little boy with a toy catalog."

"But he must have spent a fortune."

"He can afford it. And he told me that if there was anything that didn't suit, you could send Hal back into town for what you need. Or you might want to go yourself."

"No, no, this is—*perfecto*." Elena picked up a tube of paint. It was the brand she liked best. "How did he know what kind to get?"

"I believe he wrote to your father and asked."

"Esteban went to a great deal of trouble to please me."

"Yes." The older woman hesitated, as though reluctant to break a confidence, then she plunged ahead. "Stephen never was very good at expressing his feelings. Nowadays he's got a lot locked up inside himself that he doesn't let out. But there are ways you can tell...."

Elena nodded. "I know. But brief glimpses inside his private prison aren't enough for me. I plan to break the lock. Perhaps you can help."

"Try me."

"Stephen promised me that we'd talk at lunch. I want him to feel at ease. Is there somewhere we can eat where the two of us can be alone?"

Maggie looked thoughtful. "You might like to sit out in the garden in the gazebo. Even at noontime it's cool and shady—and a bit away from the house. No one would bother you there. Would that do?"

"It sounds wonderful. When does Esteban eat?"

"About twelve-fifteen. I'll send Hal up to show you the way."

"Thank you."

Maggie turned toward the door. "Is there anything else you need?"

"No. I'm fine."

"Then enjoy your morning."

"I will."

Once the housekeeper had left her alone, Elena looked around the room more systematically. It really was everything she could hope for in a studio, she mused, running her fingers over the natural bristles of the long artist's brushes. Like everything else Stephen had purchased for her, they were of the finest quality.

Even though her father had supported her talent enthusiastically, she had never been this well equipped. And in the past few years she'd had to make do with less expensive supplies.

That Stephen had made himself knowledgeable about what she liked and then bought so much for her must mean that he cared about her—even if he couldn't put his feelings into words right now. What was more important, beneath the scarred exterior he must still be the man she had fallen in love with. All she had to do was reassure him that *her* feelings hadn't changed, and everything would surely be all right.

Crossing to the large windows that dominated the north wall, she looked out for a moment. She could see the garden Maggie had mentioned and beyond it a stable and paddock. In the distance was a field of brilliant pink flowers. Farther off, live oak trees dotted the rolling hills. Behind them rugged mountains rose against the jewellike blue of the sky. It was a setting she could easily come to love. She would paint it. But right now another subject had captured her interest.

Picking up a large spiral-bound sketch pad and a piece of charcoal, she took them to the drawing table and sat down. For a few moments she regarded the blank sheet of paper in front of her. Then she set to work. Unlike many artists, she had the ability to work quite accurately from memory. Since childhood she had found that she had only to close her eyes to call up a scene in all its rich detail. At first it had saddened her to discover that other people couldn't do that. Later she had come to appreciate her special gift.

She had not allowed herself to draw Stephen from memory for a long time. She had desperately wanted the flesh-and-blood man, not a two-dimensional image, no matter how accurate. Even after her father had agreed to the marriage, she had been afraid that somehow the plans would fall through at the last moment. Until she had actually boarded the plane in Caracas, she had not allowed herself to fully believe that her dearest wish was coming true. But now the years of waiting were over. She was here with Stephen Gallagher.

It was often through drawing and painting a person that Elena came to understand her subject. The act of capturing someone on paper forced her to pay attention to the smallest details. Just as she had come to appreciate Stephen better by exploring his house, she would use her talent as an artist to increase her sensitivity to the man.

Her first rendering was of Stephen at the weight machine, his corded muscles straining as he pushed the metal handle upward. Her second showed him as he made his way along the parallel bars. With a few quick strokes, she captured the determined thrust of his injured body.

The grip of his strong fingers on the polished wood had interested her. She flipped the page and quickly sketched the isolated detail. The expression of concentration on his face had also riveted her attention. She drew that too, making a very accurate depiction of the left as well as the right side. She was so absorbed in her work that she didn't note the passage of time.

A tap at the door startled her, and she looked up to find Hal standing a bit uncertainly on the threshold.

Elena snapped the sketchbook closed. Her early studies of a subject were for her eyes alone. But more than that, she sensed that Stephen wouldn't want anyone to see the pictures. "I'm sorry you had to walk all the way up here," she said to Hal.

"No trouble at all. But you'd better come along before the soup gets cold."

"Just let me wash my hands." She held up charcoal-streaked fingers.

Downstairs, Hal pointed the way to the gazebo. As Elena walked into the garden, she stopped to appreciate the lush greenery. Graceful oleander bushes walled off an oasis where paths of irregularly cut sandstone were bordered with beds of brilliant lobelia and impatiens. In the background were carefully tended citrus and bottlebrush trees.

One sunny spot had been set aside as a rose garden. Elena paused to cup a delicate, peach-colored bloom in her hands. The fragrance was as beguiling as the color and made her suddenly remember the night so long ago when she had gone to Stephen in the garden. She lingered for a moment, breathing in the perfume.

In the next section were Maggie's garden herbs. Elena caught the pungent aromas of sage and basil as her skirt brushed the delicate leaves. Another time she would stop for a closer look. Now she was already late for her lunch with Stephen.

As she rounded a corner, she spied the wooden gazebo, shaded by a thick growth of orange bougainvillea. The setting was charming, and Elena was glad that Maggie had suggested she meet Stephen here.

At the sound of feet on the path, he looked up. Seated on a high-backed wooden bench facing the table, he was freshly showered and shaved and casually dressed in jeans and a short-sleeved, open-necked shirt.

This afternoon he made no attempt to turn his face away. The expression in his blue eyes was defiant. If he expected her to cringe the way she had yesterday, when his altered appearance had taken her by surprise, he was going to be disappointed, Elena thought. In actuality, except for the scars on his face, he looked very fit. It was a pleasure to take in the broad expanse of his chest and the powerful muscles of his arms. Smiling warmly, she slid onto the bench opposite his. Then she glanced down at her soup and laughed.

"What's so funny?"

"We're starting with gazpacho. Hal warned me to hurry or the soup would get cold."

"That's his way of having some fun with you."

"Oh, I don't mind." Elena dipped her spoon into the cold, chunky soup. "It's delicious."

"Mmm."

They each took several more spoonfuls. "Did Maggie tell you I was working in the studio?"

"Yes."

"I want to thank you. It's wonderful. But you shouldn't have gone to so much trouble. I could have picked up some supplies myself."

"I knew painting was an important part of your life. I wanted things to be ready for you."

They were silent again. Stephen reached over, placed his empty bowl on the serving cart, and picked up a large plate of open-faced sandwiches, which he set on the table between them. There was egg salad, rare roast beef, ham and cheese, watercress and cream cheese, smoked salmon.

"So many different kinds," Elena remarked.

"I guess Maggie wasn't sure what you'd like." As he spoke, he stroked his finger along his chin. Elena stared at him, her heart skipping a beat. It was one of the old gestures she remembered.

"What are you staring at?" His eyes were wary.

"When you came down to my father's estate, you used to do that . . . stroke your chin."

"Oh." Stephen helped himself to roast beef and ham and cheese. With her nerves on edge, the light soup had almost filled her up, so Elena started with the watercress.

She had hoped the two of them were going to come to some understanding out here. But Stephen seemed to be concentrating on his food. Naturally he would be hungry after the hard workout. But he had also promised that they would talk.

She stirred sugar into her iced tea and then plucked off a serrated mint leaf from the dark green sprig Maggie had provided as a garnish. Rubbing it between her thumb and finger, she released the aromatic scent. Stephen glanced up at her and then quickly returned to his sandwich. When he reached for the glass bowl of fruit salad Maggie had made for dessert, Elena cleared her throat. "I know you have to get to work soon. But before you go inside, we should speak of our marriage," she said, surprised by her own boldness.

Stephen finished spooning strawberries and cantaloupe into a bowl and took a sip of iced tea. "What about it?"

"You were angry when you found out my father hadn't told me about your accident."

His jaw tightened, but he didn't answer.

"I—I was shocked," she admitted quietly.

"I'll bet."

"My father shouldn't have done that to us. He should have had more faith in me." When Stephen didn't comment, she hurried on. "But now that I know, it doesn't make any difference to me."

"Perhaps you should wait awhile before deciding that."

"No. I would like to set a wedding date—for sometime soon."

He regarded her steadily, his blue eyes flat as water viewed from a great height. "Even if you think you want to go ahead with the arrangement—we can't marry yet. That's one of the reasons I didn't want you to come here so quickly."

"Why can't we?"

"Isn't it obvious?"

"Not to me. I know you'd like to be on your feet, but that doesn't make any difference in the way I feel about you."

"It's not just a question of *being on my feet*."

"What do you mean?"

He continued to regard her steadily, but his fingers had twisted his napkin into a rope. "Elena. I don't think you quite understand. Marriage is a very intimate relationship between a man and a woman."

She laced her fingers together in front of her. "I'm not a child. I believe I do understand that."

"In theory, maybe. But when I saw you last, you weren't very, uh, practiced in the physical aspects of lovemaking." He paused and cleared his throat. "Of course, it's been a few years. Has that changed?"

Elena felt a hot flush spreading across her cheeks and fastened her eyes on the half-eaten sandwich in front of her. She hadn't been interested in any other men. After her father had turned down Stephen's marriage proposal, she had taken refuge in her work. For weeks at a time she hadn't even left the ranch. Her art had been her life, and she had told herself that was all she needed. Now, although she was twenty-four, she was no more experienced sexually than when they had first met. "No," she whispered.

"I'm sorry. I can't hear you, *querida*. Speak up."

Resisting the impulse to take her lower lip between her teeth, she raised her head. "No. That hasn't changed," she managed in a louder voice, her cheeks fairly burning now.

He studied her face before he began to speak again. "Well, that does present some interesting problems. As you saw in the gym, I don't have a great deal of mobility. Simply rolling over in bed is a major operation." He shrugged.

"But we could still get married now! Esteban, I love you. I want to help you, take care of you."

"I can always hire a nurse to take care of me. As for marriage, I prefer to wait until I can fulfill my duties as a husband with some degree of finesse."

"I don't require finesse."

"You're in no position to make judgments."

He had ignored her words of love. She knew his clipped replies were a deliberate ploy designed to fend off any threat of her rejection. But what could she say to him now? He might be right. She knew so little of love, yet she had to make him understand how she felt.

"Esteban, back home one of my best friends, Maria Delgado, married. Very soon after that, she found out that she was pregnant. I remember we spent long hours talking about her hopes for the baby—and about her fears that it might not be perfect."

"What does this have to do with me?"

"Let me finish. I came over to her house after the child was born to bring a present, and Maria took me up to the nursery. Her little girl was hungry and she picked her up, all wrapped in a blanket. I sat with her while she nursed her daughter, watching the tender love between mother and child. I tried not to be jealous, but seeing them together hurt. That was when I thought I would never be with you again, when there was no hope of ever having your child."

She raised her dark eyes to Stephen. He sat very still, studying her intently.

"After she nursed the baby, she needed to change her diaper. When she unwrapped the blanket, I saw that the child was not perfect. She had been born with part of her right leg and her right foot missing. It was a terrible shock to me. But I looked at my friend as she leaned over the baby, cooing to her, and I could see that she didn't love her daughter any the less. Don't you understand? That's the way love is, Stephen."

His blue eyes became opaque. "That's not a very apt comparison. You knew me before, Elena. I wasn't born this way. I've changed. You think you love me. Perhaps you only love the memory of what I was."

She tried to answer, but he bore relentlessly on.

"You might come to realize that you can't really respond to a man with a crippled body—and a face that looks like a Halloween mask."

It was almost as though he hadn't listened to her at all. He was still deliberately trying to put things in the worst possible light. But his bitter words tore at her heart. She wanted to reach out to him and heal the pain she knew had prompted them. But she understood more than ever that there was nothing she could say to persuade him differently. Only actions would plead her case. Without giving herself time to think about what she was doing, she scrambled up and moved around the table. Sliding onto the bench beside Stephen, she clasped him in her arms and drew him close, pressing her face against the firm, muscled wall of his chest.

His body tensed. "What the hell do you think you're doing?"

Elena knew exactly how to make him unbend. Vivid memories flooded her mind—memories of the time long ago when he had kissed her in the garden. Lifting her face, she looked for a moment into the storm-dark blue of his eyes. Then just as he had done on that evening so long ago, she brushed her lips softly, coaxingly back and forth against his.

The touch and texture of him sent a shiver through her body, and she closed her eyes in order to savor it more fully. It had been such a long time. She thought she had remembered her reactions. But she had forgotten how exquisite something so simple could be.

When she felt him yield slightly, she tested the corner of his mouth with the tip of her tongue, then moved to explore the inward curve. His mouth opened on a groan, and his hands came up to clasp her shoulders. She felt a moment's hesitation at her own brazenness. Then her tongue pressed forward into the warm, dark interior of his mouth, skimming his teeth, exploring the inner surface of his lips. How could she have forgotten the heady taste of him? she wondered dazedly.

She felt his hungry response and knew what it meant to hold him in her power.

Then suddenly, without warning, she was no longer the aggressor. One of his hands slid upward to tangle in the dark abundance of her hair. His lips swept back and forth against hers. And then his tongue was delving more intimately— probing, exploring, curling sensually against hers. Her moan of pleasure was lost in the mingling of their breath.

It felt so right to be with him again—so perfect. Something she had kept tightly protected within her spirit unfurled.

When his lips left hers, it was to blaze a random, almost frantic path across her face—finding her cheeks, her nose, her closed eyelids in rapid succession before returning to the welcoming sweetness of her mouth.

Elena's head swam. Darts of pleasure prickled through her body. An eternity of longing had been swept away in the warm circle of his arms.

"Stephen, Stephen, *mi amor*," she murmured. The last time he had held her close like this, they had been stealing forbidden fruit, and she had been terrified of discovery. Now there were no barriers. She was to be his wife. With a joyful freedom she had never known before, she angled her body toward him and pressed closer. Her breasts were flattened against the hard wall of his chest, sending another hot wave of sensation through her body.

Stephen's hands moved urgently up and down her back, then settled at her waist. In the next moment they had slipped under the hem of her knit top. When he encountered the satiny flesh of her back, he groaned again. For Elena the gesture was startlingly intimate. She shivered, feeling the imprint of every finger like a brand of possession.

She had been right! It had been years since they had seen each other, but nothing important had changed between them. She remembered his words. *It was meant to be like this between us.* She had only to show him that her feelings hadn't changed, and he would do the same.

The realization made her bolder. She allowed herself to acknowledge how greedy she was for the hair-roughened texture of his forearms, the muscular solidity of his shoulders. Her fingers crept upward and under the short sleeves of his shirt, stroking and caressing.

She felt a shudder of response seize his body. Then abruptly, he was roughly pushing her away.

Her eyes snapped open. She was dizzy, disoriented as she stared up into his eyes. They had darkened to navy—the color of the sky before a thunderstorm. And they looked down at her with emotions she was afraid to name.

"What are you trying to do, drive me crazy?" he accused her.

In an instant he had catapulted her from bliss into confusion.

"And who the hell taught you to kiss like that?"

"I—I don't understand."

"That wide-eyed expression is very pretty. But you must admit you're quite a bit more adept than the last time we met in your father's garden." He shrugged. "It's been a long time. I guess I should have expected you wouldn't be quite so naive."

Her own anger rose to meet his. "How dare you say such a thing to me! Since you left my father's house I've been living more like a—a—nun than anything else."

"Do you expect me to believe that? After such a passionate kiss?"

"Believe what you want." She stood and faced him, her hands on her hips. "I was doing exactly what *you* taught me the night before you left the hacienda."

CHAPTER FOUR

HE OPENED HIS MOUTH to speak again, but she didn't want to hear any more of what he had to say. Turning, she dashed up the path, almost bumping into Maggie, who was in the garden gathering sprigs of cilantro.

"I thought for dinner you'd like my—" she started to say. When she caught sight of Elena's expression, the half-finished sentence died.

The younger woman averted her face and rushed past. Once inside the house, she took the stairs to the second floor two at a time. When she reached the sanctuary of her bedroom, she pulled the door closed and stood leaning against the thick wood. She was trembling.

She had been angry. Now, eyes squeezed shut, she fought to contain her tears. But the effort was futile. This afternoon she had offered Stephen her love, and he had hurled it back into her face like an Oriental warlord refusing tribute.

The stinging rejection was more than she could take. Ever since the shock of that first meeting in his office she'd felt under emotional siege—struggling to fight back loneliness, despair, anger and fear. Like grenadiers storming a fortress, they had finally broken through her defenses. She wasn't just reacting to what had happened in the gazebo— she was reacting to everything that had happened since she'd arrived. With a little sob, she threw herself onto the bed.

Giving in to the feelings had a cleansing effect. As the tears subsided, her mind grew calm. She felt renewed and almost peaceful, the way she did when she breathed the newly washed air after a torrential storm.

Finally Elena rolled over, plucked a tissue from the box on the bedside table, and blew her nose.

What did she fear most? she asked herself, and answered the question with painful honesty. Five years was a long time to cling to a memory. Since Stephen had departed, she had built up his likeness in her mind. It wasn't just the exterior of the man, but the soul. That image was engraved upon her heart. But suppose it *was* just a fantasy, a product of her own needs and desires?

The terrible possibility brought a clogging sensation to her throat. Closing her eyes, she forced herself to take a deep breath. There was no need to panic—to base any judgments on what had just happened between them. Stephen had been badly hurt. Not just physically but mentally. His body had been shattered, and along with it his image of himself.

But he wasn't a man who was used to letting someone else share his secret fears. She had to give him time. And that was what she needed, too. She hadn't wanted to admit it, but he was right. It was better if the two of them didn't rush into marriage until they understood each other better.

She might not know Stephen very well. But they were living under the same roof. She would have the opportunity to get to know him. No, she would *make* the opportunity.

And what if she found that things would never work out between them? The question sent an icy spasm through her body, and she wrapped her arms around her shoulders. Well, she had learned that she possessed a core of inner strength. If there was to be no marriage between herself and

Stephen, she would make a life for herself in her new country.

Elena swung her legs off the bed and stood up, shaking back her rich, dark hair and smoothing it with long, graceful fingers.

She could stay in her room and brood. Or she could go up to her studio and work. She chose the latter—sketching the view of the mountains outside the window as the shadow of the setting sun turned their steep slopes from light brown to deep purple. Color was one of her specialties. As she worked, she pictured the hues she would use when she turned the sketch into a painting. Alizarin crimson, viridian green, ultramarine, manganese violet. Skillfully blended, they would create a thing of beauty—the magnificence of nature transferred to canvas.

Sometime during the late afternoon, Maggie left a tray of food on a small table outside the door. Elena brought it into the studio and ate a bit of the chicken salad and fruit before setting to work again.

THE NEXT MORNING, Elena dressed in a raw silk skirt and matching blouse and made her way downstairs for breakfast before eight. Maggie was just taking a batch of golden-brown biscuits from the oven.

"Buenos días," Elena greeted her with determined cheerfulness.

The housekeeper's wrinkled face visibly relaxed. "Good morning to you, too."

Elena inhaled the tantalizing aroma of the bread hot from the oven. "Those smell delicious."

"I was hoping you'd like them."

"Can I help you with anything?"

"I've got things under control," the housekeeper replied.

"So do I."

Maggie shot her a surprised look and then gestured toward the coffee maker on the counter. "Pour yourself a mug and sit down."

Elena carried her coffee to the table. "Thank you so much for bringing me dinner. That was very thoughtful."

"I figured you might not want to be interrupted."

"Exactly." Her tone of voice warned that yesterday's encounter with Stephen in the garden wasn't a subject for discussion.

Maggie turned away and busily washed out the mixing bowl.

Elena took a sip of coffee. It was very hot—and very strong. "This is wonderful, too. We drink it like this at home."

"That's the way Stephen likes it. He used to call it my high-octane brew."

"I beg your pardon?"

After Maggie explained the joke, the two women lapsed into silence again. Elena toyed with a biscuit. Finally she cleared her throat. "I was hoping I could borrow Hal for a trip into town."

"If he can't do it, one of the ranch hands will be available. Do you want to do some shopping?" Maggie asked brightly. "That always cheers me up."

"No. I thought I might start investigating some of the local art galleries, to see where I could place my work."

"Sell your pictures? But why?"

"I may need the money."

"Elena, I can't believe..."

"But you don't know for sure. And neither do I." Elena pushed back her chair. "Where can I find a phone book? I'd like to start looking up the addresses."

Maggie capitulated in the face of the younger woman's resolve. "They're in the oak chest in the library. I'll help you figure out which places would be most convenient."

"Bien."

It turned out that Hal had been planning a trip into Santa Barbara to pick up some supplies for the ranch office. At nine-thirty he pulled Stephen's Lincoln around to the front of the house.

The short, weather-beaten man was silent until he nosed the car off the freeway. Yet Elena knew he had been glancing back at her in the rearview mirror. Finally he cleared his throat. "You know, you just lit here a couple of days ago. Isn't it rushing things to be going off on your own like this?"

"I suspect you've been talking to Maggie."

Hal didn't answer, but the red flush that spread across the back of his neck told her that she had been the subject of a discussion.

For his benefit as well as her own, she strove to project an air of confidence. "The sooner I become comfortable with my new home the better, don't you think?"

Hal sighed. "Yeah, I suppose so. But at least let me give you a little tour of the city before I let you off—so you'll know your way around."

"All right."

"I figure we can start on the mesa. Up there you'll get a good view of the whole area."

As Hal pulled into an overlook, Elena couldn't help responding to the setting. The mountains curved around the eastern edge of the small city, holding it in a lover's embrace. To the west was the blue of the Pacific, sparkling in the sunlight. Her eyes misted as she thought about Stephen growing up in such an idyllic place.

As if he had read her thoughts, Hal drove down toward the ocean, where pleasure craft bobbing in the blue water of the marina gave way to miles of sandy beach. "Steve used to come down here all the time with his father," he volunteered.

"Were Stephen and his father close?"

Hal stared thoughtfully at the traffic in front of him as he turned the car landward. "They did a lot of things together. Riding. Sailing. Fishing. Hiking. He made sure Steve could handle himself on the ranch from the time he was a boy. And he gave him responsibilities in the family business while he was still in college. Steve looked up to the old man. But his dad was—" he paused "—demanding."

"How do you mean?"

"Only the best was good enough for him. With his ranch. With his business. With his son."

"Oh."

Elena hoped that Hal would elaborate. When he didn't, she sensed that he might feel he had said too much. Instead of asking more questions, Elena turned her attention to the window again. They were in the heart of town now. The architecture was predominantly Spanish, with many buildings in the grand Moorish style. There were fountains and islands of greenery everywhere.

Hal pointed toward a used bookstore. "Steve had a lot of other interests besides the outdoors—like old books. He used to come down here every few months, right up until the—" Hal abruptly stopped speaking.

"I don't mind if you mention the accident."

"Well, I don't like to talk about it much. It was a tragedy for a man like Steve." Elena heard the anguish in his voice. Like Maggie, he cared, and he didn't know what to do about it.

"He needs to understand that his injuries don't make us feel any differently about him," Elena suggested.

"I reckon he doesn't give a damn about my opinion, if you'll pardon the straight talk. Maybe not even yours. It's what he thinks about himself that counts. And he thinks he's not the man he was."

"Do you blame me for what happened?" she asked suddenly.

Hal's head whipped around. In the next moment a car horn blared and he slammed on the brakes. "Sorry. What did you say?"

"I think Maggie may have secretly blamed me. Although I'm not sure she admitted it to herself."

"Yeah. I was angry with you at first, too. I guess for a while I sort of blamed this person named Elena Castile, who didn't think Stephen Gallagher was good enough to marry her. I needed to lash out at someone."

"I—"

"You don't have to explain. Later on I heard about your father." Hal turned around again. "If I haven't made it clear, I'm damn glad you're here."

"Thank you." *And pray God it works out,* she thought. But she didn't voice the words.

They rode for a few moments in silence. As they passed a small art gallery, Elena consulted the list Maggie had given her. "This is one of the places I want to visit."

"Elena, you've proved you've got guts. But are you sure you don't want to just come pick up those supplies with me and head back to the ranch?"

"No. I will stick with the original plan."

Bowing to her determination, Hal pulled up in front of El Paseo, a walled enclave of shops and restaurants built around a courtyard and a series of narrow, winding walkways. The whole thing might have been lifted out of an ancient Spanish city.

"This is really quite charming," Elena murmured.

"One of the tourist traps. There's a bunch of galleries inside. And I've heard the courtyard is a nice place for lunch—if you like rabbit food and quiche."

"Rabbit food is . . . salad?"

"You're learning." The older man smiled.

Elena consulted her watch. "Could you pick me up here at one?"

"Okay."

Elena opened the car door and stepped out, carrying the picture of Stephen that she had brought from home. She had no intention of selling it. But besides a few unfinished sketches and the landscape in Stephen's office, it was the only example of her work available.

"You've got the phone number of the ranch in case you need it?"

"Yes. But I'll be all right. *¡Hasta luego!*"

Still, as Elena watched the large black car drive away, she had to swallow a surge of panic. She was really on her own. Then she reminded herself how important this expedition was. Not only would she be introducing herself to local art dealers, but she would also have a chance to judge the caliber of the other artists in the area and find out what subjects were already overdone.

It took Elena about two hours to make a survey of the eight establishments within comfortable walking distance. At the first, she was so nervous under the scrutiny of the sharp-eyed proprietor that her Latin accent thickened and she actually forgot a few English words. It wasn't a good way to start things off, and she might have let discouragement overwhelm her. Instead she left with renewed determination.

Her second experience, at a gallery that specialized in local artists, was much less traumatic. The manager was impressed with the picture of Stephen. Although she couldn't promise anything from seeing one sample, she invited Elena to come back with more—both portraits and landscapes. Elena wafted out of the store on a cloud of optimism.

The fourth place she tried was an elegant gallery near the art museum. The owner was a casually but expensively dressed man in his mid-thirties, who eyed her a bit too appreciatively and introduced himself as Tom Mitchell. To Elena's discomfort, he recognized the subject of the picture.

"Say, that's Steve Gallagher, isn't it?"

Elena nodded cautiously, wondering why she hadn't anticipated that this might happen.

"A good likeness. How do you know him?"

"Are you a friend of his?" She answered the question with one of her own.

"I used to run into Steve at the horse shows out at Earl Warren Fairgrounds—and the society parties. He was also on a couple of fund-raising committees with me," Mitchell related with the enthusiasm of a man out to prove his credentials with the "in" set. "I haven't seen him around lately. Heard he had an accident."

"Yes."

"So how's he doing?"

"Much better."

"Glad to hear that." The rejoinder was mechanical. "Tell him Fiesta wasn't the same this year without him," Mitchell added, referring to the annual festival that, Elena had read, gave Santa Barbarans and tourists alike an excuse for dancing in the streets and similar revelry. "Last year he rode in the parade. Cut quite a figure in his Spanish outfit on that black stallion of his. The women loved it."

"Yes, well—"

"Damn shame about Steve. The rumor is that he's crippled now."

The casually delivered remark made Elena blanch. "That's not true. Stephen is recovering nicely."

"Well, you know how it is when someone disappears from the scene the way he did."

"No, I don't know how it is." Elena's voice was icy. Picking up the painting, she turned abruptly and hurried out the door. Once on the sidewalk, she stood for a moment, sucking in great lungfuls of air and wishing she could hurry straight back to the ranch.

As it turned out, she was glad she hadn't been able to cut her expedition short. Her best experience was at a gallery called La Paloma owned by a small, neat man with a carefully trimmed mustache and a carnation in his lapel. His name was Miles Henderson. When Elena told him she was new in town, he confided that he himself had moved down from San Luis Obispo less than a year before, because his wife eventually wanted to retire in Santa Barbara.

"Real estate's going up all the time. Margaret was right. It's a good thing we bought now."

Elena nodded.

"You'll love it here."

"I hope so."

"Where are you from?"

"Venezuela."

"Ah. Then you come from a rich artistic tradition. I'm a great admirer of Armando Reveron." He named Venezuela's most famous impressionist, who had used tropical lighting effects in his canvases to make people and objects seem to float in a warm haze.

"I have studied his work."

"How about Carlos Cruz Diaz and Hector Poleo?"

"Of course."

They chatted for a few more minutes about recent artistic trends in Latin America. Elena was pleased and surprised by the man's friendly warmth—and by how well versed he was in the culture of her country.

Finally he turned to the picture of Stephen again. "This is really very good." He tapped a long finger against his lips. "I am taking on a few new clients. Why don't you leave this portrait with me?"

"I'm sorry. It's not for sale. But I can come back with others in a few weeks."

"Then I'll look forward to seeing more of your work."

On the way back to El Paseo Elena passed a shop that sold artists' supplies. Although Stephen had equipped her studio superbly, he hadn't known that she was going to be producing a number of small- and medium-sized pictures. Perhaps she could buy the stretchers and canvas and pick them up after lunch. She opened the door of the shop and went inside.

After completing her transaction, she looked around with interest at the variety of products and materials for sale. She was thumbing through a rack of sketchbooks when she noticed that someone was staring at her from the other side of the store. Her artist's eye took in his appearance in a series of quick impressions. His sun-weathered features were rugged and not quite symmetrical. His hair needed cutting, and his clothing was mismatched, as though he had gotten dressed by pulling a random shirt and pair of slacks out of his closet. Unnerved by direct scrutiny from such a rough-looking stranger, Elena quickly glanced back at the sketchbooks.

A few moments later, when she looked again in his direction, she found his deep-set hazel eyes were still fixed on her.

To her consternation, he seemed to take her second glance as an invitation.

"Pardon me," he said, coming across the shop. "I couldn't help noticing that wonderful picture you have there. Did you paint it?"

Elena nodded tightly, noting that his pleasant tenor voice was at odds with his appearance.

"I was, uh, wondering if you might have time to talk to me for a few minutes."

Such presumption was unheard of at home. "I'm afraid not."

"Please."

Elena folded her arms across her chest, feeling suddenly alone and vulnerable.

"I'm looking for someone to give my daughter art lessons. Someone with sensitivity. Someone really good."

Sensitivity? Art lessons? This man was interested in art? That was the last thing she would have expected from someone like him. But if that was all he really wanted, why didn't he get in touch with the art department at the local university?

"I'm afraid I wouldn't be interested," she murmured, her ingrained politeness keeping her voice even.

"Please, let me take just a few more minutes of your time."

"I'm afraid not." She had already started to back away.

"Look, I know I'm handling this all wrong. I'm sorry."

"Yes." The encounter was something completely outside her experience. Heart thumping, Elena turned quickly and made her escape through the door to the street. Her hands were trembling as she started walking rapidly toward El Paseo, wishing that Hal had somehow decided to pick her up early. But he was nowhere in sight.

Still, the now-familiar old-world enclave felt like a sanctuary. Glancing nervously over her shoulder, Elena made sure that the stranger wasn't behind her. To her relief, she saw only a young couple walking hand in hand along the narrow passageway.

Selecting a table under an orange tree, she sat down and ordered a seafood salad and a glass of iced tea. By the time the tea arrived, she was feeling calmer. The fountain in the middle of the patio reminded her of the one back home at her father's hacienda. On the other side of the patio a strolling guitarist struck up a familiar Latin tune, and she smiled, unexpectedly glad that Hal had suggested this place for lunch.

Elena had just forked up a bite of crabmeat, when the rough-looking man from the art shop stepped out of a covered passageway. Elena dropped her fork to her plate with a clatter and jumped up. Then she had to bend down again to pick up her purse and the painting.

Despite the man's appearance, something about the pleading look in his hazel eyes kept her from turning and running.

He glanced down at his rumpled plaid shirt. "Damn, I wish I'd dressed better this morning. I know I look like a mess. I'm sorry to be so pushy," he continued apologetically. "But I know you're the kind of person who could help Jenny."

"Did you follow me?"

"Yes."

She started to edge away, wondering why she had been so foolhardy as to let Hal leave her downtown alone.

"Please. I'm not going to hurt you. My name is Bill Delaney. I—I should have told you I'm an acquaintance of Steve's."

She stared at him in stunned silence. Another person in town who had recognized Stephen's picture. She should never have brought it down here!

"He was in the rehabilitation hospital when my daughter Jenny was there. And I'd met him before. That portrait shows the way he looked a few years ago."

Elena nodded in silent acknowledgment, too stunned to move.

"The portrait. You're very talented . . . and you understand people."

"I—"

"My daughter needs someone like you to give her art lessons."

"But surely there are plenty of well-qualified artists in Santa Barbara who could do that, Mr. Delaney. I'm not even a teacher."

He ran a large hand through his shaggy hair. "Let me tell you about Jenny." His words tumbled out like a confession. "She's fourteen. She was in a rock-climbing accident last year. She's going to be in a wheelchair for a long time— maybe forever." He swallowed convulsively. "She's a good artist. And I want her to develop her talent. But it's going to take the right person to help her do it."

The man caught Elena's incredulous expression. "You don't have to say anything now. Just think about it. Okay? Let me give you my card."

This man had a business card?

Not only did he have one, but it was expensive-looking and printed on heavy beige stock. The card was so out of keeping with his appearance that after he pressed it into her hand, Elena stared at it for a moment without seeing the words printed in distinctive brown letters. She didn't know what he did for a living and she didn't want to know. Automatically she slipped the small rectangle into the pocket of her skirt.

"Think about it. And I won't bother you anymore this afternoon."

Before she could say anything else, he turned and hurried out of the courtyard.

Elena sat down again, her eyes glued to the walkway where he had disappeared. It was several minutes before she could think about eating the rest of the food on her plate. But the guitarist's Latin music had a soothing effect on her jangled nerves once more.

She would have liked to forget about Bill Delaney and simply enjoy her lunch. But she couldn't push him out of her mind. Was the man a typical *norteamericano*? Was he driven to such behavior by desperation—or guilt? Perhaps that was the case. Strong emotions sometimes made people do things that were completely out of character.

But there was another consideration as well. Did he really know Stephen? Or had he just seen him in the hospital and made the connection with the picture? The thought was unsettling. But whatever the case, she suspected that she didn't want to get involved with the man.

CHAPTER FIVE

THE LARGE BLACK LINCOLN reappeared exactly on time.

"Well, how did it go?" Hal asked as Elena climbed into the back seat.

She had regained enough of her equanimity to murmur, "Very well."

"Glad to hear it." He sounded relieved and pleased.

"I made some purchases. Would it be all right if we picked them up?"

"Sure."

The mention of the art store made Elena think of Bill Delaney. She decided not to talk to Hal about the strange incident.

After they had picked up the canvases, she told him about the successful interviews, surprised at her own need to inform him about her day. Perhaps it was because she was feeling proud of her accomplishments. Or perhaps it was because she knew Stephen wouldn't be waiting to greet her when she arrived back at the ranch.

"So most of them treated you pretty well," Hal summed up.

"Yes. But there is one man I didn't particularly like. Tom Mitchell."

"Mitchell. Don't tell me that creep's into art now?"

"You know him?"

"Only from what Steve used to say about him. An ass ki—" He stopped abruptly.

"What?"

Hal laughed. "That's one American idiom I'm not going to teach you. Let's just call him a, uh, status seeker. He didn't give you any problems, did he?"

"No. Not really. I just didn't think he was very nice."

"He isn't. You probably want to stay away from him. So, did you get any ideas about what you're going to paint?" Hal changed the subject.

"Well, not Mission Santa Barbara. And not the courthouse. I saw dozens of those. And seascapes. I think I'll stick with the garden and the mountain scenery around the ranch—and try some portraits."

The favorable reaction to the painting of Stephen had given Elena a needed boost. She had gone into town, wondering if her work would win a good reception. Now she felt as if she had a definite goal. She was full of energy that afternoon. First she took her sketchbook out to the front patio and worked on some scenes that would translate into small, intimate landscapes.

There were also the new sketches she had drawn of Stephen. She intended to turn at least one of them into a painting, too. But for the time being she put that project aside. Working on a picture of Stephen was simply too painful.

It was late afternoon when Elena finally put her tablet and pencils away and went to her room. She had intended to relax and read for a while before dinner, but the sound of breaking glass from the patio below caught her attention. It was followed by a muttered curse.

The voice was Stephen's, and Elena was drawn to the window. Without adjusting the half-opened shutters, she had a good view of the area below. Stephen, dressed in a short terry robe, had apparently been maneuvering his wheelchair to the edge of the swimming pool. One of the wheels must have knocked over and broken a tumbler left beside a chaise lounge. Jagged shards of glass lay in a semi-circle around the chair.

Maggie had also heard the crash. In a moment she came hurrying through the French doors to the patio. "Let me move you away from there, before you cut yourself," she offered.

"My arms still work. I can do it myself," Stephen snapped, jerking on the chair wheel. It spun backward, crashing into another of the chaise lounges. He winced, then cursed again.

From her vantage point, Elena pressed her flattened hand against her mouth. Probably Stephen had jarred his injured leg. She could imagine that it hurt badly. She could also imagine his frustration.

¡Dios mío! What twisted logic could have convinced her father to hide this from her? she wondered. How could he have been so insensitive, so shortsighted? He had been afraid she wouldn't want to marry Stephen if she knew about his injuries. He hadn't realized that Stephen might reject *her*, because she hadn't come here under the terms he'd specified.

She was aware now that Stephen had been watching carefully for her reaction when she first came into his office. And her shocked expression must have cut him like the hot pain of a razor-sharp knife. If only she'd had time to prepare herself! Or was that just wishful thinking? Maggie had had plenty of time to prepare herself for dealing with Stephen—and that didn't seem to make things any easier.

Fathers, she thought bitterly. Hers and Stephen's. If only they'd thought about what they were doing to their children. Or maybe they hadn't cared.

Her own father had needed obedience from those around him. Sometimes he'd made his will felt through subtle pressure. If you did what he wanted without an argument, life was tolerable, even pleasant. If you defied him, you were almost always sorry later. Her mother had tried to stand up to him at first. But he'd made her life miserable, and finally she'd left the ranch for good.

When Eduardo Castile had lost his fortune, it had only gotten worse. With no more real power, he'd been desperate to prove that he still counted for something. Elena had understood his anguish. Despite everything, she'd tried to help him cope. But he hadn't been able to accept her solace. That was part of the reason she knew she wasn't going back—no matter what the circumstances. She'd decided that, even before she'd walked into Stephen's office and discovered just how Machiavellian her father had been.

She shook her head. From what Hal had said, she guessed Stephen's father probably hadn't been as bad. But he'd set rigid standards for himself. And he'd taught his son to demand too much from himself. That had been hard on him even when he'd been in superb physical shape. Now he couldn't even walk, and a simple trip from his bedroom to the swimming pool was a major undertaking. No wonder he couldn't cope with that kind of life.

Elena watched Maggie adjust her expression. Ignoring Stephen's outburst and making no further attempt to help him, she calmly went back into the house and reappeared a few moments later with a brush and dustpan.

"Don't walk barefoot on this side of the patio," she admonished as she began to sweep up the glass.

"Oh, I won't. Haven't you noticed I'm not walking anywhere?" His voice dripped with sarcasm.

Maggie blanched. Instead of answering, she bent and began cleaning up the glass as quickly as possible.

When Maggie finally turned to go back into the house, Stephen stared after her for a few minutes, his hands clutching the arms of his chair so tightly that the knuckles stood out in bloodless relief. Then he glanced toward his room, as if debating whether to give up the afternoon's expedition and go back inside. Instead he sighed with weary resignation before looking around to make sure there were no other obstacles in his way.

Elena's fingers gripped the windowsill as she continued to peer through the half-open shutter. As Stephen maneuvered himself quickly along the edge of the pool, his right side was turned toward her. She couldn't see the scars on the left side of his face or his injured left leg.

A long time ago she had stopped torturing herself with thoughts of what might have been or what could have happened in her life. But now, just for a moment, she allowed herself to wish away the terrible injuries. My God! If her father had allowed them to marry in the first place, none of this would have happened.

But there was no point in hungering after what might have been. The real question was whether Stephen could come to terms with the way things were now.

Elena watched as he undid the terry robe and draped it over the back of the chair. He had made it clear in the gym how he felt about her looking at his partially clothed body. Now she told herself she should move away from the window and go about her own business. Her feet didn't obey the command.

Much of the patio area was now in shade. But the rays of the afternoon sun slanted onto the concrete at the far side of the pool. Stephen had maneuvered himself into that patch of warmth and brilliance. Because the shadows around him were dark, it was almost as though his body were being set off by a spotlight—like a religious figure in a medieval painting. But, as Elena's heartbeat began to quicken, she acknowledged that her thoughts were far from religious.

She had never seen Stephen with so little on, but during the time they had been separated, Elena had pictured him like this. Having studied the human form as part of her training in technique, she had been well equipped to speculate. The superbly developed musculature of his chest and shoulders was what she had imagined. Somehow she hadn't been prepared for the thick mat of hair that swirled across his chest and tapered to a dark line that drew her eye down to his black bathing trunks. They emphasized his narrow waist, lean hips and obvious masculinity.

There was a metal bar above his head, supported by two wooden posts. Grasping it, he pulled himself up and out of the wheelchair in a quick, easy motion.

As he stood supported by the bar, Elena had an even better view than in the gym of the scars that crisscrossed his left leg like a road map. And she could see some others that had previously been hidden by his shirt. One slashed across his abdomen, and another tunneled through the hair of his chest and disappeared around his left side. The scars told more eloquently than words just what Stephen had been through. That he had made so much progress already was a testimony to his fortitude and courage.

As Elena watched in fascination, he arched his back and the focus of her attention shifted. The sun had painted the red highlights in his hair with glints of crimson and burnished the skin of his shoulders. The muscles of his chest and arms rippled as he flexed them. On another occasion they would surely have commanded her attention. This afternoon she was much more conscious of his lower body. His posture had stretched the knit fabric of his bathing suit tightly across a swelling in the front.

Elena sucked in a sharp breath. It was impossible to take her eyes from that provocatively virile raised outline. How would Stephen look completely unclothed? she wondered.

She had never thought about his body in such explicitly sexual terms. But as she secretly stared down at him, she felt the blood begin to rush hotly in her veins. She shivered, remembering the feel of his man's embrace—hard and warm and exciting.

She closed her eyes, too abashed to look at him anymore, but couldn't keep a host of sensations from flashing back—from that night so long ago and from yesterday, when she and Stephen had kissed in the garden. In her imagination she knew again the heady taste of the man she loved. There had been open hunger in his kiss, and she had responded to it.

As she relived the experience, she flicked out her delicate pink tongue and stroked it along the curve of her own lip.

"Stephen," she whispered. His name was a shaky plea.

The ache of longing brought her to a new level of awareness. She remembered the crisp texture of the hair on his forearms. Did that thick hair on his chest feel the same way? she wondered dreamily, her fingers flexing in anticipation.

She had never felt quite this way before. She didn't know what was happening to her. But suddenly it seemed as though she had awakened from a long, dreamless sleep. Every pulse point was pounding to life, demanding a response that she didn't know how to satisfy.

Feeling utterly vulnerable, she called his name again—this time more loudly. Like a hidden spring bubbling to the surface, she felt her love for Stephen welling up inside her. Silently she acknowledged that she wanted—needed—to belong to him in every sense that a woman could belong to a man. Now she didn't know if that love would ever be fulfilled.

The realization was almost too much to bear. Without warning, her knees turned to rubber. As she swayed forward, she grabbed the window ledge to steady herself.

When she finally opened her eyes again, Stephen was sitting on the side of the pool, his feet dangling in the water. With a stern admonition, she kept her mind from straying as it had a moment ago. It was much safer to concentrate on Stephen's legs as he kicked up little splashes of water. Droplets had caught in the dark hairs of his calves and thighs, reflecting the sunbeams in tiny flashes of light.

She had noticed the state of his left leg in the gym. Was it her imagination that it seemed a bit better this afternoon? He was putting so much effort into getting well. How long would it be before he was able to walk?

As she watched, he flattened the palms of his hands against the concrete and levered himself into the turquoise water.

When he took several steps along the side of the pool, the change was instantaneous and almost miraculous. On land he had been forced to hold himself up with the strength of his arms and shoulders. In the water he didn't appear handicapped at all. It was impossible to tell that one leg wasn't bending fully, because the fluid motion of the water around him cushioned all his movements. She watched as he exercised the injured limb for several minutes. When he was satisfied, he kicked off and began to stroke slowly through the water.

While the left leg didn't churn up water with nearly the force of the right, the difference was not terribly important. It was obvious that he was a strong swimmer. He cut through the water with a natural grace, reached the far end of the pool and turned to start back. She felt herself smile. He looked strong and virile and very much at home in his environment.

"Beautiful," she murmured in appreciation, for the first time daring to hope that he might make something close to a full recovery.

She wanted to rush out of her room, hurry down the stairs and join him beside the pool. She wanted to tell him of her joy at seeing him like this—of her confidence in his returning abilities. Then she remembered the cold look he'd given her when she'd first gone into the gym. If he hadn't liked her watching him then, he certainly wouldn't appreciate her observing him uninvited now.

She was coming to grips with that, when a far more distressing thought struck her. She knew from Maggie that he had set a timetable for his recovery. He hadn't met it. He had wanted to be on his feet when she arrived. When he finally walked, would it be too late for the two of them? Would he already have become too bitter?

As she stared down at him, torn between conflicting emotions, Stephen came to a stop at the deep end of the pool and rested in the water, his arms moving in lazy circles. He appeared quite tranquil. But the anxiety of her thoughts was too much and she turned quickly away, pulling the shutters firmly closed.

THE MOVEMENT CAUGHT Stephen's attention. His head swung toward her window, and he looked up, his eyes carefully searching the blank expanse of green shutters. When he saw nothing more, he turned and thrust his shoulders into the water again and began to stroke with almost savage intensity.

He hadn't been able to see her behind the closed shutters. But he had felt her staring down at him, as surely as he might have felt the heat of the sun on his face. Then she had called his name, sending a shock wave of desire through his body.

He hadn't known it was possible to want a woman so much that the blood pumped in your veins like molten fire, and the pressure building up inside you was like a volcano ready to erupt. He hadn't wanted to feel that way. Not now. Not when he was like this. At least during the day he had trained himself not to think about the way she had been in his arms—soft and warm and exciting—innocent, yet ripe with untested passion. He had been doing all right. Then she had kissed him in the garden with all the sweetness he'd remembered, and the intensity of his need for her had come slamming back, like a two-ton truck crashing into a stone wall. He hadn't known how to deal with it. So he had struck out in anger at the woman who was the cause of it all—Elena.

He balled his large hand into a fist and pressed it against his lips in an effort to hold back the emotions that were welling up inside. Slowly he brought himself under control.

His father had taught him self-reliance and a respect for men with strength of character. It had seemed a sensible way to live. The idea that he could want another person so much, need another person with such a degree of intensity struck at the very core of his being. The fact that in the end she might turn away from a man with his diminished capacities made him feel as though a sharp knife were twisting in his guts. It was worse than all the physical pain he had endured since the accident.

Over the past five years, he had built up a likeness in his mind of Elena Castile—not just of her exterior, but of her soul. That image was engraved upon his heart. But suppose it was just a fantasy, a product of his own needs and desires? Suppose he was simply fooling himself?

She traveled thousands of miles to marry you. Alone.

Did she have a choice?

She says she loves you.

How could anyone love you now?

She didn't just say the words. She tried to show you. She took you into her arms, and you pushed her away.

Uttering a muffled curse, he pounded the surface of the pool, his fists raising geysers of spray and sending waves slapping against the sides. Then he turned and again began to cut furiously through the water, as though he could outdistance the devil that was chasing him.

CHAPTER SIX

IT MIGHT HAVE SEEMED impossible for two people to live in the same house and not run into each other. But Stephen and Elena managed it. The choice was not hers, and she felt her spirit dying a little from the isolation. She ached to reach out to the man she loved. Yet she sensed his need to distance himself from her for now. If he required time to adjust to her presence here, the best thing she could do was give him that breathing space.

So she looked for other ways to be close to him.

"What do you have there?" Hal asked one afternoon. He had come upon Elena sitting under an ironwood tree with a worn volume open in her lap. She held up a copy of *A Connecticut Yankee in King Arthur's Court* for him to see.

"How did you settle on that?" the ranch foreman asked quizzically.

"It looked like *someone* had read it. I was hoping it was Stephen."

Hal brushed back a gray lock of hair with a callused hand and leaned against the fence rail. "Oh, he read it all right. Under protest."

"Are you going to tell me the story?"

"Mmm-hmm." He grinned as he remembered the incident. "Steve was supposed to do a report on it in high school. But he told me he thought it was the dumbest book he ever read. So, instead of working on the assignment, he came down to the stable to ride Storm Dancer." Hal paused for effect. "The old man caught him. Grounded him for a month as punishment. And before you ask, 'grounded' doesn't mean buried. It means 'confined to quarters.'"

"I see."

"Why are you looking so relieved?" Hal questioned.

Now it was Elena's turn to grin. "Because I was hating the book—and hoping that it wasn't something Stephen had liked."

Maggie, too, was a source of stories about Stephen's childhood. Sometimes they talked while Elena helped the housekeeper prepare dinner.

With fine attention to lovingly remembered detail, she told Elena about the tree house he'd built with scrap lumber, the prizewinning heifer he'd raised, and the speeding ticket he'd borrowed the money from her to pay—so his father wouldn't find out.

"Was he afraid of his father?" Elena asked.

Maggie put down the potato she was peeling and looked out the window toward the distant mountains. "Not afraid. I guess he never liked to disappoint the old man."

The comment confirmed what Hal had told her earlier.

Other times, Maggie made an effort to focus Elena's attention elsewhere. And since she had lived all her life near Santa Barbara, she was genuinely awed by tales of Elena's travels.

"Which did you like better, the Louvre or the Prado?" she inquired one afternoon as they both sat sipping tea at the kitchen table.

Elena thought for a moment. "It's hard to compare them. The Louvre has a broader collection—more sculpture and even some furniture. But the Prado has more paintings. Of course, the Louvre has the *Mona Lisa*," she added. "But the Prado has Goya and El Greco, except that you have to go to Toledo, where he lived, to see some of his most famous paintings.''

Maggie shook her head. ''What a life you have. There aren't many people who can casually make that kind of comparison.''

''I guess I never thought it was anything special. Travel was just something my father thought was important for my art education.''

The story Maggie liked best came from London. Elena and her duenna had been shopping at Harrods and were meeting her father at the nearby Victoria and Albert Museum.

''Since we weren't going to have too much time at the museum, I asked one of the guards what we should see,'' Elena related. ''He told me not to miss the 'spice' exhibit.''

Maggie lifted a questioning eyebrow.

Elena grinned. ''I was expecting jars of cinnamon and cloves, and I must have looked dubious, because he said, 'You know, the rocket ships and the satellites.' ''

Maggie burst out laughing. ''I guess he had a real cockney accent.''

''He certainly did.''

It didn't take long for the two women to get to know and like each other. And Maggie played a big part in introducing Elena to the conventions of American life.

''I see we're almost out of flour,'' she observed one morning as she put away her baking supplies. ''And we also need milk, eggs and fresh vegetables. Want to come to the store with me?''

''I'd like that.''

The supermarket was large and modern, and completely out of Elena's experience. ''I thought it was a store for groceries,'' she remarked. ''Why do they sell patio chairs and linens? And there's a whole aisle full of cosmetics.''

Maggie laughed. "Good old American enterprise. The management is hoping the shoppers will buy them along with their sugar and bananas."

"I didn't expect to find so many of the things I like to cook with," Elena observed as she set a package of black beans in the shopping cart.

"Oh, we're pretty progressive here in California."

"You're teasing me."

Maggie struggled to repress a grin. "Are you going to make soup with those beans?" she asked.

"No, more like stew."

"Sounds interesting."

"Later in the week I'll make my shredded pork with sweet potatoes."

Maggie reached for several cans of green chilies. "Is most Venezuelan cooking hot and spicy?"

"Not really. We use a lot of garlic and cilantro—coriander—for seasoning. And root vegetables with interesting flavors."

As they stood in the checkout line, the conversation inevitably turned to the topic that had been hovering in their thoughts that morning. "My cooking is getting in a rut," Maggie remarked. "When I ask Stephen what to fix, he says he doesn't care."

"What did he use to ask for?"

"He always loved my spaghetti sauce. And my barbecued ribs." She paused for a minute. "And apricot tart for dessert."

"You stay with the cart. I'll go back and get some apricots. This afternoon you can teach me how to make it."

Maggie took a different route home so she could stop at the farmers' market for some additional produce. As they passed a row of shops on Hollister, Elena looked up in surprise as the name Delaney's Outfitters leaped out at her. She was reminded of Bill.

"What kind of store is an outfitter's?" she asked Maggie.

"Camping gear. Mountain climbing equipment. Stephen used to shop there." She paused and shook her head. "The owner, Bill Delaney, has had some bad times, too. His daughter, Jenny, was injured in a climbing accident about the same time Stephen was hurt. They were out alone in the Sierra Nevada. Bill had to carry her out himself. The rehabilitation hospital isn't very big. I used to see them there when I'd visit Stephen. Bill would take Jenny out on the patio in her wheelchair."

"Bill Delaney started a conversation with me when I was in town a few days ago. He said he knew Stephen and that he wanted me to give his daughter art lessons."

"I can bet he didn't make a very good impression. I always thought he looked like he'd just climbed out of a rumpled sleeping bag with his clothes on."

"That's a good description."

"But under that unkempt exterior he's—" Maggie was clearly searching for the right words "—a good person. You ought to have seen him up at the hospital with Jenny. He was always bringing her some funny little present to try to cheer her up. What did you tell him?"

"I said I'd have to think about it, but I was sure I didn't want to have anything more to do with him. It was such a strange experience. He just came up and started talking to me. Perhaps you can tell me some more about him."

"Well, he was pretty broken up about his daughter. Blames himself for the accident, although it sounded to me like bad luck rather than negligence."

Maggie filled her in on more details. Bill Delaney was divorced, and Jenny had been a big part of his life for a number of years.

"Perhaps I should reconsider," the young woman mused.

"You'd be wonderful for Jenny. And it would be good for you to get to know some other people in town."

That afternoon, Elena retrieved the business card from the skirt pocket where she'd stuffed it. When she called, Bill Delaney wasn't home, but the woman who answered the phone said she'd give him the message.

She expected the man to get back to her that day, but he didn't call. Perhaps he had changed his mind. Or perhaps it was best that she not get involved with him, after all.

Putting the Delaneys out of her thoughts, Elena tried to concentrate on her own work. Sometimes she could lose herself in her painting. But that wasn't possible now, not when she had to fight another overpowering emotion—homesickness.

She had wanted to marry Stephen with all her heart. Yet despite her world travels, her father's estate had always been home base. The idea of leaving everything beloved and familiar and traveling thousands of miles alone to a new country had been frightening. She had coped with the anxiety by focusing on the life she would have with Stephen. It would be warm and close and very loving. Even when she had told herself how important it was to develop as a painter, deep down she had longed for a relationship with one special man. When Stephen Gallagher had walked into her life, she'd known that he was that man.

But things were not working out. Stephen's energy was going into fighting his own battles. Elena couldn't begrudge him that. She admired his courage. She even understood why he wouldn't let her help him, although his lack of trust in her hurt. And because he wouldn't reach out to her, she couldn't ask for what she craved from him. That meant her own needs for comfort and reassurance were going begging.

She longed for some familiar touchstone, some link to the life she had left behind. So one morning she dressed in boots and jeans and a flannel shirt and wandered down to the stable.

The low wooden building was a quarter of a mile from the main house. As Elena stepped through the wide door, a smile curved her lips as she felt the straw underfoot and heard the sounds of the horses in their stalls. Even the earthy smells seemed to welcome her. Why hadn't she come down here before? she wondered.

A short, dark man who had been forking clean hay into an empty stall stopped and tipped his hat. "You must be Miss Elena."

"Yes."

He glanced at her scuffed boots and jeans. "Did you just want to have a look around, or do you want to ride one of the horses?"

"I'd love to ride."

"Then I'd better get Hal."

A few moments later, the ranch foreman appeared. "It's good to see you down here," he greeted Elena warmly.

"I was thinking about riding this morning."

"Steve's horse could use a workout. I usually take him out. But I haven't had time for the past few days."

As he spoke, he led her over to a stall containing a sleek black stallion. The big horse tossed his head inquisitively as the newcomer approached.

"Oh, he's beautiful!" she exclaimed, reaching out to stroke the silky muzzle. "What's his name?"

"Storm Dancer."

"Hello, Storm Dancer," she crooned, continuing to gentle the black horse.

He responded with a whinny.

She brought out a carrot from her pocket, broke it in half and offered the larger end to the horse. He took the treat without any hesitation.

"Well, it looks as if you've got him literally eating out of your hand," Hal observed. "Should I have him saddled up?"

Elena smiled as she fed the rest of the carrot to the stallion. "I'd love that, if Stephen wouldn't mind. I know how my father was about his favorite mount. He didn't let anyone else ride him."

"Oh, Steve's not like that. In fact, before you arrived, he told me you'd probably be coming down here. He said you could handle any horse on the ranch."

"He did?" Here was more evidence of how Stephen felt about her—even if he couldn't tell her himself.

Hal sent the stable hand to get a beautifully tooled western saddle from the tack room.

"How many horses does Stephen have?" Elena asked the ranch manager while they waited.

"Fifteen. All excellent stock. Raising and showing them is a sideline of his. If he'd give me the go-ahead, we could have one of the best breeding stables in the state."

Elena couldn't miss the mixture of pride and wistfulness in Hal's voice.

The stable hand interrupted the conversation as he returned with Storm Dancer. A few moments later Elena found herself on the stallion's broad back.

"I'd like to see how you handle him," Hal said.

Elena walked and then trotted the black stallion around the paddock. "You're not going to take Stephen's word for my riding ability, are you?" she questioned.

Hal scuffed his boot against the dirt. "Look, I don't want to smother you, but—"

"I hope not!"

"Sorry, another idiom."

"That must mean 'act overprotective.'"

Hal sighed. "I'd feel pretty rotten if anything happened to you while you're in my charge."

"Of course. I do understand."

"But I reckon you and Storm Dancer are going to get along fine," he pronounced as he opened the gate.

Elena turned in the saddle to look back at him. "What trail should I take?"

"There's one that leads down toward the arroyo and circles back. You might want to try that one."

"¡Muchas gracias!"

With a pleased grin, she urged Stephen's mount out of the stable yard. It felt wonderful to be astride a horse again after so long—and on such an exuberant animal. It made her feel closer to Stephen to be sitting on the strong back of his horse.

Testing Storm Dancer's power and training, she guided him into a trot and then a canter. He responded beautifully, as though the two of them had known each other for years. Elena's grin widened. Since she'd been old enough to sit a horse, she'd loved the joy and freedom of taking out a spirited mount into the countryside. Now she drew in a deep breath of the clean air and tossed back her head, looking up at the feathery clouds floating lazily in the blue sky.

The path ran downward into a small canyon, where pungent bay and eucalyptus trees grew on either side of the trail. Here were huge sandstone boulders, testimony to the landslides that had once helped shape the area. Among the rocks grew a tall stand of fennel and white-plumed pampas grass. Elena slowed Storm Dancer and twisted in the saddle to get a better look, delighted with the rugged beauty of the setting. She would paint this, too.

Her fingers twined themselves in the reins, and she suddenly realized just how much she had missed their familiar feel. From now on riding was going to be a regular part of her routine, she promised herself.

OVER THE NEXT FEW DAYS Elena kept her word, riding Storm Dancer every morning. She also spent a great deal of her time sketching or painting the local landscape. The work went well, she thought, perhaps because she used it as an outlet for her emotions. She was particularly interested in the dense patches of deep pink flowers she could see from her bedroom window. Hal, who had a wide knowledge of the flora in the area, told her they were fireweed.

"Do they get the name from their color?" Elena wanted to know.

"Maybe. But they also like ground that's been burned. We had a brush fire up there in the hills a few years ago," he added.

"So close to the house," Elena murmured.

"Nothin' to worry about. Steve got it under control pretty quickly."

Despite its origin, she couldn't help but be drawn to the beauty of the fireweed. Several times Elena took her easel to the edge of the field and painted the tall, erect plants with their spires of pink flowers. They made a wonderful contrast with the blue of the sky and the earthy color of the hills.

She also began a portrait of Stephen, as he had looked that morning in the gym. It was much too personal a statement for her to take down to the gallery with her other pictures. But working on it gave her the sense of connection with Stephen that she needed.

On Friday she made a second trip into town with Hal, this time to the Department of Motor Vehicles, where she picked up the study booklet for the written driver's test. If one of her goals was independence, she didn't want to ask somebody else for a ride every time she wanted to leave the ranch.

When she returned it was almost lunch hour.

"I'll be ready to eat as soon as I wash up," she told Maggie.

"Your tray will be out on the veranda."

"*Gracias.*"

She had gotten into the habit of eating the noon meal on the wide porch on the other side of the house from her studio. It gave her a view of a meandering stream shaded by oaks and bay trees.

When she pushed open the door, she saw that her lunch was sitting in the usual place. But on the corner of the tray was an exquisite cut-glass vase, filled with a small bouquet of deep pink flowers. She recognized them at once—fireweed. Propped against it was a square white envelope with her name lettered across the front. It was in Stephen's handwriting.

Barely daring to breathe, she walked closer. Then, with trembling fingers, she reached for the envelope and drew out a folded sheet of notepaper.

> I've watched you riding Storm Dancer and painting out on the hillside among the fireweed, and wanted very much to join you.
>
> Esteban

Her vision suddenly blurred, and she realized she was reading the note through a film of tears. Sitting down, she clutched the folded sheet of paper in her hand. It wasn't exactly an apology. Yet for a man like Stephen, those simple words were more eloquent than an elaborate peace offering.

What's more, they told her something very important that wasn't written on the paper. Stephen had been willing to risk her rejection to let her know that he had missed her. With shaky fingers she stroked the velvety petals of one of the flowers. She couldn't imagine that Stephen had asked someone to pick them for him. Yet how had he gotten his wheelchair into the meadow?

He had made the first move. She longed to go to him at once. Then she pictured him eating lunch in the gazebo where they had had their last meeting. Too much had happened between them out there. Perhaps it would be better to wait until later in the day.

Elena spent a restless afternoon, hardly able to paint. Finally she gave up and went back to her room. Stephen usually worked until five. Then he went out to the pool. She might as well wait there, since she wasn't getting a thing accomplished.

Taking her bathing suit from one of the bureau drawers, she held it up. It was plain black and very simple in style, the kind of modest swimsuit her father had insisted that she wear. She had seen much more stylish ones in the shops in Santa Barbara, and had thought about buying one. But she wasn't sure she had the courage to wear something slit up the sides and plunging in the front. Perhaps the suit she had was best, after all.

She was sitting on one of the chaise lounges by the pool, wearing a long robe over her bathing suit and trying to read a book, when the door near Stephen's bedroom opened. Looking up, she was just in time to see him come onto the patio. Her heart gave a lurch, and she stared at him wonderingly. He wasn't in the wheelchair, but was leaning on a pair of crutches, his left side turned slightly away from her.

Though he was trying hard to keep his expression neutral, he couldn't hide the look of triumph on his face.

Her own countenance lighted up. "How wonderful."

He grinned, obviously pleased with himself as he made his way slowly across the concrete. It was almost the grin she remembered from the happy time so long ago. Stopping a few feet away, he looked down at her. His expression had become tense. "You got my note."

"Yes." She wanted to say something bright and cheerful that would ease the awkwardness. She wanted to leap up and throw her arms around him. Instead she gripped the sides of the chair and gazed at him. He turned fully toward her, as though by showing her his scars, he was issuing another challenge. Did he still expect her to flinch?

She held her ground, but her heart had begun to pound so violently that she wondered if the frantic beating showed at the front of her bathing suit. She resisted the impulse to look down and see.

After what seemed like endless moments he spoke again. "I missed you."

"I missed you, too."

The silence lengthened once more.

"I thought about you a lot this week."

"I did, too."

"Are you comfortable here? Have you been all right?"

"Yes." Her hands made an ineffective little gesture. "I love the ranch. And Storm Dancer,"

He nodded. "Hal was impressed with your horsemanship."

She nodded, wondering if any topic of conversation was going to last more than two sentences. "Did you pick the fireweed yourself?" she blurted.

"Yes."

You waited until you were out of the wheelchair. The words went unspoken. She watched his Adam's apple bob. Was he as nervous as she?

"Maggie said you made the apricot tart I had for dessert a couple of days ago."

"Yes."

"It was good. And the black bean stew. That was good, too."

"Thank you. I wanted to cook some of the things you like—and show you some of my favorites."

He nodded and cleared his throat. "It gets cool here in the evenings."

"I've noticed."

"If we're going to swim, we should do it before it gets chilly."

"You're right."

He laid down his left crutch before untying his robe. She could see that getting out of the garment standing up was going to be a difficult maneuver.

Automatically she sprang to her feet. "Can I help you?" Then she wished she hadn't been so quick to offer. He might not want any help.

He hesitated. "Thanks."

She crossed the few feet of patio that separated them. It had been such a long time since she'd stood next to Stephen—a week since she'd been close to him at all. Her hand trembled slightly as she helped him slip his arm through the sleeve. When he grasped her shoulder to steady himself, she closed her eyes. She stood still as a statue, but a statue with tingling, sensitized nerve endings. Through her own robe she felt his strong fingers branding her skin. As he struggled to free his arms from the sleeves, the pressures changed, sending little zings of sensation down the nerve paths.

With her eyes closed, every other sense strained to compensate. The familiar scent of his body seemed to swirl around her. His breath was a warm caress on her cheek.

She heard rather than saw him toss the robe across one of the loungers. He picked up his crutch again and released her shoulder. She didn't have to open her eyes to know that he was now standing next to her all but naked, just as she had seen him from her window.

In her mind she saw the broad chest, flat belly, hard thighs and even more intimate details. And the scars that had become such a familiar part of him.

The moment stretched taut. When he cleared his throat, her eyes snapped open. Her face was level with his shoulders. She couldn't raise her head to meet his eyes. Instead her gaze became tangled in the thick hair that matted his chest. It swirled around his dark nipples, drawing her eyes to the dark circles. They were flat and hard. She dared not let her inspection slide lower. It was one thing to see him like this from a distance. Up close, the impact was almost overwhelming.

"Are you going to get undressed?"

Her head jerked up. "What?"

"You can't swim with your robe on." His voice was husky. His blue eyes seemed to burn into her dark ones like lasers.

"I know." Her fingers fumbled with the cord. They felt thick, immobile.

"Let me." Steadying himself with the crutches, he leaned forward. When his fingers brushed hers, she tried not to tremble. He unfastened the tie and slowly parted the fabric, the flat of his hand brushing her midsection, making the flesh under her suit quiver. For a moment she stood there, her lower lip between her teeth. Then, turning slightly, she tore off the robe and let it drop over the arm of a chair.

She hadn't known it was possible to feel a man's gaze as surely as you could feel the caress of his warm hand. She learned it now. In response, her skin bloomed with a delicate flush.

She knew he was as aware of her state of undress as she was of his. He had never seen her like this. Did he think her legs were too thin? Her waist too thick?

Were her breasts too small? She fought to stop herself from folding her arms protectively across her chest. She told herself the reaction was ridiculous. The suit was modest by American standards. Yet she couldn't squelch the feeling of exposure. Beneath the knit fabric, her nipples beaded.

HE ACHED with the impact of her beauty. She was so perfect. The knit fabric of the suit concealed very little. Her breasts were high and firm and perfectly rounded. God, the nipples were erect—delicate beads that begged for his attention. He clenched his hands in an effort to keep from reaching out to those soft mounds, cupping them, lifting them, gently squeezing them.

A more enticing notion struck him, and he compressed his lips. *Don't even think about how they'd feel against your tongue,* he ordered himself.

Concentrate on something else. Her waist. It was so small. He could probably span it with his hands.

The gentle curve of her thighs was just as seductive. The creamy softness of her shoulders. Her long, graceful arms. The sum total of her. He had imagined her like this. Thinking about her had given him something to cling to through the long night of his despair.

Now here she was, standing in front of him, trembling slightly. She was such a beguiling combination of innocence and sensuality, vulnerability and strength. He longed to reach out and pull her against him, clasp her so tightly that her warm flesh flowed into his own.

DON'T STAND HERE like an idiot. Say something, her mind commanded. "This is such an old-fashioned suit."

"I didn't notice." His voice was thick. As though it were happening in slow motion, she watched as his hand stretched out toward her. His finger touched the strap on her left shoulder, then traced lightly along the edge to the top of her breast, searing her skin with sudden heat.

She made a small "Oh" sound in her throat and swallowed convulsively. Unspoken feelings simmered below the surface. She was almost overwhelmed by their intensity. From deep inside her the love that she felt for this man welled up and overflowed in a tide of longing.

She swayed toward him. His hand went to her chin, stroking, caressing. He was going to tip her head up, kiss her. Her lips parted slightly. A tight knot of anticipation coiled in her stomach.

The moment seemed to last forever. Or perhaps it was only an instant.

He snatched back his hand and angled his body away from hers. "I think I'd better get in the water." His voice wasn't quite steady.

"Oh." Her vocabulary seemed to have shrunken to minuscule proportions.

He turned and used the crutches to lower himself to the side of the pool.

She watched as he pushed off and began to stroke quickly through the water, the way he had done that first day when she had seem him out the window. Somehow she knew now that he was aware she had been watching.

CHAPTER SEVEN

FOR THE FIRST TIME since Elena had arrived, she and Stephen would be eating together that evening.

"The dining room is so large," she told Maggie as they fixed the meal together. "Is there somewhere else we could sit?"

"Stephen's been eating in his office. But that won't do for the two of you. How about the library? It's cozy. And you could sit at the table by the window."

Elena pictured the room. "That would be perfect."

Another first, she thought as she prepared for the occasion with special care. After brushing out her long dark hair until it shone and dabbing on a bit of makeup, she slipped into a simple, but exquisite cotton dress decorated with Indian embroidery.

As she inspected her reflection in the mirror, she admitted to herself that she was nervous. There were important issues she and Stephen still had to discuss, and she could sense how strongly he wanted to avoid them.

When she came into the room, he was standing by the fireplace, wearing dark slacks and a crisp blue shirt. As was his habit, he had turned so that his right side was facing her.

You don't have to do that, she thought. *I'm comfortable with the way you look.* But she sensed he wasn't quite ready to believe those words.

At least his stance was easy. One crutch was propped against the mantle. In his free hand he was holding a wineglass.

He couldn't disguise the warmth of his gaze as he took in her appearance. "You look lovely."

The compliment made her skin glow. "Thank you."

"I broke out a bottle of Corton Charlemagne for the occasion." The wine was in a bucket of ice near the table. Stephen set down his glass and reached for the crutch.

"That's all right. I can pour my own," Elena offered.

He hesitated.

"You don't have to do everything."

"Maybe not now. But I will."

"Esteban, you don't have to prove anything to me."

"How about to myself?"

She caught the tension in his voice. Perhaps it was time to change the subject. After she'd poured herself a glass of wine, she turned back to Stephen. "I'm having a wonderful time with Storm Dancer. I can't wait until we can ride together again."

"I'm not quite ready for that yet."

"There's no hurry. I've been doing other things, too—like getting acquainted with Santa Barbara. It's a charming place."

"Hal's kept me advised of your trips."

"Oh. Did you ask him to report back to you?" She couldn't keep a note of reproach out of her voice.

His own tone was defensive. "What you do is my business."

Elena swallowed, wondering why they were suddenly at odds. "I told him that I'd like to get a driver's license," she continued more evenly. "What do you think?"

"It makes sense. I can't have one of the men dropping what he's doing every time you want to go into town."

She found herself tilting her chin upward. "I had that same thought."

"Have you done much driving?"

"Quite a bit on my father's estate."

"Hardly the freeway. It may take a little time to get used to the speed—and the traffic."

"Hal told me you started off on the ranch roads yourself, in an old Jeep."

"That's true."

"I was hoping you might be able to give me some lessons. Since the ranch is private property, I won't need a learner's permit out here, so I could get started right away."

Stephen took a long swallow of wine. "I haven't driven a car in months."

"You don't think you could manage it?"

"I can manage!"

"Then maybe tomorrow after lunch we could go for a practice drive."

She had neatly maneuvered him into having to admit a weakness or acquiesce. He chose the latter, but not entirely graciously. "Not tomorrow. I have some work that won't wait. But the next day. And if we end up in a gully, you'll have nobody but yourself to blame."

"I consider myself warned."

Maggie arrived with the food, and Stephen seemed relieved by the interruption. Elena wondered if he was taking longer than necessary to maneuver himself into his chair. As he sat down, he muttered something under his breath.

"What's the matter?" Elena asked anxiously.

"Nothing!"

"Elena made the beef burgundy," the older woman announced before she left them alone again.

Stephen took a bite. "Very good."

"If you tell me what else you'd like to have, I could learn to make it," Elena suggested.

"That's not necessary. I do have a housekeeper."

"I like doing things for you."

"I'm not used to being taken care of."

"Do you always have to put things in terms of your accident?" The words slipped out before she had a chance to think.

He laid down his fork with a clank of metal against china. "I'm afraid it's the paramount factor in my life right now."

Elena poked at her meat.

Stephen had begun to push his own food around the plate. Was he just being polite when he said he liked it?

"Did Hal tell you an art dealer is interested in my work?" Elena asked, hoping to fill the silence.

"Mmm-hmm."

"He hasn't actually accepted anything yet. But I'll be going back in a few weeks."

Stephen eased back in his chair and took a sip of his wine. "What did you bring along for a sample?"

Elena swallowed. "Why, uh, a picture of you I painted back home."

"Of me?"

"On horseback. Galloping toward the hacienda."

"You mean before the accident." His face was pale, and there were lines of strain across his forehead.

"Of course before the accident." For a moment she thought guiltily about the new pictures of him she had started. Then she put them firmly out of her mind. What she painted in private was her own business.

"If you had asked, I wouldn't have given permission to take that picture." He looked angry, but there was something else in his expression, too.

"The picture belongs to me."

"Did you bring it to remind yourself of what I used to look like?"

"As far as I knew, you looked the same."

He laughed hollowly. "That's right. How could I have forgotten about your father's little deception?"

Elena sucked in her breath. She knew they had to talk about that again, but calmly. Not like this.

Stephen wadded his napkin and laid it on the table. "I'm sorry. I'm afraid I'm not very good company tonight."

"Why is that?"

"I don't care to discuss it further."

He reached for his crutches, pushed back the chair and pulled himself to a standing position. As his left foot hit the floor, he grimaced.

Elena eyed him with concern. "Stephen, are you in pain? Is that what's wrong?"

"I said I don't want to discuss it." Without further comment he turned and slowly made his way out of the room. His hands were clamped around the grips of the crutches so firmly that the knuckles had turned white.

Elena's chest tightened as she watched him leave. He was stubborn and proud. As far as he was concerned, any setback in his physical progress was a sign of weakness. She should have realized what was wrong tonight. But what good would that have done her? she asked herself.

It was very late that night before Elena was able to fall asleep. After Stephen left the table, she went up to her room and tried to read. But her mind refused to concentrate on the mystery novel she'd taken from the library. She kept remembering the tangled sheets she'd seen on Stephen's bed that first morning, when she'd explored the house.

She got up and went over to the window. Stephen's room was just off the patio. Although the shutters were drawn, she could see that the light was on. Was he also trying to read?

Or was he tossing and turning, trying to get comfortable? The image made her squeeze her eyes shut and clench her fists. She wanted to do something for him—if only he would let her. Larry had told her that massaging Stephen's leg helped control the pain. If she learned the proper technique, she would be able to take over when the therapist wasn't available. Tomorrow she would ask Larry to show her.

THE IDEA HAD SEEMED like a good one the night before. Yet as she stood outside the door of the gym the next morning, dressed in sweatpants and a T-shirt, she felt her resolve wavering. If Stephen was still feeling antagonistic, she was better off turning around and going back to her studio to paint.

However, while she was debating what to do, Larry looked up, saw her and grinned broadly. "Hey, stranger. Long time no see. Come on in."

She glanced over at Stephen, who was sitting on a high stool, working out on the arm press. He didn't skip a beat as he pulled the handlebars down, but his lips compressed into a thin line.

"Where have you been?" Larry inquired, striding across the polished wooden floor.

"Painting—riding—and getting acquainted with Santa Barbara."

The physical therapist eyed her outfit discerningly. "Did you come to join us in a workout?"

"No. But I was wondering if I could take you up on your earlier offer to show me how to massage Stephen's leg."

"Sure."

Her gaze flicked to the man in question. He had stopped working the machine and was leaning on the handlebars, staring coldly at her.

She ignored the unspoken hostility and continued to address Larry. "Stephen was in a good deal of pain last night at dinner. It was frustrating not being able to help him."

The therapist turned toward Stephen. "You didn't say anything about that this morning."

"I don't have to report every little ache and pain to you."

"I don't think it was so little," Elena murmured under her breath. Stephen's sharp look told her that he had heard.

Larry stroked his chin. "It probably wouldn't be a dumb idea to give you a work-over now. And I can show Elena what I'm doing."

"I'd prefer that you didn't."

"And I'd prefer to be able to ease your discomfort," Elena cut in.

"She's right," Larry added. "I'm not always around when you need me. It would be great if she could give you a treatment when I'm not here."

Stephen scowled as he looked from one to the other. Finally he shrugged and reached for his crutches.

A few minutes later he was lying on the padded table at the side of the gym. Larry stood beside his left leg. Elena had moved to the end of the table, where she could watch the procedure.

Although Stephen was wearing more than he had been at the pool yesterday, Elena discovered that she was just as aware of his body. She reached out to steady herself against the end of the table as he shifted to a more comfortable position, clasping his hands behind his head so that he could easily view the proceedings. She couldn't meet his inquisitive gaze.

"The muscles in Steve's legs tend to knot up and go into spasms. There are two techniques that seem to give him relief," Larry was saying.

She forced herself to focus on the words. *Give him relief*.

"Move your left leg over this way," Larry requested.

Stephen obediently complied, and Elena followed the movement.

"Sometimes all it takes is general rhythmic pressure. Other times circular rhythmic pressure is better," Larry continued.

"Circular rhythmic pressure," Stephen repeated. "You'll probably be good at that, Elena."

"Why?" she questioned, flushing slightly.

He shrugged. "I imagine your wrist gets a workout when you're painting."

Larry interrupted the interchange to explain a few more details.

"It sounds quite technical." Elena forced her voice into a neutral tone. Her phrasing had become stiff, the English harder to cope with.

Larry seemed determined to ignore the byplay between the man on the table and the woman who stood at his feet. "It's not that difficult. Let me show you." He looked inquiringly at Stephen. "Where does it hurt?"

"My calf—and my thigh."

Elena blanched. She hadn't realized she'd be touching him so close to the edge of his shorts.

"The area of the calf is smaller, and it will be easier to pinpoint the problem, so let's start with that." Larry unknowingly came to her rescue. He reached down and ran his thumb along the area indicated. When he touched a particular spot, Stephen winced.

"Okay. Got it."

The therapist turned to Elena. "I'm going to apply a fair amount of pressure with the heel of my hand—not on the spot that hurts, but *around* it in a clockwise motion. A couple of seconds and then release. And then repeat." Despite herself, she watched in fascination as he began to do just that, using his body weight for extra leverage.

After a minute or two he gestured to his pupil. "You try it."

"All right." She heard the quaver in her voice and hoped that Larry hadn't noticed. She didn't have any illusions about Stephen. She knew beyond doubt that he was enjoying her discomfort. In fact, he was using it to punish her for insisting on this lesson. But she could hardly back out now.

After changing places with the therapist, she glanced at Stephen's face. He was watching her intently. She thought she could detect amusement in his blue eyes. She swallowed and reached out to run her thumb along his calf the way Larry had. His hair-sprinkled leg might be scarred, but the skin was so warm and alive that her own flesh tingled at the intimacy of the contact. She knew she was flushing slightly.

At the same time, despite his mocking attitude, Stephen tensed. If Larry hadn't been standing there watching them, she would have pulled her hand away, as though her fingers had just come into contact with a hot light bulb. Although this exercise had been her idea, she hadn't really been thinking of what it would entail.

"Feel anything?" Larry asked.

"*¿Qué?*" Now she was starting to forget to speak in English.

"Do you feel the knot?"

"*Sí.*"

"Apply pressure around it. Press and release. Press and release."

She did her best to follow the instructions, imitating the clockwise motion that Larry had used. But as she leaned over Stephen, she was conscious of the way the pressing motions thrust her breasts forward toward him. Why had she worn a T-shirt? she wondered. Why hadn't she selected a loose-fitting blouse?

"Good," her instructor said approvingly. "But don't slide your hand along his skin. Lift it up when you move to the next spot."

Elena jerked up her hand.

"Easy does it." Larry patted her arm. "You're too tense. Just relax. You're not going to injure him."

So that was what Larry thought was making her nervous. She wasn't going to set him straight. Drawing a shaky breath into her lungs, she tried again.

"That's right," the therapist confirmed. "How does it feel?" he asked Stephen.

"Nice. I mean better." His voice had roughened slightly. His lids were half-lowered, veiling the expression in his blue eyes. But she knew from her own reaction that he was looking at her breasts.

"If this doesn't help, we go to direct pressure. I'll show you that, too." They switched places again. This time, instead of using his palm, Larry rotated his thumb on the painful spot.

Stephen sucked in a sharp breath.

Elena looked anxiously at the therapist.

"This particular technique hurts a bit," he admitted. "But it's effective. You don't want to work so deeply that you cause extreme pain. It's a matter of judgement. Usually you can feel the knot or spasm begin to loosen up and start to disappear. Or Steve will let you know that it's feeling better."

He let her practice that application as well. Then he looked at Stephen. "Well, buddy, shall we work on the thigh?"

"I think Elena needs to get back to her painting. Perhaps you could just take care of it yourself." She heard the tightness in his voice.

Couldn't Larry feel the electricity crackling in the air? Elena wondered.

"Thank you for the instruction. I think I understand what to do," she added quickly.

Larry didn't protest, and it was with relief that she exited the gym and headed to her studio.

BILL DELANEY had been sitting at his desk, folding and unfolding the pink message slip. For the third time that morning he reached for the phone, then drew back his hand.

When he'd talked to Jenny about art lessons, she hadn't exactly been enthusiastic. But it was usually that way with her these days. He remembered how she'd been chomping at the bit to get out of the hospital. And for the first few weeks at home, she'd been like a puppy—eager to reacquaint herself with everything. But after the novelty of being able to play her records and watch videos again had worn off, a sort of gray fog had settled around her.

She didn't snap the way she used to when he asked her to straighten up her room. In fact, she didn't show much emotion at all. She didn't want to invite any friends over. She didn't want to try anything new. And she particularly didn't want to meet anyone who hadn't seen her in her wheelchair.

Maybe he had detected a spark of interest when he'd mentioned art lessons. Then he'd started talking about Elena Castile, and Jenny's expression had closed—like a clam snapping shut.

Well, what harm was it going to do to try? The worst he could do was waste Elena's afternoon. And he was willing to risk that for his daughter.

With more decisiveness than he really felt, he reached for the phone again and dialed.

"Ms Castile?"

"Speaking."

"This is Bill Delaney. I'm sorry I didn't get back to you sooner, but I just returned from a business trip and found out you phoned. I was wondering if you'd be able to come out to the house and meet my daughter today."

"I'm not sure—"

"Please. Say yes."

"It's very short notice."

"I realize that," Bill apologized.

"I'd need to see if someone here could drive me."

"I could come out and get you."

"All right," Elena agreed. "Do you need directions to the ranch?"

"I know how to get there. Ms Castile, this means a lot to me." He went on to tell her a bit more about Jenny. "So how about lunching with us?" he concluded.

"I'd like that."

"Then I'll see you around twelve."

As Elena ended the conversation, she was smiling—until she thought of Stephen. Would he be expecting her at lunch? Perhaps she should check with him. Then she firmed her lips. She didn't want to go back into the gym. Besides, he would probably be busy this afternoon.

Instead she told Maggie about her plans.

"Wonderful," the housekeeper commented. "I think you may get as much out of this as Jenny will."

"Please tell Stephen where I've gone. And that I'll be back in time for dinner."

Elena spent the rest of the morning working in her studio. She had been painting steadily, and three pictures were ready. When they were dry enough, they could be framed.

About twenty minutes before she was due to be picked up, she put some art supplies into a small carrying case. Then she returned to her bedroom, cleaned up and changed into a green cotton skirt and a matching knit top.

Promptly at twelve a blue car rounded the curve of the driveway and pulled up in front of the hacienda. Elena was surprised to see that it was a well-kept Volvo. Apparently Bill Delaney was more concerned about the appearance of his car than of his person.

However, when he got out Elena could see that he had made an attempt to spruce himself up a bit. His brown hair had been trimmed, and his shirt and slacks were at least in the same color range.

As he came around to greet Elena, a broad smile spread across his suntanned face. The salutation was so warm that Elena couldn't help responding in kind.

"I'm so glad you're eating with us," he declared.

"It will be a change of pace for me."

"Well, let's get going then."

He ushered her into the car and started the engine. Elena set her case of art supplies on the floor. As she reached to fasten her seat belt, she glanced toward the house. Stephen was standing just inside the doorway, leaning on his crutches. The expression on his face made her fingers freeze, and the metal buckle snapped out of her hand.

"Here, let me help you," Bill offered, leaning over her to grasp the seat-belt catch and click it into place. Elena sat rigidly beside him, staring straight ahead.

"Is something wrong?"

"No, nothing."

"You're not still thinking that I'm a nut, are you?" Bill questioned. "I . . . I still can't account for my behavior that afternoon. But when I saw you and the picture of Stephen, I just knew you were the right one to teach my daughter."

"Stephen's housekeeper, Maggie, helped me make up my mind. She told me something about you and Jenny."

"I hope she said I was a solid citizen, despite the fact that I don't look much like a fashion plate. I never could get very interested in clothes."

Elena nodded, only half listening. She was fighting the impulse to turn and look back at Stephen as the car made its way down the driveway.

Bill cleared his throat. "About Jenny...she may not seem glad to see you at first. So don't be put off by her lack of enthusiasm."

Elena made an effort to concentrate on the man sitting next to her. There was nothing she could do about Stephen now, anyway.

"She hasn't been very comfortable with new people," Bill went on.

"Stephen's like that, too," Elena murmured.

Bill and his daughter lived in a modern wood and stone ranchero just south of Santa Barbara. The house was up in the mountains with a breathtaking view of the ocean.

Jenny was out on the sunny patio. She was a beautiful girl with pale blond hair, and soft brown eyes that reminded Elena of a fawn. She felt a painful squeeze in her heart as she saw that the teenager was sitting in a wheelchair. Bill had mentioned that his daughter was fourteen. Small and thin for her age, she looked very young and fragile.

Jenny regarded her uneasily. Stephen had reacted in a similar manner, Elena recalled. Seeing the response again made her realize how devastating such injuries were to even the strongest personality.

These thoughts went through Elena's mind so quickly that her smooth progress across the terrace was not impeded. Coming over to Jenny, she smiled and stretched out her hand.

Bill made the introductions. "Elena, this is my daughter Jenny."

"I've been looking forward to meeting you," Elena declared.

The girl's expression was carefully neutral. "Why?"

Elena was hardly prepared for the question, but she smiled again as she answered. "I don't know many people in Santa Barbara. Your father told me you were interested in art. It's one of my interests, too."

"I don't know where he got that idea."

"Jenny!"

There was a moment of awkward silence. Jenny turned her chair away from the two adults and sat looking down toward the ocean that was barely visible in the distance. Bill waited another moment. Then he went over and put a hand on her shoulder.

"Why don't you tell Elena what we've got planned for lunch?" he prompted.

When she didn't answer, he went on. "Mrs. Matthews is off today, so I thought we could make pizza. I got the dough from a shop. But we're going to do the sauce and topping ourselves. We haven't baked it yet, so you can have it with the works, if you want."

"I guess I don't know what the works are—I've never had pizza before," Elena answered.

Jenny looked over her shoulder. "You've never had pizza?" she asked incredulously.

"I don't think the cook on my father's ranch had heard of it."

"Where are you from, anyway? The moon?"

Elena laughed. "Sometimes I feel that way. There's so much I don't know about American culture. But I'm from Venezuela."

"What are you doing here?" Jenny asked.

"I came here to marry my fiancé, Stephen Gallagher."

Jenny looked as if she'd forgotten that she didn't want to be interested in this visitor. She opened her mouth, as though she were going to ask another question. Then she abruptly closed it.

Elena turned to Bill. "I'd love to learn how to make pizza."

"Then come on in the kitchen."

Without asking, Bill wheeled Jenny inside the house. But his daughter didn't offer to help make lunch. So while he made the sauce, Elena chopped the green pepper and onion and sliced the mushrooms. Jenny watched from a corner.

"We've also got anchovies, pepperoni and shrimp," Bill explained.

"Well, I'm brave enough to try them all."

"Anchovies, yuk!"

Both adults looked at Jenny.

"We'll leave them off yours," Bill told her with a smile.

While the pizza baked, Elena gave the Delaneys a somewhat abbreviated explanation of how she had come to this country.

"My dad told me Stephen is in a wheelchair like me. He says he was in the hospital when I was, but I don't remember him," Jenny said.

Elena nodded.

"And you want to marry him, anyway? If I'm still in this wheelchair when I grow up, I wonder if anyone will ever want to marry me," the teenager added wistfully.

Elena and Bill looked at each other across the girl's head, both deeply affected by the pensive voice and unguarded comment.

The large, rugged man knelt beside his daughter, bringing himself to her height. "With the right person, that won't matter. He'll see all the things that make you special."

Elena turned away and pretended to check the plates and napkins laid out on the counter. But it was several moments before she could see through the film of moisture that had unexpectedly clouded her eyes. She hadn't known these people for very long, and her first impression of Bill hadn't been favorable. But now she could see he was a unique individual. And she could also see through the barricades that Jenny had erected around herself. No wonder her father was so determined to insure that her life was as full as he could make it.

"The pizza's almost ready," Bill announced. "If Elena will carry out the soft drinks, I'll bring the food."

Without being asked, Jenny reached for the plates and napkins on the counter and put them into her lap before wheeling herself toward the door.

They ate on the patio in the warm California sunshine. Elena was delighted with the novelty of the meal. But it wasn't easy to keep up a conversation with Jenny. She answered questions in monosyllables. And she didn't introduce any topics of her own.

Instead of probing, Elena addressed herself to Bill and let Jenny concentrate on the food.

They talked about Elena's impressions of Santa Barbara.

"It's a beautiful city—not just the architecture, but all the flowers—and the setting, too."

"The tourist literature says it's the place where the mountains meet the sea."

"Oh, Dad. That's just propaganda," Jenny interjected.

"In this case, it's not an exaggeration," Elena pointed out.

After they'd finished eating, Elena pushed back her chair. "I've been wanting to do some portraits. But I haven't found anyone to sit for me. Bill, would you mind if I make some sketches of you?"

"Well . . ."

"Please. You'd make an interesting study."

After a bit more coaxing, Bill agreed. While he made himself comfortable on the chaise lounge, Elena retrieved her supplies from the car. Then she settled into a chair on the other side of the patio and set to work. She knew Jenny was watching from a distance, but she didn't urge the girl to come see what she was doing.

Finally Jenny wheeled her chair across the patio and peered over Elena's shoulder. "Gee, that looks just like Dad."

"I'm glad you think so."

There was a moment of silence. "I'd like to be able to draw that good—I mean well."

"Mmm," Elena murmured noncommittally.

Jenny was silent for another moment, then she cleared her throat. "Do you think you could teach me?"

"It depends on how much ability you already have."

"She's very talented," Bill interjected.

"Oh, Dad."

"Really." Bill got up to bring out some of his daughter's drawings and paintings.

"Well, your father hasn't overestimated your abilities," Elena said, as she looked through the pictures. One was a view from the patio and another was of the bookcase wall in the living room. "These are quite good,"

"I did the one of the bookshelves last year. Do you really think they're good?"

"I wouldn't say it if I didn't think so."

Jenny nodded, trying not to show her pleasure at the praise. It was wonderful to see the change in the girl. But

Elena could tell that the unaccustomed activity of the afternoon had tired her out.

Elena packed up her supplies. "I've had a wonderful time, but I should be getting home."

"I wish you didn't have to go."

"I can come back, and we can start some art lessons."

"Could you?" Jenny couldn't keep the eagerness out of her voice.

"I should check with Stephen about what day would be best."

"But you will come back?"

"I promise."

On the drive back to the ranch, Bill turned to Elena. "You've handled things just right with Jenny."

"I thought at first she wasn't going to respond to me."

"Thanks for not giving up."

"I've had a lot of practice lately."

Bill shot Elena a sidelong look, but she didn't elaborate.

"I'm glad I came," she said instead. "Today really was my pleasure. And you're right. Your daughter is talented." Elena paused. "I guess the last six months have been hard for you."

"Yes. I realize I must have looked pretty shaggy the first time I saw you. But sometimes getting my hair cut is the last thing I think about."

"How do you manage everything?"

"Mrs. Matthews, the housekeeper is a great help, but it's still difficult at times."

At the ranch, Bill pulled up in front of the hacienda.

"I'll call tomorrow and let you know about a date for Jenny's first lesson," Elena told him.

"Fair enough." He got out of the car and went around the door for his passenger.

When she stepped out, he surprised her with a quick hug. "Thank you again, Elena."

She was somewhat flustered, but recovered quickly. "I'm looking forward to next time."

CHAPTER EIGHT

ELENA WAS SMILING as she watched the Volvo pull away. The afternoon had been good for her. As she turned toward the house, she saw Stephen standing in the shadows of the entrance, just as he had been when she left. He was leaning forward on his crutches, his body rigid, his blue eyes glittering like reflective bits of glass.

"I see you and good old Bill Delaney have gotten pretty friendly. How long have you known him?"

"Esteban. You startled me."

"I'll bet." There was a dangerous edge in his voice. "I said, how long have you known him?"

"I . . . I met him last week."

"I wouldn't have thought Delaney was your type. Where did the two of you meet, anyway?"

She stared at him.

"Don't tell me he picked you up?"

"Picked me up? *No comprendo.*"

"It's a little hard to get through to someone who can barely speak the language."

She felt the blood drain from her face. "I'm...I'm trying to improve my English."

"Great."

She wanted to turn away. But she held her ground, unwilling to let him attack her with a meaningless change of subject. "You're making a grateful gesture into something that it isn't."

He snorted.

"Señor Delaney was just thanking me for agreeing to give his daughter art lessons."

He didn't respond, but a muscle twitched in his jaw.

She knew what direction his irrational thoughts had taken. He considered himself inadequate, and so he was torturing himself with the assumption that she might turn to some other man. The idea was ridiculous. But she had also come to understand that when he was in this kind of mood, nothing she could say would have any effect. He had to cool down before they could have a sensible discussion. Her chin in the air, she tried to make her way past him. He shifted to block her passage. The movement was jerky. His foot came down hard and not quite flat on the tile floor.

She saw the stabbing pain reflected in his face. His muttered expletive was colored with agony.

"Stephen, what's wrong?"

"What the hell do you think? My goddamn leg."

"Let me help you—" She reached out toward him.

"Don't you know by now that I don't want anybody's help, least of all yours?" A flush spread across his cheeks, and he turned away awkwardly.

Since arriving at the ranch, she had held herself under tight control. Now something inside her seemed to break loose. "You coward!" she shouted after him. "The way you deal with a situation you don't like is to run away. And you use your pain as an excuse. Don't you realize that your behavior is self-destructive?"

Stephen halted, every muscle in his body rigid. The pain it cost him to turn around was obviously terrible.

"What could you possibly know about it?" he challenged.

"I know what I see. I know what I feel."

She saw his shoulders quiver. "This is pointless." Instead of continuing the conversation, he limped down the hall and disappeared around the corner.

The rest of the afternoon passed in a mercifully numb blur. Elena wasn't surprised when Stephen didn't appear at dinner. And the two bites she tried of Maggie's excellent cottage pie felt like wet cement in her throat. After taking her plate back to the kitchen and scraping the contents into the garbage disposal so that Maggie wouldn't know how little she'd eaten, Elena went up to her room and mechanically got ready for bed. But when she had showered and slipped into a short satin nightgown, she stood looking at the turned-back spread and blue pillows. Her mind craved the oblivion of sleep, but she knew her body wasn't going to cooperate.

That afternoon at the Delaneys', she had felt drawn into the warm circle of their close relationship. Bill might be rough around the edges, but he loved his daughter, and she knew she could depend on that love.

Seeing them together had made her realize even more strongly than before what she wanted with Stephen. Perhaps the frustration of not being able to communicate with him was why she'd lost control. Every time she tried to have a meaningful conversation with him, he withdrew. Practically the only thing she was sure of was that he wanted her physically. But although she, too, could feel that link between them growing stronger, it wasn't enough to satisfy her craving for something more substantial.

Still, she didn't want to examine her doubts tonight. Perhaps the thing to do this evening was to go downstairs and simply relax in front of the television. That would be an easy way to occupy her mind, and she might even improve her English. Quickly she donned a robe.

After turning on the TV, she discovered an old Cary Grant movie just starting on a cable channel. It was one of her favorites, although previously she had seen it dubbed into Spanish.

Curling up on the sofa, Elena allowed herself to get caught up in the story. A time or two, when it seemed as though Cary and Ingrid Bergman were not going to be able to work out their complicated relationship, she had to brush a few tears away. But by the end, she was smiling at the warmhearted resolution. It was just a movie, she knew, but it touched her romantic spirit. Feeling almost rejuvenated, she stood up and stretched.

She was just heading quietly through the darkened hall when she heard a muffled exclamation. She froze, the hairs on the back of her neck prickling as she peered into the shadows.

Then she realized that the sound had come from Stephen's bedroom. Tiptoeing in that direction, she stopped outside the door and listened intently. A faint light shone from inside. She could hear Stephen tossing about. A few moments later he muttered another richly expressive oath.

Indecisively she raised her hand. Perhaps she could help him. Or perhaps he didn't want her help. He had said as much this afternoon. But she knew by now that he didn't always say what he meant. Quickly, before she could change her mind, she rapped her knuckles against the wood.

"Who the hell is that?"

"Elena." Without waiting for him to tell her to go away, she turned the knob and stepped across the threshold.

The room was softly lighted by the lamp on the bedside table. Stephen had pushed himself to a sitting position in bed. The blanket was on the floor. The sheet was tangled around his legs. He was wearing only a pair of Jockey shorts. Reaching down, he snatched at the sheet and suc-

ceeded in pulling it up around his waist. But it had come
untucked at the bottom of the bed, leaving his feet and lower
legs uncovered.

"Get out of here."

Her heart clogged her throat. He looked so defiant—and
so elementally male—except that the feet protruding at the
bottom of the covers spoiled the picture. They made him
look vulnerable. That was what helped her muster the
courage to remain in the room.

His eyes bored into her; his expression was sardonic. Once
before she had felt his gaze as vividly as she might feel his
touch. Then it had made her body quicken. Now it was
frightening.

She stood her ground as he treated himself to a slow inspection of her satin robe.

"Don't you wait for an invitation before coming into a
man's bedroom in the middle of the night?"

"I heard you—"

"Cursing?" he supplied with a hollow laugh.

"Yes. Does your leg hurt?"

"How did you guess?"

She closed the door and was suddenly struck with the
vivid knowledge of how a lion tamer must feel when he steps
into a cage with an infuriated animal and shuts the gate behind him.

Her stomach was in knots, but she didn't allow herself to
betray her disquiet. Instead she glided serenely across the
room until she was standing beside the bed.

"Let's see if we can do something about the pain. Where
does it hurt?" she asked calmly.

His lips had been about to form another acid comment.
Instead he gaped at her, his mouth still open.

"Where does it hurt?" Elena repeated.

"The same places as this morning," he answered, his tone several degrees milder than it had been a moment ago.

With the matter-of-factness of a nurse tending some anonymous patient, she reached out and straightened the tangled sheet, neatly folding it back to bare his calves. She stared at the scarred, hair-sprinkled skin she had exposed, flexing and unflexing her fingers uncertainly. From under lowered lashes she glanced at Stephen's face. His blue eyes dared her to continue.

Taking a deep breath, she reached out and touched him. At the first contact of her fingers against his warm skin, she faltered slightly and hoped he didn't detect the hesitation. Briskly she began to search for the knot of muscle that was causing him pain.

"There." His voice had roughened.

"Yes. I feel it." Her own voice had risen half an octave. It was one thing to practice this under Larry's watchful eye. It was quite another to be alone with Stephen in his bedroom.

She began to work around the spot as she had done that morning, trying to keep her mind neutral. This was a leg. Just a leg. Never mind that it was Stephen's leg. Never mind that touching his flesh sent little prickles of sensation right to her nerve endings.

After a few minutes she could feel some of the tension leave him. "Better?"

"Yes. Thanks."

She glanced again at Stephen's face. His head was propped on the pillow. His eyes were closed.

"Does your thigh hurt, too?"

"Mmm."

With quivering fingers she slowly rolled up the sheet, baring more of his masculine leg to her inspection. She was careful not to uncover the white cotton fabric of his shorts.

Massaging his muscles had seemed like a good idea only a few minutes ago. Now she felt almost light-headed.

"Can you show me where?" she whispered.

He sat up and took her hand. For a moment he simply held it, his thumb stroking across the soft skin of her palm, trailing invisible sparks of sensation in its wake. She knew he had felt her quiver.

He looked at her hand as though he had forgotten what he was supposed to do with it. Then he pressed it against a spot about three-quarters of the way between his knee and the edge of the sheet. The contact was so personal that she had to force herself not to snatch her fingers away.

"There."

"I feel it." Her voice was far from steady. She wished he would lie down again. His face was so close as he sat there regarding her, his lips slightly parted, his eyes cobalt pools in the dim light.

She felt him studying her, her hair, her face, her bosom, as though he could see its exact shape through two layers of fabric—thin, silky fabric.

To work on the tight muscle, she had to lean over and put her weight into the treatment. As she pressed firmly against his skin, she felt her unemcumbered breasts sway, as though they were straining toward him.

She hadn't known a thigh could be so hard. The texture intrigued her fingers so that she almost forgot what she was supposed to be doing.

"I heard the television."

"I hope it didn't disturb you."

"It wasn't loud." He paused. "What were you watching?"

"An old movie." The plot had fled her mind.

"I thought about getting up. I decided you probably didn't want my company."

"You thought wrong."

He abandoned the attempt at conversation. She could hear his breathing quicken. Or was it the accelerated rhythm of her own breathing that she felt? She knew he was still studying her from under half-closed lids.

Her hand moved rhythmically, mindlessly. *Press and release. Press and release.* There was nothing erotic about this, she told herself. She was like a doctor giving a medical treatment. But then why was her heart pounding so wildly? Why was her skin flushed? Why did she feel herself coming undone?

The knot of taut muscle seemed to be breaking up, but she sensed a new tension gathering within Stephen.

"Are you all right?" She didn't recognize the high, reedy quality of her voice.

"No. Actually the point of discomfort has shifted somewhat."

"Where? Would a massage help?"

"I wouldn't try it if I were you." As he spoke he captured her wrist, lifting her hand off his leg. In the next moment he was pulling her down onto the bed beside him. Her eyes widened in a mixture of alarm and anticipation as his arms came around her, gathering her firmly against his bare chest. His arms locked around her and held her to him. Then his mouth closed over hers with a fierce, almost harsh possessiveness.

The kiss had a potency that made her head whirl. She could do no more than respond to the urgent pressure of his lips, the audacious thrust of his tongue as it plundered the warm, sweet hollow of her mouth.

Suddenly she understood that this was the way it was supposed to be between men and women. She had been telling herself that the strongest thing she felt between them was physical desire. Well, perhaps that was the way to communicate with him, after all. The thought was swept away by a wave of feeling almost as soon as it had formed. Dizzily she clung to him, pressing closer, glorying in the contact.

He growled deep in his chest. The primitive sound fueled her own response.

Although he was the aggressor, she feasted on the kiss. Every nuance was intoxicating—the silky sliding of his tongue against hers—the hardness of his teeth as he drew back slightly to nibble at her lips.

"Elena."

Eagerly she captured the word, drawing it inside herself. She had wanted this from him, this primal demand that acknowledged surrender even as it laid claim.

"Esteban. *Mi amor.*"

Although he relinquished her mouth, the need to taste, to touch, to sample was still rampant. His lips traveled urgently over her cheeks, her chin, her forehead. Hers were no less greedy. And she had never been bolder. Without thought of anything but experiencing him, she slid her tongue over the midnight growth of beard on his chin, delighting in the roughness of the texture. She nibbled at his eyebrows, flicked out her tongue to test the feather softness of his lashes.

He quivered under her touch, telling her without words that his feelings were as strong as hers.

Her eager fingers smoothed over his bare shoulders, sought out the corded muscles of his arms.

When he spoke, his lips moved against the warm spot where her head met her neck. "This afternoon I shouldn't have said those things to you. I didn't mean them."

"I know."

"I kept thinking about you while I was trying to work. Finally I gave up and went outside to wait for you. When I saw Delaney put his arms around you, I couldn't think straight.''

"It's all right. I understand. I shouldn't have said what I did.''

"You were right.'' His voice was heavy with pain.

"No. You're no coward, Esteban. You have the courage of ten men.''

"*Querida*. I don't deserve you.''

"Don't say that about yourself.''

For long moments he simply held her, his hands ranging up and down her back and caressing the silky skin of her arms. Then he drew in a deep, shuddering breath. "You'd better leave.''

"I can't.''

"I don't think you quite grasp the implications.''

She tightened her arms around him. "Don't ask me to leave you, *mi amor*. Not now. Not this time. I love you too much.''

She felt the frantic beating of his heart—or was it hers? On a tremulous sigh, he found her lips again. This time he kissed more tenderly, savoring the sweetness she so gladly offered. He rubbed his lips back and forth against hers, then stiffened his tongue, stroking the corners of her mouth before delving further.

Her murmur of arousal was apparently his undoing.

"Elena, sweetheart, I've got to touch you.''

His hands opened the front of her robe and pushed it off her shoulders. Mindlessly she shrugged her arms out of the sleeves. Stephen's hands came up and cupped her breasts through the silky fabric of her gown, lifting and kneading.

He groaned, his lips nibbling along her neck as his thumbs stroked back and forth across her hardened nipples.

The incredible pleasure of it was almost too much for her to bear. She whimpered deep in her throat. Her whole body throbbed with awakening sensations. She felt hot and shivery—as though she had a fever and a chill at the same time.

Soft endearments tumbled from his lips. He pressed his face into the warm valley between her breasts, moving back and forth so that he nuzzled first the side of one and then the other. Inside her something seemed to liquefy.

Her hands went to the back of his head, clasping him to herself, her fingers running through his thick, springy hair.

When he finally lifted his face, his pupils were dilated. Taking her hands, he folded them and brought them to his lips. His teeth gently worried her knuckles and then his tongue caressed them.

She heard him draw another deep breath into his lungs. "Elena, holding you, kissing you like this is driving me crazy. Very soon I won't be able to stop."

"I'm not asking you to stop." The words were bold, yet her voice quavered.

He traced his thumb regretfully along her lips. "Sweetheart, I told you I could hardly move around in bed. It's still true, and that isn't the way it should be for you the first time."

"Stephen, that doesn't matter. I want the same thing you want."

"Don't!" He closed his eyes and sucked air into his lungs as though he were a drowning man who had finally broken the surface of the water.

God, he wanted to strip that gown off her body and then lie back and pull her against himself. He ached to tease those taut nipples, to bury himself in her softness. He could hardly move. But if she were on top, they could manage it. He clenched his teeth at the thought of her moving above him, her body fluid with passion.

He wanted her so much that he felt like a time bomb ready to explode. But it shouldn't be that way for her. Not the first time.

Yet the thought was still so tantalizing that it almost shredded his control. "Elena, I can't get up and walk out of here. You have to do it. Please."

She leaned over and pressed her forehead against his. "I love you. Don't send me away this time. I'll do anything you want me to. Truly. Anything." Her words expressed unfulfilled passion and hinted at tears.

"I know that, *querida*." His voice was rough with his own powerful emotions. "And I know I'm asking something very difficult of you now. But I think if you stay, we'll both regret it later."

For an endless moment her gaze locked with his. She understood her power. She could pull him back into her arms and force the issue. But instinct told her it would be the wrong thing to do—for him, if not for herself.

Quickly she slid down from the bed. Her legs were rubbery, but she managed to walk away from him. Not until she reached her own room did she realize that her robe was still lying on his bed.

THE SMELL OF MORNING COFFEE and muffins wafted through the house as Elena hurried toward the kitchen. When she reached the doorway, however, she stopped in surprise. Stephen had always been in the gym when she had breakfast—but not this morning. Today he was sitting at the table dressed in navy sweat clothes, his large hand wrapped around a coffee mug.

"What are you doing here?"

A slow smile curved his lips. "I live here."

"I mean, why aren't you working out this morning?"

"I was waiting to talk to you first." His expression was enigmatic. "Are you going to sit down?"

Then she realized what was different. He wasn't turning his head away to block her view of his scars. Nor was he challenging her. He was simply looking directly at her. Her heart began to thump as she joined him at the tale.

Without being asked, Maggie brought her a cup of coffee and a plate of muffins with butter and jelly. Then she bustled out of the room, mumbling something about needing to fold a load of sheets from the dryer.

When the housekeeper had retreated, Stephen reached over and covered one of Elena's hands with his. His palm was warm from the mug. He didn't speak at once, and Elena had the odd impression that in some important way he was seeing her for the first time.

"Thank you," he finally murmured, his voice so low that it seemed to wrap the two of them in intimacy.

"For what?"

"Coming to my room to work the kinks out of my leg last night . . . For leaving when I asked you to."

She looked down at their hands on the table. "I'm glad you let me help. I'm even more glad you let me get closer to you."

"So am I." His fingers folded themselves around the underside of her hand, and he clasped it tightly for a moment before taking a slow sip of his coffee. "It's not easy for me to say how I feel. I guess I'm not used to taking that kind of risk."

Tears glistened in the corners of her eyes. She had prayed for words like this from Stephen, but she had almost given up hope. Now she didn't dare speak above a whisper, for fear her voice would break. "Yes, it's a risk. It is for me, too."

"You do it so well." He cleared his throat. "Despite that stupid crack I made about your English."

"I told you I understood."

"I'm damn lucky that you do. It was a pretty cheap shot."

This time it was Elena who gripped his hand.

"You communicate so easily—in any language," he added huskily. "I thought it came naturally to you."

"No. I'm not used to sharing my private feelings, either." She drew in a deep breath. "But I do know something about the tragedy of people not really understanding each other. My parents ended up separating, because they couldn't tell each other how they felt about the things that are important in life."

"I didn't realize that."

"There's a lot you don't know about me."

"Yes, and I want to know everything. But talking about myself is going to be harder." He cleared his throat. "I . . . I never really got a chance to study my parents' relationship. My mother died when I was very young."

"How terrible for you."

"I survived."

"By making yourself tough."

"My father had a lot to do with that. He wanted to make sure I was self-sufficient. That's why—"

"Why it's so hard for you to accept the accident or anybody's help," she finished for him.

"Yes." He looked into his coffee cup. "Bill Delaney can walk without crutches," he said quietly. "When I saw him with you, it made me think of all the things I can't do."

"But I'm not in love with Bill Delaney. I'm in love with you."

"Sometimes it's hard for me to believe that."

"Don't ever doubt it."

They sat without speaking for a few moments, their hands twined together. But it was a different kind of silence from the long pauses that had punctuated their earlier conversations.

"Can I ask you something?" Elena finally murmured.

"You just did," he joked.

"I mean something serious."

He nodded.

"The picture in your office—the one I painted. How did you get it?"

"I've been waiting for you to get around to that." He paused. "If you'd asked me a few days ago, I would have been embarrassed to tell you."

"And now?"

"I had it commissioned, *querida*."

Her eyebrows shot up in surprise. "But I thought it was for a collector in my country."

"I was devious. I was afraid your father might not let me buy it if he knew. And having something you'd painted meant a great deal to me."

She stared at him, knowing how hard it must have been for him to tell her that.

"I'm glad you were able to get it then," she managed. "I wish I had known. It would have given me a sense of connection with you, when you were so far away."

Under the table Stephen's foot slid forward and pressed against hers. They sat that way for a long time. Finally he took one last swallow of the now-cooling coffee. "Larry is waiting for me. I'd better get over there."

"Will I see you at lunch?"

"Yes." He hesitated. "Would you like a driving lesson after that?"

"That would be wonderful, if you have the time."

"I'll make the time."

"I'll see you later, then. Have a good workout."

He reached for the crutches that were propped against the kitchen wall behind his chair, then stopped, half turning back in her direction. "By the way, I put your robe away in the bottom drawer of my bureau, where Maggie won't stumble upon it."

Her cheeks reddened. She'd forgotten all about the robe. Now she could just imagine what the housekeeper would think if she had come across it. "Thank you," she murmured.

"It was the least I could do under the circumstances."

When he stood up, it was with what seemed to Elena like a new buoyancy. She watched as he made his way around the pool and into the gym. Long afterward she sat with her eyes still focused on the doorway through which he had disappeared.

CHAPTER NINE

THE REST OF THE MORNING sped by. Elena had intended to work on the paintings she was taking down to Miles Henderson. Instead she set a picture of Stephen on her easel. It was one she had begun sketching that first day she had gone into the gym. All the details of his physical appearance were in sharp focus—the scars on the left side of his face—the wasted muscles in his left leg. Looking at the image, she could see how much progress he had made in the few weeks she had been here.

Should she abandon the study now that he was better? she wondered. No. She wanted to show Stephen as she had first seen him on arriving at the ranch, because now more than ever, the portrait symbolized the indomitable spirit that had kept him going through the long months of pain and uncertainty.

Stephen had asked Maggie to serve lunch in the garden. Elena couldn't help wondering why he had chosen that location. He answered her unspoken question as soon as she stepped a little hesitantly into the gazebo.

"This is a lovely spot. I don't want the two of us to avoid it because I acted like an ass the first time we ate here."

Her eyes traveled from the regretful expression on his face to the bouquet of fireweed in the center of the table. Then she gracefully slid onto the bench opposite Stephen.

Maggie had made a taco salad. After they had served themselves, Stephen looked across the table. "My work schedule has been pretty busy, but I'm thinking about taking some afternoons off. I'd like to spend them with you, if that wouldn't interfere with your painting.''

Her eyes twinkled. "I believe I could spare you some time.''

"Good." He stirred sugar into his iced tea. "You haven't talked much about your painting, but then I haven't exactly given you the opportunity. How is it going?''

"Very well. I should be ready to take some canvases down to La Paloma Gallery soon." She told him a little bit about Miles Henderson's interest in her work.

"That's wonderful," he complimented her.

"Yes. I was very pleased.''

"How do you feel about showing work in progress? Do you allow visitors in your studio?''

"It depends on the canvas—and on the visitor. I'd feel funny about someone like Miles Henderson coming by. That would be like meeting him in my underwear. But I'd love to have you come see what I've been doing.''

"Ah, meeting you in your underwear, that does open up interesting possibilities," he teased.

Her hands fluttered above her plate. "Stephen, I didn't mean—''

"I know you didn't. But I couldn't resist." He took a sip of his iced tea. "I do want to see what you've been doing. The problem is, I can't manage the stairs very well, and the studio is at the top of the house.''

"Yes. I understand." Setting down her fork, she looked across at him. "About the afternoons. I told Bill Delaney I'd let him know about Jenny's art lessons." She paused. "Is there a . . . a problem about that?''

"Do you mean, 'Can I control my insane jealousy?' ''

"I wouldn't put it quite like that.''

His expression became serious. "I tried to say it this morning, but couldn't quite manage. One of the things that worried me most was that you wouldn't want to marry a man quite so battered as I am."

Elena had realized that instinctively. Now she scrambled out of her seat and came around the table as she had done the first time they had lunched here together. Sliding onto the bench, she pressed her head against his shoulder and clasped her arms tightly around him. "I haven't changed my mind about wanting to marry you. But I think you might have figured that out last night."

"Yes." His hands glided up and down her back, drawing her even closer. For a long moment he was silent, the stroking of his fingers conveying his emotions. When he finally spoke, his voice was very low but steady. "Last night, after you left, I did a lot of thinking. I admitted to myself just how much you mean to me. And I realized that in a way, I've been testing you—trying to see if I could drive you away."

"But why would you do that?"

"Fear—that you were going to leave."

She tilted her face toward his. "That doesn't make sense."

"In a kind of crazy way it does. If I didn't have anything else to lose, then I couldn't be terrified of losing it anymore."

"Well, I'm afraid you can't drive me away."

He bent his head, and his lips came down on hers in a kiss that told her more than words ever could. Seconds passed before they broke apart.

"Elena. Sweetheart. When I first met you, you were so young and innocent, but I sensed you had great strength of character. These last few weeks I've come to realize just how wonderful you are." His hands stroked her hair; his lips nuzzled the side of her face, the curve of her ear.

She didn't know quite what to say, so she closed her eyes and snuggled against him, enjoying the closeness, the sensuality of his lips and hands.

"I dreamed of being with you like this," she confessed at last.

"I did, too." He continued to hold her as though she were a precious, fragile treasure. Then he shifted her body slightly away from his. "But Maggie is going to come back in a while and wonder why we haven't eaten her lunch."

"I didn't think of that." Reluctantly she moved back to her own seat.

"This way at least I get to look at you," he consoled himself. "You're very beautiful, you know. And your cheeks have such a becoming blush right now."

Elena felt the flush deepen. "I'm not sure how to respond to comments like that."

"Oh, I think you're learning." He grinned as he picked up his fork and began to eat.

They had come to a new understanding. Elena felt like a ship's captain who had navigated a long, rocky channel into much calmer waters. Yet she knew instinctively that the rest of the trip wasn't going to be all smooth sailing.

"So are you ready for that driving lesson?" Stephen asked as he put down his napkin.

"I hope so."

"I have a few calls to make. Why don't you go and tell Hal we'll need a car."

"All right."

A few minutes after she had consulted the foreman, a sleek silver Porsche appeared at the front door of the hacienda.

Stephen, who had come out to the driveway, hobbled over and stood looking at the vehicle as though meeting an old friend after a long absence. Then he ran his hand along the gleaming silver fender with obvious pleasure. "Hal, you've kept this baby in wonderful condition for me."

"Just making sure it would be ready whenever you wanted it."

Elena looked at the vehicle and then from one man to the other. It was obvious that Stephen had very strong feelings about his automobile. Suddenly the idea of taking a driving lesson in it had almost no appeal.

"Is there, uh, some other car we could use?" she inquired.

"Not unless you want to take a shot at the Jeep or the Lincoln."

"Uh, I guess not."

Stephen dug the keys out of his pocket and handed them to her. "Climb in."

"Good luck," Hal called as he headed back to the ranch office.

"Thanks."

Elena gazed at the sports car and then at the curving driveway, hemmed in by flower beds and adobe walls. Beyond lay the ranch road, flanked by fields of coyote brush and brown grass. At least if she made a mistake out there, she wouldn't hit anything.

"Aren't you going to drive?" she asked as Stephen opened the passenger door. "Just until we get out of the yard, where it's more open."

He shook his head. "You won't learn anything that way. My dad always said that the way to teach a kid to swim was to throw him into the pool and see if he could make it to the side. He taught me to drive the same way when I was fourteen. Let's go."

Gingerly Elena opened the door and slid behind the wheel. She peered uncertainly at the instrument panel. Some of the dials and gauges were recognizable. Others were totally unfamiliar.

It took Stephen a few moments to stow his crutches in the back and lower himself to the passenger seat.

"It feels fantastic to get back in here," he said, more to himself than to Elena. Taking a deep breath, he reached behind himself for the seat belt. Then he turned to Elena. "You said you've driven on your father's place."

"Yes."

"Stick shift or an automatic?"

"Mostly an automatic. But he did give me a few lessons on a manual."

"Good. Then you know where the gears are and how to work the clutch."

Elena hadn't been very good with the clutch. "It's been a while," she said tentatively. "Maybe if you drove first, you could show me—"

"Don't worry. It'll come right back to you, and I'll be sitting here if you have any problems. Try running through the gears now." Elena depressed the clutch and worked the lever into the various positions.

"Fine," Stephen said approvingly.

"What's that gauge?" she wanted to know, pointing to the dashboard.

"The tachometer. But you don't have to worry about it. Go ahead and start her up."

She turned the key and pressed the gas pedal. The powerful car bucked forward, then the engine died.

"You're in first gear. You want to start off in neutral—unless you keep the clutch depressed," Stephen observed dryly.

Elena shot him a nervous glance. "Sorry, I forgot. Couldn't we, uh—?"

He put one hand on her shoulder. "You're tense, that's all. Just relax."

She sighed, put the car into neutral and turned the key again. This time she got the vehicle started.

"Good," Stephen said as he listened to the soft purr of the engine. "You'll love driving this baby."

"I hope so," Elena muttered under her breath. She depressed the clutch again and shifted cautiously into first. Letting the pedal up at just the right rate was the tricky part, she remembered. Unfortunately she didn't get it right. Again the car bucked forward—and continued to buck and kick down the driveway like a runaway bronco. It was heading toward a low adobe wall that marked the edge of the lawn.

"The brake! For God's sake, put on the brake!" Stephen bellowed.

Terrified and confused, Elena looked down at the floor pedals. The car nosed off the driveway and onto the grass.

"Jesus!"

Her foot came down hard on the brake, and the car slammed to a halt in a flower bed, inches from the wall. Driver and passenger were thrown toward the windshield, then snapped back by their seat belts. For a moment there was silence; Stephen leaned his head against the headrest and dragged a deep breath into his lungs.

Elena eyed him apprehensively as his face twisted. Then, to her amazement, he began to laugh. She watched in stunned silence as he wiped tears from his eyes. "I believe my father would have been against throwing the Porsche into the swimming pool."

"I beg your pardon?"

"When Dad taught me to drive by the sink-or-swim method, we were out in the Jeep on a nice, flat ranch road."

"You mean like the one out there, where I wanted to start off?"

"Mmm, yes."

"Why were you laughing just now?"

"It was either that or treat you to some colorful language you don't deserve." He looked at the wall, then craned his neck to survey the path they'd taken across the lawn.

"Maybe I should stick with Storm Dancer. I could ride him into town. Although I didn't notice any hitching posts along State Street."

"You're kidding, I hope."

"Yes."

"I, uh, don't suppose you know how to put the car in reverse, do you?"

"No."

"Good. Because I don't believe I'd like you to attempt it—not so close to this wall."

"You're sure you're not angry?" she asked uncertainly.

"Naw." He put an arm around her shoulder and drew her toward him across the console. "But we won't speculate on my state of mind if you'd actually creamed the car."

"Creamed? Like creamed vegetables?"

They stared at each other. Stephen started to laugh again, and this time Elena joined him.

The next day when she came out for her driving lesson, a new Camaro was sitting in the driveway.

"It's an automatic," Stephen explained.

"But a new car. You shouldn't have."

"I wanted to. Besides, it's better that than turning you loose on the Porsche again."

"Well then, thank you—I think."

LATER IN THE WEEK Elena gave Jenny her first art lesson. Again Bill Delaney came to pick her up. This time, Stephen was waiting with her when the blue Volvo pulled up in front of the house. His expression was only slightly guarded as the car door opened, but Elena felt his body tense. Casually she laid a hand on his arm.

"Good to see you looking so fit!" Bill exclaimed, reaching out to shake the other man's hand.

Stephen shrugged. "I expected to be off the crutches by now."

"You can't push it too fast. I know that from Jenny. She had a couple of real setbacks."

"How is she?" Elena asked.

"Trying to act blasé, but I can tell she's excited about seeing you again."

"I don't want to keep you then," Stephen interjected. He looked at Bill. "Don't bring Elena back too late."

"I won't."

Bill was silent as he nosed the car down the ranch road. After turning onto the highway, he shot Elena a glance. "I think you've done wonders for that man."

"He did it himself."

"Physically, maybe. But I'm referring to his attitude. In the hospital, he was the terror of the nursing staff."

"That isn't too difficult to imagine. He has a hard time accepting his condition."

"And he isn't really comfortable around people," Bill added.

"Because of his face, mostly."

"I know. Jenny is that way, too, about the wheelchair."

"Is she going to walk again?" Elena couldn't stop herself from asking.

"That's the damnedest part. We don't know yet. She has a lot of nerve damage. The doctors said it could go either way."

"The waiting must be hard."

"Yeah." He drove on in silence for a few moments, then turned to Elena. "You know, we haven't even discussed what you're going to charge for the art lessons."

"Do I have to charge you?"

He laughed. "You may be a wonderful artist, but you're no businesswoman."

"Yes. But last time I got as much out of being with Jenny as she did."

Bill turned onto the winding road that led to his house. "That's quite a compliment."

"It's true."

"Nevertheless, I'd feel better if I were paying for your expertise." He named a sum. "Would that compensate you for your time?—on a per hour basis, of course."

Elena countered with a lower figure.

"This isn't the way the negotiations are supposed to go."

"I know. If my duenna heard me now, she'd ban me from the marketplace."

He shook his head. "Then let me pay you what I suggested."

"If it makes you feel better."

On this visit, Elena met Mrs. Matthews, the woman who kept the house in order and took care of Jenny when Bill was at work. After exchanging a few pleasantries, they went in search of Elena's student. Jenny was waiting in the studio her father had set up in a spare bedroom. Although she was obviously eager for her art lesson, there were still a few awkward moments when Elena came into the room.

Jenny was seated in her wheelchair behind a low easel. "Dad said if I was going to be serious about my work, I should have a studio."

"That's a good idea," Elena murmured.

"He says this room has northern light—and that's good for artists," she explained to her teacher.

"Mmm-hmm."

Finally Jenny gestured toward the easel in front of her. "I want to show you what I've been working on.... I'm not sure you'll like it."

Elena came around to look at the picture. It was an acrylic portrait of a dark-haired young woman.

"Why, that's me!"

Jenny puffed out her chest. "You can tell!"

"Of course. You did that from memory?"

The girl nodded.

"Well, then you have real talent. And I'm flattered that you chose me as a subject."

Bill was standing in the doorway. Elena saw him beam, then quietly retreat down the hall.

"You're so pretty that I wanted to paint you. But it's not quite right."

"Let me show you some techniques that will help," Elena offered, settling down opposite the girl and picking up a soft pencil and sketch pad. "Some artists think of the head as egg-shaped. Others begin with a cube or a triangle. Then they attach the parts like the eyes, ears, nose and mouth according to a certain set of average proportions."

"That's sort of what the book I used said to do."

Elena nodded. "But using a formula doesn't work very well, because each person's head is different. No one is really 'average.'"

"True," Jenny agreed.

"It's better if you indicate the skull with a very simple outline—using a circle or an oval. Then look at the person you're drawing and establish the center of the face with a line. I'll use you as a model to demonstrate what I mean." As she spoke, Elena began to work. "Now I'll sketch in a line where your eyes will go, then the bottom of your nose and your mouth. That way I'll have the unique proportions of your face." Elena reached across and gave Jenny another pad and pencil. "Why don't you try starting another portrait of me, using that technique? That way we can work together."

"Good. Then you can help me when I get stuck."

Elena smilingly agreed. "But remember," she cautioned, "portraits aren't just a matter of technique. You have to try to capture the essence of the person, not just a set of features. Do you understand what I mean?"

"I think so."

They were both so absorbed in their work that it was a surprise when Bill came back an hour and a half later.

"I hate to break this up, but I promised to get Elena home to her fiancé."

"You live with him?" Jenny inquired.

"I've lived in his house since I came up here to Santa Barbara. But I don't, ah—"

"You don't have to answer impertinent questions from nosy teenagers," Bill said, coming to her rescue.

"I was just wondering, because Carol used to stay here sometimes with Dad—before my accident. When she was here, his clothes matched better." She shot her father an impish look.

Elena didn't know what to say. "I'll see you next week," she told Jenny and then made a quick exit to the car.

It was a few minutes before Bill joined her.

"Sorry," he apologized. "You never know what these kids are going to come out with."

"I understand." She laced her hands together.

"Carol and I were going to be married. We would have been last January, if Jenny hadn't taken that fall."

"Bill, you don't have to explain anything to me."

"I know. You're about the least judgmental person I've ever met. But sometimes I wish I could explain it to myself." He sighed. "Maybe I drove her away by being so wrapped up with Jenny after the accident."

"You were terribly worried about your daughter."

"But I didn't have much time for Carol when Jenny was in the hospital. That was what she told me when we broke up." He paused. "Although I sort of wondered if part of it was that she couldn't cope with the idea of a stepdaughter in a wheelchair."

"I'm sorry."

"I've come to terms with it. Maybe I made an unconscious choice. Or maybe it was something that would have happened, anyway. Sometimes a man and a woman think they know each other, but they don't really."

"In my country, people would rarely talk so openly about anything so personal. And certainly not on such short acquaintance."

"Have I offended you?"

"Oh, no. That's not what I meant at all," she assured him quickly. "I'm...I'm glad that you think of me as a friend."

"It's easy to trust you because you're so understanding. I just wish I could do as much for you as you've already done for Jenny. There's a big difference in her just since last week."

"Bill, you've done more for me than you realize." She shook her head. "Things can be so overwhelming. Sometimes I feel as though I'm a visitor from another century, not just another continent."

He reached over and patted her hand. "I know it must be discombobulating, being thrust into the middle of a strange culture."

"Discombobulating. I don't know the word, but it certainly sounds right."

"Well, you're coping beautifully as far as I can see."

Bill was silent for the next few miles. As they pulled into the driveway, he turned to Elena. "I've been thinking. I'm on the fund-raising committee for the rehabilitation center. We're having a meeting Sunday night to organize things. Why don't you come?"

When Elena looked doubtful, he went on. "We could use someone like you. But you'd benefit, too." He hesitated. "I've sort of gotten the impression from things you've said that you haven't had a chance to get out much. The committee would be a good way to meet some nice people."

"I'll have to think about it."

"If you decide to go, I'll be glad to give you a ride."

"Let me see what Stephen thinks."

When Elena stepped out of the car and turned toward the house, she spotted Maggie's bulky figure blocking the doorway. "Is something wrong?"

"Nothing," the housekeeper reassured her quickly. "Sorry I gave you a start, but Stephen wanted me to catch you as soon as you got back." As she spoke, her face broke into a broad grin.

Elena shook her head. "I have the feeling that the two of you have been up to something."

"Not me. Stephen."

"Where is he?"

"Down at the stables. He told me to ask you to change into jeans and riding boots."

Elena looked at the housekeeper inquiringly. "What exactly does he have in mind?"

"I guess you'd better ask him."

It took only a few minutes to comply with Stephen's request and make her way down to the stable. When she opened the door and stepped inside, she had to stifle a surge of disappointment. Nothing seemed particularly out of the

PLAY
HARLEQUIN'S

LUCKY HEARTS
GAME

AND YOU COULD GET

- ★ **FREE BOOKS**
- ★ **A FREE BRACELET WATCH**
- ★ **A FREE SURPRISE GIFT**
- ★ **AND MUCH MORE**

**TURN THE PAGE AND
DEAL YOURSELF IN** →

PLAY "LUCKY HEARTS" AND YOU COULD GET...

★ Exciting Harlequin Superromance® novels—FREE
★ A bracelet watch—FREE
★ A surprise mystery gift that will delight you—FREE

THEN CONTINUE YOUR LUCKY STREAK WITH A SWEETHEART OF A DEAL

When you return the postcard on the opposite page, we'll send you the books and gifts you qualify for, absolutely free! Then, you'll get 4 new Harlequin Superromance® novels every month, delivered right to your door months before they're available in stores. If you decide to keep them, you'll pay only $2.74* per book—that's 21 cents below the cover price and there is no extra charge for postage and handling! You can cancel at any time by marking "cancel" on your statement or returning a shipment to us at our cost.

★ Free Newsletter!

You'll get a free newsletter—an insider's look at our most popular authors and their upcoming novels.

★ Special Extras—Free!

When you subscribe to the Harlequin Reader Service®, you'll also get additional free gifts from time to time as a token of our appreciation for being a home subscriber.

HARLEQUIN "NO RISK" GUARANTEE

★ You're not required to buy a single book—ever!
★ As a subscriber, you must be completely satisfied or you may cancel at any time by marking "cancel" on your statement or returning a shipment of books at our cost.
★ The free books and gifts you receive from this LUCKY HEARTS offer remain yours to keep—in any case.

If offer card is missing, write to:
Harlequin Reader Service, 901 Fuhrmann Blvd., P.O. Box 1867, Buffalo, NY 14269-1867

ordinary. But the man who was cleaning out one of the stalls stopped and gave her a knowing look.

"Where can I find Señor Gallagher?"

He pointed toward the paddock.

As soon as she reemerged into the afternoon sunlight, Elena spotted Storm Dancer. But it wasn't the horse that riveted her attention. Her eyes were drawn to the rider jauntily sitting astride the stallion.

"Hi." Stephen's greeting was deceptively casual.

"Hello yourself."

Not to be left out of the conversation, the big animal bobbed his head and nickered a greeting.

"I see my horse now has divided loyalties," Stephen observed with a note of mock disapproval.

"And I see you've already begun reeducating him about who's the boss."

"Mmm-hmm. But we won't talk about what it took to get me up here."

Concern flickered in her dark eyes. "Is it really all right for you to ride?"

"Yes. In fact, I've already taken a couple of practice turns around the paddock."

The groom, who had been standing in the shadows of the stable, took his cue and emerged, leading a palomino filly.

Elena turned and stared at the other horse.

"What do you think of her?"

"Stephen, she's beautiful."

"I was hoping you'd think so. Her name's Windemere. She's three years old—and quite a match for Storm Dancer."

Elena walked over to the filly and stroked her caramel-colored forelock. She responded with a soft, nickering sound. After taking a few more minutes to get acquainted, Elena swung herself into the saddle and looked at Stephen.

The groom opened the gate and Stephen turned his mount. When Storm Dancer walked onto the brown grass, Windemere followed.

Stephen glanced back at Elena and grinned. Then he leaned over and smoothed his fingers across the black stallion's neck. It had been a long time since she had seen him like this—carefree and glad to be alive. This was how he'd been on those rides across her father's estate.

"You're remembering." His voice held a note of certainty.

"Yes."

"Even that first time we rode together, I wanted to bring you up here, show you my ranch."

She felt a lump forming in her throat and simply nodded.

"Hal says you usually ride down into the canyon."

"Mmm."

"Then let's try the other direction."

"Into the hills?"

"Yes."

He made a clicking sound with his tongue and lightly flicked the reins. Storm Dancer started off at a trot. Just as Hal had once watched her and the black stallion, Elena now observed the big horse and his rider carefully. They moved in concert. She'd had no trouble controlling Storm Dancer, but it wasn't the same. Horse and man moved together, almost as though the former were reading the latter's mind.

Stephen increased the pace to a canter. Then he leaned forward and gave the powerful stallion his head. Storm Dancer kicked up his heels and galloped joyfully across the sun-drenched landscape. Windemere followed.

The two magnificent animals pounded across the rolling hills. Elena threw back her head as she had done on her first ride here, glorying in the feel of sun on her shoulders and the wind in her hair. But more than that she was awed by the knowledge of what these simple pleasures must mean to the man beside her.

As they approached a clump of live oak trees, Stephen slowed the pace. By the time they reached the filtered shade of the broad boughs, he had slowed his mount to a walk.

Elena brought Windemere abreast of the stallion. ''That was wonderful.''

''Yes.'' His grin was jubilant. ''I've been cooped up in the house so long. Now I feel like one of the Spanish conquistadors.''

''I'll bet none of them had a horse quite like Storm Dancer.''

He nodded. ''You don't know what it means to me to ride like this with him again.'' He turned Storm Dancer in the direction from which they had come, and Elena followed suit.

''I'd like to get down and walk around.'' He shook his head. ''But I'm afraid I need the fence to climb back up.''

''This is fine.''

''When I was a kid I used to come up here early in the morning and sit in the shelter of one of these trees. If you're very quiet, you can see deer up here at dawn, drifting through the brush like shadows.''

''Oh, I'd love to do that with you.''

He nodded. ''Or we could pack a lunch. Maggie used to do that for me, too.''

Elena looked around. Below them were the gently rounded hills. Above was the chaparral dotted with sage and the dark, twisted shapes of manzanita bushes. It was so different from the lush greenery of her former home, yet she had come to love it just as deeply. ''This must have been what it was like before the Spanish came,'' she murmured.

"That's what I used to pretend—that the modern world didn't exist."

"I used to do that, too, on my father's estate."

"And then a jet plane would fly over and spoil the illusion."

She nodded.

He maneuvered Storm Dancer beside Windemere, so that their riders sat knee to knee. Elena smiled at him, and for a little while they sat looking at the landscape.

An airplane high in the blue sky finally broke the silence.

"But the world does exist," Elena whispered.

"Yes." Stephen glanced up at the white trail of jet exhaust. "And we'd better start heading back before it gets dark. I don't want Hal to send out a search party."

CHAPTER TEN

THAT EVENING Elena helped Maggie carry the dishes to the kitchen after supper. "Go on back and relax with Stephen," the housekeeper said, shooing her out of the room. "I'll finish up."

"Are you sure?"

"Go on."

Elena let Maggie persuade her. Over the past few days, she and Stephen had gotten into the habit of making a fire in the library fireplace every evening. Because she had discovered that his leg felt better stretched out, she'd come up with the idea of spreading a quilt on the floor in front of the couch and bringing down several of the cushions to lean against. It was a cozy place to sit and talk.

Now when she entered the book-lined room, Stephen had already lighted the fire and made himself comfortable.

"Shall I take your boots off?"

"Please."

Kneeling by his feet, she eased off first one boot and then the other. Through his socks she could see him wiggling his toes.

"Ah, freedom."

She smiled and nodded. It was a pleasure to see him enjoying such simple things again.

"That apple pie of yours was wonderful. I keep thinking about whether I should have another piece."

She sat back on her heels. "Why not?"

"I don't want to ruin my figure."

"I hardly think you're in any danger. You're still under-weight."

"Bad habits have a way of creeping up on you."

"What about an after-dinner drink instead?"

"Sounds good." Stephen started to push himself to a sitting position.

Elena put a gentle hand on his shoulder. "I'll get them. What would you like?"

They had reached an understanding about her doing things for him—at least some things.

"Surprise me."

She came back in a few minutes with two miniature snifters. After handing one to Stephen, she lowered herself to the quilt beside him.

He sniffed the amber liquid and then took a sip. "Cointreau. You're learning my tastes."

"I want to do that." She settled down next to him and took a sip from her own glass. "When I was a little girl, there was a cough medicine that Anna gave me that reminds me of this."

He chuckled. "Cough medicine! So that's what you think of my choice in liqueurs."

"Cough medicine can taste good."

"Ah, you're a master of diplomacy, as well as an accomplished painter, a good cook, an excellent rider—and a passable driver."

"I'm doing much better with the Camaro and I've passed my learner's test. Hal is going to take me out on the freeway in a few days."

"I'm just teasing." He closed his eyes and leaned back against the pillows, crossing his long legs at the ankles. Elena understood the importance of the simple gesture. It meant that his body was limbering up.

"Do you want to play The Game?" Elena murmured.

As a way of getting to know each other better, they had invented an activity that they first called, "The Game of Best and Worst" and then simply, "The Game." It had been a device for starting difficult conversations. As they had gotten to trust each other more fully, the topics had become more revealing.

"The Game, hmm?"

"Yes."

"All right."

"It's my turn to start. Which of your accomplishments pleases you the most?"

Stephen smiled. "Did you spend all day thinking of that one?"

"Stalling no fair. Just answer the question."

He thought for a moment. "My father gave me Storm Dancer when I was seventeen and he was just a colt—told me that he would be my responsibility. I raised him and trained him, and I'm pretty proud of him."

"You did a wonderful job."

"Did you expect that answer?"

"I've come to realize that what you care about most is right here at this ranch."

He squeezed her shoulder. "Yes, right here."

She looked over at him. "You know, Hal would love it if Rancho Palo Colorado were a bigger part of your professional interests."

"He told you that?"

"Not in so many words. But I could tell."

"I've been thinking about it, too. But right now isn't a good time to make any major changes—not when I'm running the corporation from out here."

"You haven't talked much about your business."

"I didn't want to bore you to tears."

"No, I'd love to hear."

He settled more comfortably into the cushions. "All right, you asked for it."

For the next half hour she listened in fascination, occasionally asking a question.

Finally he stopped and smiled. "I see you're still awake."

"Don't be silly. I'm interested in everything about you."

"Okay. But it's my turn to ask a question now."

"All right."

"What was the worst thing about your childhood?"

"Now you are making me pay for my question, aren't you?"

"No. I want to know the answer."

"I don't have to think about it. I know it was my mother's leaving. You know how it is when you're a child. You see everything in terms of yourself. I thought it was somehow my fault, that I'd driven her away."

Silently he reached for her hand, but didn't interrupt.

"It was only later," she continued, "that I really understood. It was the relationship with my father that had made it impossible for her to stay."

He pressed her fingers tightly in his. "You don't have to tell me any more about it now."

"No, I want to talk to you about the things that made me the person I am. Stephen, I was always afraid of my father. He was a man who needed to control everything around him. I was afraid of his temper. I know now that my mother was, too."

"Did he ever . . . hit you?"

She looked down at the muted pattern of the quilt. "Sometimes."

"Tell me!"

"The worst times were with a strap."

Stephen muttered something in a low and dangerous-sounding tone.

"Not very often," Elena rushed on. "One time I'd taken a book from the library and left it out in the rain. Another time I was showing an expensive cut-glass ornament to a friend and dropped it."

His hands had balled into fists. "He did that to you because of things that could be replaced?"

"Yes. But you have to remember, I come from a place where the owner of a large estate is like the lord of a manor. That's the way *he* was raised."

"That's no excuse." He was silent for a moment, thinking. "I understand some things better now. What about that night you came to me in the garden? What would he have done if he had caught you?"

She shuddered. "I don't know."

"I didn't realize what a risk you were taking, *querida*." He drew in a deep breath. "I'm sorry you had to live that way."

"Some good came out of it. It made me a more disciplined person. And then my mother's leaving was what made me throw myself into painting. It was a way to express the emotions that were bottled up inside."

His fingers sought hers again. "But you're so warm and giving. How did you learn that?"

"Anna was loving with me. Even when my mother was still there, Anna treated me like the daughter she never had. She was the one who wiped away my tears when I skinned my knee and gave me little rewards for a good report card." Elena lowered her voice to a whisper. "And she was the one who held me and let me weep the night after you left."

Stephen put his arms around her. "Oh, *querida*. If only..."

They both struggled to control their emotions. In soft tones she told him more about her relationship with the old woman.

"I'm glad you had her."

Elena nodded. "And Stephen, despite what you may think, my father wasn't all bad. He could be generous—on his own terms."

For a few moments they sipped their drinks. "And your mother?" Stephen finally asked. "You never say much about her. Did she keep in touch with you after she left?"

"Maybe she wanted to. At least I hope so. But I think my father forbade her to write to me."

"You just said—"

"I know. He was a hard man to understand."

"Didn't he realize what you must be feeling?"

"He had to cope with his own sorrow—and the failure of his marriage—as best he could." Elena took another sip of her drink and looked across the small room at the dancing flames. "Stephen," she murmured, "I've told you things I've never told anyone else."

"I'm glad you feel you can. It's true for me, too."

After setting down her glass on an end table, she turned and gently traced the curve of his lips with her index finger. Eyes still closed, he smiled.

"In some ways I feel very close to you. But in others it's as if you're farther out of my reach."

"What do you mean?"

"Since that night I came to your room, you've hardly kissed me. Why not?"

His lids snapped open, and she found herself suddenly drowning in the sea-blue pools of his eyes.

"Not because I don't want to, *querida*."

The tone of his voice warned her not to pursue the subject. She couldn't stop herself. "This afternoon Jenny asked me if I were living with you. Stephen, she's a fourteen-year-old girl.''

''They grow up fast in Southern California.''

''I was embarrassed—for the wrong reason, I think.''

''You shouldn't be.''

''Bill said that, too.''

''You told *him*?''

''He was there when she asked me.''

''I see.''

She slid down beside him on the quilt, so that her head was even with his. ''Stephen, I want to be close to you in every way. I know I'm very—'' she searched for the right word ''—inexperienced. But is there something I'm doing wrong?''

He swore softly under his breath. ''You're not doing anything wrong, sweetheart.''

''Then what is the matter?''

''Let's talk about something else—like the Federal Reserve Board prime lending rate. I heard on the news that it went down again today.''

''Esteban, I don't want to talk about the Federal Reserve Board.''

His eyes had darkened to cobalt. ''Believe me, it's safer than the subject you've started on.''

''Why?''

''We're treading on dangerous ground again.''

''Perhaps I'm trying to tell you that's what I want.''

His gaze swept over her devouringly. She saw that he had wadded handfuls of the quilt in his fists, as though to keep himself from reaching out to her.

Neither of them moved, although it cost her a great deal of effort not to turn away.

"All right." His voice had thickened. "I try not to think about kissing you, because when I do, I think about what else I want to do with you."

"What do you want to do?" The question came out high and reedy, like wind rustling through dry grass—grass crisp as tinder, ready to ignite at the smallest spark.

His gaze traveled to the front of her blouse and lingered there. In response she felt her nipples harden.

"That night when you came to my room, I could see your breasts through your gown. They're very high and very sweetly rounded. I keep thinking about how beautiful you look. But I want to do more than see you. I want to touch you—and not just through a layer of silky material." As he spoke, his fingers twisted more tightly in the fabric of the quilt.

It was unbelievable that mere words could have that great an effect. It was almost as if she felt his hands hot and insistent on her naked skin. She sucked in her breath. "I think you're right. Maybe you shouldn't tell me any more," she managed to say.

The reflection of the flames danced in his eyes. He might have been a savage alone with his mate in the wilderness. The camp fire was their only protection against the creatures lurking in the night.

"Oh no, *querida*," he rasped. "You're the one who insisted. Now you're going to hear it all. I know how warm and soft your breasts will be, because I've caressed them so many times in my fantasies. For months I only had those fantasies. They helped me fight for my life, gave me something to want badly enough to stay alive. But the fantasies didn't stop when you arrived. Having you here only made the wanting more intense."

She waited, afraid of what he might say next, yet aching to hear the words.

The firelight flickered on the planes of his face, softening the scars, but accentuating the intensity of his expression. "And your nipples," he continued with deceptive quiet. "I know just how it will be to circle them with my thumbs—take each hard pebble into my mouth—feel your body quickening to my demands."

She saw the tension in his body like a bow pulled taut. Her own was almost too much to support.

Her head flopped against his shoulder. She pressed her open mouth against his shirt, biting into the fabric, seeking intimate contact. Her body had grown rigid, yet at the same time was liquid with sensation.

He continued to study her. "You feel it too, don't you?"

Did he mean that her whole body felt as though it had reached flash point—that she throbbed with the need for something still beyond her grasp? "I want..." Her throat was so constricted that it was impossible to say more—to describe what he had done to her with the power of his words.

His eyes burned in the darkness. "So do I, *querida*. So do I."

Finally he let go of the quilt and tangled his fingers in the thick darkness of her hair. "So silky. So alive," he murmured.

"Yes, please touch me, Stephen. And don't turn away when I reach for you."

She wouldn't have believed that the expression on his face could have grown more primitive. But it did. "*Querida*, you don't know what you're asking. When I lie there in the dark fantasizing about you, I think about taking your hand, showing you precisely how much I need you."

For a moment he was very still. Then he captured her hand. At first he simply held it. Then, with a growl deep in his throat, he pressed her palm against the front of his slacks.

A tiny gasp of desire escaped her lips. She had thought about him like this, but the reality was far more potent than her virginal imaginings.

He felt stiff and immense, pulsing with life. She knew she should snatch her hand away. But she acknowledged that she had secretly wanted to know the feel of him, experience the power she felt under her palm. Of their own accord her fingers began to move over him, discovering, stroking.

He closed his eyes and sucked a deep, shuddering breath into his lungs as he arched into her caress. "Sweetheart, you don't know how good that feels," he murmured. Then, as though he had suddenly realized that this was not his fantasy but reality, his eyes snapped open again.

"My God, Elena! Don't! I want you so much, it's driving me insane."

"Please, let me give you whatever you want."

He ignored her words. With trembling fingers he pushed her hand away, even as he struggled to a sitting position. "But it always comes down to the same damn problem—my goddamn legs that I have to drag around like slabs of dead wood."

Despite his protestations, he scrambled to his feet with more agility than she had ever seen him display and snatched his crutches from the edge of the couch.

For a moment he stood beside the quilt, looking down at her, his gaze hooded. "Don't count on sipping coffee with me tomorrow morning, *querida*. I don't believe I'm going to be ready to face you at breakfast."

IN FACT, she didn't see him at all during the next few days. True to his word, he was already working with Larry when she came down to breakfast.

"He grabbed a cup of coffee and went over to the gym," Maggie explained. "Said he didn't want anything else—and not to expect him at lunch, either."

The housekeeper gave the young woman at the table a speculative look. "Did the two of you have a fight?"

Elena's mug clattered against the table, sloshing brown liquid onto the polished surface. Grabbing a napkin from the holder, she began to wipe it up.

"Sorry. It's not my place to ask."

Elena looked at the housekeeper's worried face. "Maggie, I know how much you care about Stephen."

"Not just Stephen, you, too."

"Thank you." She was silent for a moment. It was so hard not having anyone to talk to about some of her deepest anxieties. Yet there were certain personal things she didn't feel comfortable confiding—even to someone as close to her as Maggie had become. Perhaps it was her experience with Anna that made her hold back. They had been close in so many ways. But when it came to sexual matters, her old duenna had failed her. Sex simply wasn't something Anna had felt comfortable talking about. Maggie was of the same generation, and she had never been married. Trying to talk to her about what had happened last night would probably just embarrass the two of them.

"Is there anything I can do?"

"No. We have to work it out for ourselves." She paused. "It's not always going to go smoothly with us. Stephen's still concerned about his physical problems. Even with me."

"I know."

"But we *will* work it out. I'm convinced of that now."

"That's what I was hoping you'd say."

ELENA SPENT the weekend painting and practicing her driving on the ranch roads. But she still found her thoughts turning to Stephen when she least expected it.

Partly to get her mind off her problems, she called Bill on Saturday afternoon. "If you're still willing to take me to that meeting tomorrow, I'd like to go."

"I was hoping you would."

"I don't have my driver's license yet, just my learner's permit. Will you be able to pick me up?"

"I'll be glad to."

The meeting was at the home of Mary Falconer, a wealthy widow who had been active on the rehabilitation hospital's board for several years.

Elena couldn't repress a broad smile when Bill picked her up. He was actually wearing a subdued gray sport coat and tie and a clean white shirt.

"This must be a special occasion."

"Oh, I can get dressed up when the need arises."

As they drove south, Bill began to talk animatedly about the group's fund-raising activities. But as Elena tried to analyze the enthusiasm in his voice, she began to wonder if he was really so stimulated by the idea of helping the rehabilitation center. Was there perhaps something else about tonight that he was looking forward to?

It reminded her of their first meeting at the art supply store. Something was going on that she didn't understand yet. But with Bill, she knew she was bound to find out sooner or later.

Mary Falconer's lavish Spanish colonial mansion was high in the hills above Santa Barbara in the well-to-do area known as the Riviera. As they pulled into the wide, circular driveway, Elena's attention shifted away from Bill.

"Are you sure I'm going to fit in?" she asked her companion anxiously.

"Don't worry about it. You'll be perfect." He patted her hand reassuringly before opening the door and coming around to help her out of the car.

As soon as they entered the house, they were greeted warmly by the hostess herself. "Bill has told me so much about how you've helped Jenny," she informed Elena.

"I haven't done very much."

"More than you realize. And I'm sure you'll be a real asset to our committee."

"I hope so."

Before turning to greet another guest, Mary pointed the way to an enclosed terrace that provided a magnificent view of the city below. Elena looked around at the group of prominent businessmen and other prosperous local residents who were already assembled.

Seated on the couch was Tom Mitchell, one of the gallery owners she'd met on her first trip into Santa Barbara— the one who'd recognized the picture of Stephen she was carrying and made some remarks about his disfigurement. The comment had set Elena's teeth on edge. She would have been happy to never see the man again. Now here he was.

Quickly she turned away, pretending to be interested in the view. But her attention was immediately caught by an attractive, delicate-looking blonde standing by one of the broad windows. The woman was looking out into the darkness, seemingly absorbed by the view of the twinkling lights far below. But as she heard footsteps on the tile floor, she turned and glanced into the room. Shock registered on her features. Elena saw that she was staring at Bill, and he was staring back at her. In a few swift strides he crossed to her.

As Elena watched the pair stood gazing awkwardly into each other's eyes, then began to speak in low tones. All at once she realized that this must be Carol, the woman Bill had been dating when Jenny had had her accident.

She knew she shouldn't be listening to their conversation, but couldn't help herself.

"Carol." He sounded as if he were dredging up air from the bottom of his lungs just to say her name.

She looked pale. Fragile. Her hand fluttered. Then she brought it quickly back to her side. "Bill."

He shifted his weight from one foot to the other. "How are you?"

"I've been okay. How's Jenny?"

"She's doing much better."

"I'm glad."

Bill cleared his throat. "I wondered if you were going to be here tonight."

"Oh."

"I—"

She leaned forward slightly. "What?"

"Nothing."

Elena saw Bill gesture awkwardly with his hands. She had the odd sensation that the spoken conversation represented only the surface of what this man and woman wanted to communicate to each other. She held her breath, wondering if they could really let each other know what they were feeling. But after a few more moments of chatting, Bill nodded curtly and turned away. Maybe it was just too public a place for a private discussion. Or maybe they were each afraid to take the chance of reaching out.

Before she could speculate any more, Elena became aware that someone was standing in front of her. It was Tom Mitchell, and there was no way to avoid talking to him without being rude.

"Well, well, the very attractive Elena Castile. How nice to see you here."

"Mr. Mitchell."

He glanced questioningly down at her bare left hand and then up at her face. "No ring. Are you still engaged to Steve Gallagher?"

The question was so presumptuous that Elena almost turned away. But for some reason she wanted this man to know that things were going well between Stephen and herself. She tilted her chin so that her eyes met his. "Of course."

"Great. How is he doing?"

"Very well. We were out riding the other day."

Mitchell looked surprised. "He is doing better than I'd heard."

"Yes."

"I suppose his injury got you interested in the rehabilitation hospital."

Bill, who had come up behind Elena, answered the question. "I told her about the meeting. Now if you'll excuse us, there's someone I want Elena to meet."

Taking her elbow, he led her across the room.

"Thanks," she whispered when they were out of earshot.

"You didn't look as though you were having a particularly good time."

"Neither did you."

Bill shrugged, but didn't say anything more. Instead he introduced Elena to a short, slender man with thick gray hair and darkly tanned skin. There were deep lines around his eyes. They crinkled when he smiled, which Elena soon discovered was often.

"Elena, I'd like to introduce Sam Goldner."

Goldner offered Elena his hand. "So nice to meet you."

"Sam owns the Santa Ynez Ranch just south of town. It's a very exclusive resort that was originally purchased as a getaway by a group of silent film stars. They'd come up from Hollywood whenever they had a chance.''

"How interesting."

"He's agreed to donate a long weekend in one of his plushest cottages this year."

Bill had explained on the drive over that the committee would be organizing its second auction to raise funds for the rehabilitation center. Last year they'd offered everything from a harbor cruise dinner party to fifty-two fresh flower arrangements delivered weekly from a downtown florist. The response had been gratifying. Everybody who'd attended the event had had a wonderful time, and the committee had raised almost $100,000. They hoped to do even better this year.

"Steve and I used to get in some deep-sea fishing together. I've missed him," Sam told Elena.

"I hope the two of you can go out again sometime soon."

"He must be better, then. I'm glad. I was worried about him."

"Yes, he's much better."

The threesome chatted for a few more minutes until Mary Falconer invited everyone into the dining room for some light refreshments.

Elena had met so few people since coming to the States that she had worried about how she would fit into a group of *norteamericanos*. But she needn't have feared. Everyone seemed eager to put her at ease. Moreover, her natural charm and the quiet good manners instilled by her upbringing made it easy to get along with the assemblage.

By the time the meeting began, she felt as though she was among friends.

"We already have a nice list of items to auction off," Mary announced. There were exclamations from the group as she named a cruise to Mexico, a dinner party catered by one of the town's most exclusive restaurants, and a custom-designed gold necklace from a jeweler on Rodeo Drive in Los Angeles.

"Mary arranged for that herself," Bill whispered. "She's one of their best customers."

But the fund-raiser still needed additional items, and the chairwoman went on to urge everyone to go out and do some soliciting. It wasn't something Elena could easily imagine herself doing.

"Start with the people who value your patronage," Mary urged.

Well, that left her out, Elena thought. The only place she'd shopped with any regularity so far was the grocery store. And she suspected a case of oranges wasn't going to create quite the excitement of a necklace from Rodeo Drive.

Mary discussed some additional techniques. "Point out the tax advantages of contributing," she suggested. "And the advertising value. And don't forget that anybody who contributes gets a free ticket to the gala—which gives them the opportunity to spend money on somebody else's contribution."

That brought a laugh from the crowd.

It was almost 10:00 p.m. by the time the meeting broke up.

"Well, what did you think?" Bill asked as he helped her into the car.

"I liked almost everyone. You're right. It was a good way to get to know some people. But I'm overwhelmed. Do you think someone as new in town as I am is really going to be much help?"

"Of course."

They exchanged impressions of the meeting for a few moments. Then Elena gave Bill an inquiring glance. "That pretty woman named Carol. Is she the one you used to date?"

"Yeah."

"She seemed glad to see you."

"I wasn't sure. How could you tell?"

"The way she looked at you. The way her hands fluttered."

"I asked Mary to invite her to the meeting." He looked embarrassed. "Maybe she just—you know—felt funny about seeing me again. That could be it."

Elena didn't think so. Slanting Bill a look, she saw his lips were set in a firm line as he watched the road ahead. She would have liked to keep him talking, but had never felt comfortable prying into someone else's life. And who was she to be offering advice, anyway? she asked herself. She didn't even know how to put her own life in order.

When Bill dropped her off at the ranch, she thanked him warmly for the evening out. But her steps were heavy as she made her way up the stairs to her bedroom.

WHEN SHE CAME DOWN to breakfast the next morning, Stephen was at the table. As Elena slid into the chair opposite him, Maggie made a hasty exit from the room.

Stephen fiddled with his knife for a moment, then cleared his throat. "I'm sorry about the other night."

"You warned me."

"I shouldn't have started talking to you like that. I'm sure I shocked you."

"I didn't mind." She laughed uncertainly. "No, I'll be honest. I liked it."

His laughter mingled with hers. "Now I'm the one who's shocked."

"Well, since I've forgiven you, you have to forgive me."

"Sweetheart, I think I'm getting the best of the bargain."

Stephen reached out and twined his fingers with Elena's. "Not even knowing that I had made a fool of myself could keep me away from you."

"You didn't—"

"What would you call it?"

"My being stupid enough to pursue a subject you had warned me to drop."

"Mmm. So you're going to let me off the hook."

Her eyes twinkled. "Like a wiggling fish."

He grinned back at her. "Exactly."

"That reminds me. I met your fishing buddy, Sam Goldner, at the committee meeting I went to with Bill."

"Sam. I haven't seen him since that trip we took to Baja California. How is that old devil?"

"Old devil? What else did the two of you do together besides fish?"

"Well, let's just say he's one of the best cardplayers in Southern California." Stephen relaxed in his chair. "So tell me who else was at your meeting."

Elena smiled at him across the table. It had been a long time since she'd seen him in such a good mood. And it was wonderful to be talking so easily with him again. She told him who'd been at Mary Falconer's, describing the plans for the auction and the prizes they'd already gotten.

"And what about your plans for today?" he finally asked.

"I want to finish up another landscape for Miles Henderson. And then in the afternoon I'm going to give Jenny Delaney another lesson."

"How's she coming along?"

"Very nicely." Elena told him a bit about the girl's blossoming abilities and then asked about his own plans.

"Unfortunately, I have to take care of some things that have come up at work. So I won't be seeing you again until dinner."

"I understand." She looked at him inquiringly. "Is there something else you want to say?"

"Why do you ask?"

"Your mood . . . your expression."

"And what is my expression like?"

"Like a little boy who isn't sure he can keep a secret."

Stephen laughed. "Sweetheart, sometimes I wish you couldn't read me so accurately." He paused. "There *is* something else. But I'd rather wait a few more days."

CHAPTER ELEVEN

THREE DAYS LATER Elena awoke a little earlier than usual. The covers had slipped away from her shoulders, and her skin felt chilled. After pulling the blanket up again, she glanced drowsily at the small clock on the table beside the bed. She was about to close her eyes once more and snuggle deeper under the covers when the feeling of being watched drew her gaze to the opposite side of the room. She had become so used to having the top floor of the house completely to herself that she had gotten into the habit of sleeping with her door ajar. Now to her sleepy amazement, she saw Stephen standing propped against the doorjamb, looking at her warmly. Despite the early hour, he was dressed in jeans and a blue cotton shirt that she had never seen before.

She smiled lazily. "Am I dreaming? Or is that really you?"

"I don't know. Perhaps I'm still asleep and it's my dream."

"It's too early in the morning for me to cope with anything that complicated."

He smiled back at her and then his face grew serious. "Your door was open."

She started to push herself to a sitting position, realized that the maneuver would expose the top of her nightgown and grasped the edge of the covers so that she could drag them up with her.

"I should have asked if I could come in. But I was enjoying the view—and I didn't want to wake you."

All of a sudden she remembered the conversation they'd had a few days ago. "Did you want to talk to me?"

"Mmm-hmm."

He started across the floor, and she realized suddenly that he wasn't using crutches. Instead his right hand gripped the handle of a dark wooden cane.

"Stephen!" And then a new thought struck her. "You walked up the stairs! Your knee must be much better."

"Yup." He looked pleased with himself. When he reached the bed, she shifted slightly to give him room to sit down. After putting aside the cane, he took her up on the offer. She could see that his hair was damp from the shower.

"You're up early."

"I have been for the past few days. I've been practicing on the steps. This morning I decided to see if I could make it all the way to my old room."

She reached over and squeezed his hand. "I guess that was one of your goals."

"Mmm-hmm. Actually it meant something very important to me."

She waited, hardly daring to breathe.

His blue eyes sought her dark ones. "Elena, I've been telling myself for weeks that when I could walk upstairs to the second floor, I'd be in good enough shape to ask you to marry me."

She stared at him, wondering if she had really understood the words.

"Perhaps I'd better rephrase the statement as a question. Will you marry me?"

She reached up and joyfully clasped her arms around his neck. "Oh yes, Stephen. Yes, I will."

He let out the breath he had been holding. "Well, that's a relief."

"Did you really think I'd say no?"

"After the way I've acted, I had my doubts."

"And I was beginning to wonder if you'd ever ask."

"Elena, I've been rough on you and I'm sorry."

"Not any rougher than you have been on yourself."

"That's no excuse."

"I understood."

"*Querida*, I love you so very much. I would have been a fool to let you slip away."

She drew back and looked at him, her vision suddenly misted by a film of tears that was making bright prisms of light play in his hair. "That's the first time you've said that to me."

"I know. I've wanted to so many times. Saying it out loud was the final risk."

"*Mi amor.* I love you so much."

His arms tightened around her. His fingers glided over the silky skin of her back. His lips nibbled along the line where her dark hair swept back from her face.

When he lifted his head, their gazes locked.

"*Querida,*" he murmured. "I shouldn't be here in your room, but I couldn't stop myself from looking in. You were so tantalizing and so trustingly asleep."

She nodded wordlessly, feeling the sudden tension of the moment.

His eyes focused on her lips and his fingers stroked across her cheek, smoothing the tangle of her hair.

With arms that weren't quite steady, she reached up to clasp his broad shoulders. He was solid, real, vital.

Somewhere below them a door slammed.

Stephen's hands stilled, and his head turned toward the half-open window.

Warily Elena followed the direction of his gaze. As they both listened intently, Maggie's voice drifted up from the patio. "What are you doing here so early this morning?"

"Checking the equipment," Larry answered. "Have you seen Steve around?"

"I think he's upstairs. Want me to look for him?"

"I'll let you know."

Elena felt Stephen's body stiffen and heard him mutter an oath. In the next moment he had moved away from her.

She looked up at him, her lips quivering. Tenderly he smoothed his thumb across them. "Sweetheart, I don't want to snatch a few moments alone with you in your bedroom, hoping Maggie isn't going to come upstairs."

Unable to keep from touching him, she trailed her fingers across his cheek, watching the rapid rise and fall of his chest and wishing with all her heart that Larry hadn't chosen this morning to show up early.

His hand came up to press against her fingers. For a few minutes neither of them spoke. Then Stephen laughed self-deprecatingly. "Considering the state of my willpower, I think we'd better make it a rather short engagement. What do you think about getting married next Thursday?"

She gulped, her practical woman's mind suddenly taking over. "That's only a week away. How can I get ready in a week?"

"There won't be much for you to do."

Her brow wrinkled questioningly. Back home the weddings of her friends had been elaborate affairs that had taken months of planning.

He ran a hand through his damp hair. The gesture brought her eyes upward to the vivid scars that still ran up from the left side of his jaw into his hairline.

"I—" He searched her face for understanding. "*Querida*, forgive me. I should do things right—invite the people you've already met in town and introduce you to the rest of the people I know—let them have the pleasure of meeting my beautiful bride. But I haven't been comfortable with crowds since the accident. I'm not going to be able to handle a big wedding."

She nodded. "Esteban, you don't have to apologize. I understand. It would be hard for me to meet a bunch of new people on my wedding day. I'd love to have a simple ceremony right here at the ranch."

"Are you sure you're not just saying that? You won't be disappointed?"

"Of course not. Really, it's a relief to hear you say that we don't have to have something elaborate. There will be plenty of time to meet your friends later. The only ones I'd want to invite are Maggie and Hal—and Jenny and Bill. Can they come?"

"Yes. Certainly."

"Then it's settled."

"And the only responsibility you'll have will be to get a dress." His eyes caressed her face. "I know it's short notice, but I want to see you dressed in traditional white, with a train. If anyone should marry in a long white dress, it's you."

She looked at him shyly. "I . . . I brought my mother's wedding dress with me. It's very beautiful. Would you mind my wearing it?"

"I think that would be perfect." Then his expression changed, and he drew back and shook his head. "What a blithering idiot I'm turning into. I bought you an engagement ring, if I can remember where I put it." He began to search the various pockets in his shirt and pants. In his right jeans pocket he finally located a small velvet box, which he handed to Elena. Inside was a fiery white, emerald-cut diamond ring.

"It's beautiful."

With hands that were none too steady, Stephen took it out and slipped it onto her trembling finger.

"I'm so happy."

"I am, too." He looked at the ring. Then he turned her hand palm up, pressing it against his lips. "You belong to me."

"For always."

He smiled tenderly. Then a new thought struck him. "Before our children ask where we got engaged, we're going to have to make up some story and stick to it."

"Out in the gazebo in the garden."

"Perfect, but what were you wearing?"

She looked down, her eyes inspecting the bodice of her lavender nightgown. She knew his gaze had followed. "Why, uh, a lavender dress."

"Are you going to be able to tell that whopper with a straight face?"

"I hope so."

"I'll never forget the color of your gown. I'm not so sure I'll be able to say the word 'dress' without choking."

"Then let me tell them."

"And just how many children are we going to have?" he asked suddenly.

Her hands fluttered helplessly. "Why, uh . . ."

"I was an only child."

"You know I was, too. It was lonely."

"That was why I was hoping we'd have at least two."

She nodded wordlessly.

He held her hand for a moment longer and then eased himself off the bed. "I think we've had enough excitement for one morning. I should let you go back to sleep."

"I can't possibly."

"Then why don't we go down and tell Maggie?"

"She's going to be thrilled—and furious that you're giving her such short notice."

"No, my dear. *We're* giving her. We have to start off with a united front."

"Yes."

"Then I'll let you get dressed."

SINCE IT WAS such a special morning, Elena brought out one of her nicest outfits. It was a handmade white knit sweater and matching skirt.

"Well, don't you look radiant," Maggie said when Elena walked into the kitchen.

Stephen looked up appreciatively. "I'll second that comment."

"He's been sitting here for the past twenty minutes, grinning like a bird dog with a brace of pheasants," Maggie observed. "But he informed me he wasn't going to say anything until you arrived."

Elena held up her left hand, and Maggie stared at the ring.

"You mean you've finally made it official!" she crowed.

"Mmm-hmm."

"Fantastic!"

"The wedding is next Thursday."

The housekeeper took that piece of news with more equanimity than either Stephen or Elena would have given her credit for.

"I can't believe the two of you." She chuckled as she filled their coffee mugs. "When you make up your minds, a body can hardly keep up."

"I'd like you to make the arrangements," Stephen said.

Maggie reached into her apron pocket and brought out the notepad she used for grocery lists. "Let's see, we're going to need flowers, refreshments, a photographer—"

"No photographer!" Stephen cut in.

Maggie shot him a quick look.

"I'm sorry. I'm just not ready to have my picture taken."

"That's all right," Elena murmured. "We understand."

Under the table Stephen reached for her hand and squeezed it. *Thanks,* he mouthed silently over Maggie's bent head.

Men didn't realize what went into getting ready for a wedding, Elena reflected later that day—even a small, hastily conceived wedding. Despite Stephen's assurances that there wouldn't be much for her to do, Elena was drawn into serious consultation with Maggie on a myriad of details. Where did she want to hold the ceremony? Where should they serve refreshments? What kind of flowers did she want? What was Stephen going to wear?

Late in the morning, however, she remembered that there was something else she had to take care of. Her paintings. Miles Henderson had asked when she could bring some down. Could she possibly deliver them before the wedding, or would she have to wait until afterward? Perhaps if she looked to see what was actually ready, she could make a decision.

"Do you mind if I go up to my studio for a while before lunch?" she asked Maggie.

The housekeeper gave her a sympathetic look. "I've been working you like a slave driver all morning, haven't I?"

"It's all right."

"Well, why don't you go on up there now? I'll have lunch ready at the usual time for you and Stephen out in the garden."

"Thanks."

As Elena passed the phone, she thought of Jenny. They had a lesson next week that she was going to have to cancel—and the one the week after. She had better take care of that before it slipped her mind again.

She picked up the phone and dialed. "I'm sorry, but we aren't going to be able to work together for the next few weeks," she explained to her new pupil.

"Elena, I was counting on it."

"I know. But I hope you'll understand. Stephen and I are getting married."

The disappointment in the teenager's voice turned into a squeal of delight.

"All right! Are Dad and I going to be invited?" she asked with her characteristic frankness.

"Of course. I know the ceremony is going be next Thursday, but I'll have to tell you later about the time."

"I'm glad you're getting married." The teenager's voice had taken on a wistful note.

"Jenny, what is it?"

"I wish Dad were getting married too—to Carol."

Elena wasn't sure how to respond.

"I shouldn't have said that, I guess," Jenny added.

"I like the way you say what you think."

"Really?"

"Yes."

Jenny asked how Stephen had proposed, and Elena told her the story they'd concocted that morning. She was glad they were talking on the phone, because she knew her face was flushed.

After putting down the receiver, she closed her eyes for a moment. Her thoughts still focused inward, she climbed the stairs and started down the hall to the studio. The door was open, but she was so preoccupied that she almost bumped into Stephen, who was standing in the middle of the room.

"What are you doing up here?" she asked in surprise.

He didn't turn around. "Maggie said I could find you here."

"Of course. I'm sorry. I don't seem to be able to think straight this morning."

"I came to see your work."

There was an odd, strained note in his voice.

"Don't you like any of the pictures?" she asked anxiously.

He stepped aside, and she came face-to-face with two portraits, both of Stephen. Then she understood what was wrong. She had been going to put these canvases away until she thought he was ready to see them.

One showed him straining at the bar of the exercise machine. In the other he was relaxing in the filtered sunlight of the garden. Both showed him full face. Under Elena's skilled brush, the scars on the left side somehow stood out in more lifelike detail than in reality. The picture in the gym showed him in shorts, the shrunken muscles of his left leg another testimony to his injuries.

"Why in the hell did you do this?"

"I . . . I wanted to show your spirit."

"My humiliation." He almost spat out the word.

"No, Stephen. Never that. Your ability to conquer adversity."

"Dammit, Elena. Don't you understand anything? You were so ready to forget about a wedding photographer. I thought you knew what I was feeling. Now I see why you didn't need a photograph, because you had these."

"Stephen, *por favor*. Let me explain. I do understand."

"That's hard to believe."

"I paint what I feel. This is how you made me feel. Can't you see your courage, your vigor?"

"Vigor! Are you joking?" He laughed derisively and gestured toward the paintings. "My God, did my leg look like a piece of shriveled rawhide? And is that the way you see my face? Like something out of a Salvador Dali nightmare?'' As he finished speaking, he whirled to confront her, his features contorted with anger.

She tried again. "Stephen. I told you painting is a way for me to get in touch with my emotions. It's something deep within my soul. Painting you was the only way I could get closer to you, when you wouldn't let me past the barriers you had set up between us. Don't you understand? That was all I had.''

He ignored her impassioned words. "It's enough to have to look in the mirror every morning. I don't need a record of what I've gone through. Get rid of them.''

"I can't.''

"Well, if you can't, I can.'' He looked wildly around the room for some way to destroy the paintings. His gaze settled on the palette she had left by the easel. The rounded board was covered with irregular splotches of wet paint that she had been mixing for a picture of the ranch at sunset. Picking it up by the hole in the middle, Stephen advanced toward the portrait of himself in the gym.

Seeing what he was going to do, Elena sprang forward. *"¡Esteban, no!"*

"Oh, yes.'' As he raised his hand, she moved between him and the picture. For a heart-stopping moment he loomed over her, a dark figure whose face was filled with anguish. Elena stood her ground.

Instead of striking the portrait, the palette in his hand came down against the delicate stitchery of her white sweater. It stuck to the nubby fabric, then slid downward. He loosed his grasp, and the palette fell away, leaving gobs of Venetian red, cadmium yellow and manganese violet across her shoulder and chest.

For a moment Stephen stared at her, as though unable to comprehend what had happened. Then he whirled and hobbled out of the room.

It was several moments before Elena could move. She heard his footsteps as he clumped heavily down the stairs. She felt the wall reverberate as the door slammed behind him. Running to the window, she saw him heading for the stable.

She sank to her knees and pressed her face against the hard surface of the windowsill, feeling as though the world had just turned upside down. She had painted his valor and determination. He had looked at the portraits and seen only pain and humiliation. Was he right? Should she destroy the pictures? Pushing herself up, she crossed to the jar of utensils beside the easel. She closed her fingers around the handle of a palette knife, then opened them again. No. She couldn't destroy her work. Not when it meant so much to her.

A flash of movement from the window caught her attention and she looked out again. Stephen had saddled Storm Dancer. Minutes later she saw the black stallion and his rider gallop out of the stable yard and down the trail, raising a cloud of dust behind them.

"What in the name of creation was that? It sounded like the roof falling in," Maggie said, panting. She had come rushing up three flights of stairs to the studio and stood in the doorway, her chest heaving and her skin flushed from the unaccustomed exertion. When she caught sight of Elena's face—and the ruined sweater—her mouth fell open.

The younger woman averted her gaze. "I can't talk to you now."

"Elena, please. Let me help."

"Don't you understand? *No puedo hablar.* I can't talk." It was the first time she had ever raised her voice to Maggie.

For a frozen second the housekeeper didn't move. Then she backed out of the room and made her way down the stairs again, her head bowed.

When Elena was alone once more, she looked around her studio. She had spent so many happy hours here. Now she felt the walls pressing in around her like a deflating balloon. She had to get away—and away from the house.

With a kind of desperate energy she began to sort through her paintings. Some were still so wet that removing them would smear the paint. The rest, including the two portraits of Stephen, she leaned against the wall by the door.

The picture on top was one of the first landscapes she had completed. She had depicted the blazing pink expanse of fireweed on the hillside above the ranch. Now Elena looked at the oil painting and gasped. It was as though some evil magic had changed it. She seemed to be viewing the picture through an eerie mist that blocked out its light, absorbing and hiding the vitality of the colors. This couldn't be the landscape she had painted! Somehow the bright pink of the fragile flowers had bled away, leaving a muddy quagmire of raw umber. The brilliant ultramarine of the sky had become a dirty swath of burnt sienna.

Elena stood and stared at the picture. Then, not daring to breathe, she stepped forward and reached out, smoothing her fingers across the painted surface of the landscape. The brush strokes were familiar, undeniably her own.

But the colors? What had happened to the vibrancy of the colors? Could there be something wrong with the pigments she had used? Could they have changed so drastically in a few weeks? No, that was impossible. The color of paint might change over the years, but not so quickly and hardly ever so hideously.

Heart pounding, she forced herself to take several deep, calming breaths. She had seen paintings like this before. In the Prado in Madrid. They were like the harsh, murky scenes the great Spanish painter Goya had produced during the last few, depressing years of his life. Standing in the basement gallery, she had felt the great painter's despair reaching out to her across the centuries. She'd been deeply disturbed that an artist of such soaring talent could sink into such melancholy. Now she was seeing her own work in the same terms.

Pressing her hands to her eyes, she waited a few seconds before looking at the picture again. Nothing changed. This had to be an illusion, a terrible vision born of her own despair. She stood staring at the picture, trying to understand. Nothing like this had ever happened to her before, not even in the lowest depth of her misery back home.

Now more than ever she knew she had to get away from this place. Her mind was churning as she dashed down the stairs to her bedroom and threw open the closet doors. It took only a few more minutes to bundle some clothes into a suitcase. Then she retrieved the Camaro from the garage and pulled it up to the front door. After tossing her suitcase into the passenger seat, she went back for the canvases. Transferring them all took several trips. By the time she finished, Elena was breathing hard.

Maggie, who must have heard her hurrying up and down the steps, appeared in the front hall. "What in the world are you doing?"

The younger woman stared at her. She wasn't sure how to answer the question. She hadn't thought that far ahead.

"Please, don't do anything foolish," Maggie begged.

Elena shook her head. All she knew was that she had to get out of here. "I must leave."

"Please. Just try to calm down. Let me go find Stephen."

"No, no Esteban." Without waiting to hear more, Elena pushed past the housekeeper and fled to the car.

Her movements were jerky as she started the engine and slammed the gear lever into drive. She almost hit the gatepost as she careered out of the yard.

CHAPTER TWELVE

THERE WAS ONLY one place she could think of going—Bill Delaney's house.

But Elena had driven only on the ranch and lightly traveled secondary roads. Now she resolutely headed for the freeway. When she reached the on-ramp, the dizzying speed of the traffic ahead was suddenly terrifying.

She had been crazy to try this, she thought, looking frantically over her shoulder. Perhaps she could back up.

But a harsh beep from the car behind made her realize that there was no way to go except forward. Clutching the wheel with hands that felt as though they had turned to stone, she pressed the accelerator.

Elena hugged the extreme right lane, keeping her eyes straight ahead as faster cars whizzed past. A line of tractor-trailers passed the Camaro, their vibrations shaking it back and forth. Bloodless lips clamped together, Elena silently recited a prayer and concentrated on holding her small vehicle steady.

As she drove, she kept imagining herself getting pulled over by a police officer, who could somehow detect her lack of a driver's license from a glimpse of her face. When he saw her sweater, he'd probably assume that she had escaped from a lunatic asylum.

Her death grip on the wheel didn't slacken until she had taken the Montecito off-ramp. As she nosed the car up into the hills past walled estates and oleander-screened haciendas, she wondered what she was going to say. She had come to think of Bill as her friend, but perhaps she was presuming too much on the relationship now.

As she pulled into the parking area behind his house, she spotted him immediately. Dressed in green plaid Bermuda shorts and a clashing, red-striped shirt with a rip in one sleeve, he was washing the blue Volvo.

"Well, this is an occasion. Does it have something to do with the wedding, by any chance?" he called out cheerfully, turning off the hose. Then his brow wrinkled. "Say, how did you get here? I didn't think you had a driver's license yet."

"I don't."

Bill took a good look at the woman who had climbed out of the Camaro and stood trembling in the driveway. "My God, what happened to you?"

"¡Ay! Bill." Her anguish had been frozen inside her. Suddenly it was impossible to hold it back. Even as the first sobs racked her body, the big man was striding forward. Heedless of the paint slathered across her sweater, he took her into his arms and led her gently to a bench under the orange trees.

"Elena, it's all right, Elena," he soothed. "Tell me what happened, honey."

"I—" The syllable was choked off by the force of her misery. Bill didn't try to get her to pull herself together. Instead he simply held her, murmuring reassuring words and rocking her as though she were his daughter, letting the emotional storm run its course.

"Better?" he asked finally.

"No. But I can't go on weeping like that forever." The admission was punctuated by a hiccup.

Bill patted her back. From the pocket of his Bermuda shorts, he miraculously produced several clean tissues. "Here."

Elena nodded her thanks and blew her nose. "I'm so embarrassed."

"It happens to everyone at some time or another. You should have seen me after Jenny's accident. I was a basket case. Every time I thought I had myself under control, I'd start bawling again."

She nodded shakily.

"Can you tell me about it?"

Elena's gaze was riveted to Bill's chest. "*¡Madre de Dios!* I've gotten oil paint all over you. Oh Bill, I'm so sorry."

He laughed. "Don't worry. When Jenny saw me this morning, she said my shirt was a candidate for the rag pile." His expression sobered. "But what happened to you? You look as though you got into an altercation with the paint-mixing machine at the hardware store—and lost."

"No—with Esteban."

"*He* did that to you?"

"It wasn't what he intended. He was trying to destroy one of my pictures, and I couldn't let him. I stepped in the way."

Bill's hitherto calm features darkened. "Has the man gone crazy?"

"He was upset. He hadn't been up to my studio until today, and he saw—" She stopped and stood up. "The portraits are in the car. Perhaps I should show them to you."

Bill followed her over to the Camaro and watched as she shuffled through the canvases in the back. Slowly she drew out the two pictures of Stephen and propped them against the side of the car.

After studying them for a few moments, Bill whistled. "I see what you mean."

"Then you think he was right—that I shouldn't have painted them? That it was an invasion of his privacy?"

"I didn't say that."

"What *are* you saying?"

"These portraits are certainly very graphic, and very powerful. But I have to assume Steve couldn't recognize what you intended."

"And you can?"

He pursed his lips. "I think so. They show a man with iron determination, a man striving to overcome a handicap by brute force."

She looked down at the hands that had executed the pictures. "Thank you."

"You're a very talented painter. I didn't realize how talented until now."

"For all the good that does me. But maybe you can't be a successful artist if you're happy. Some of my best work was done when I thought I was never going to see Stephen again."

"And some of it had been done since you got here, too, I'll wager."

"You're right. I guess I'm so confused I don't know what to think anymore."

Bill hesitated. "What did Stephen see in the pictures?"

"Shame. Humiliation."

"I suppose he's still too close to what happened."

Elena nodded. Then, after several moments of silence, she cleared her throat. "Bill?"

"Yes."

"I couldn't stay out at the ranch. I...I threw some clothes in a suitcase and put the pictures in the car, without really knowing what I was going to do next. There wasn't anywhere else I could think of to go except here."

"You're welcome to stay with me and Jenny as long as you like."

"I don't want to impose on you."

"Don't be ridiculous. Jenny and I will both be glad to have you."

"Even if I'm not very good company."

He shrugged. "Don't worry about that."

"Bill, Stephen asked me to marry him this morning. Now I don't know if I can," Elena blurted.

He smoothed his hand across her shoulder. "Don't make any hasty decisions about that, either."

"I'm not going to. That's one reason I had to get away from the ranch—so I could figure out what to do." She shook her head. "I thought I understood Stephen. Now I wonder if I ever really knew him."

After installing Elena in the spare room, Bill went to tell Mrs. Matthews that they'd be having a houseguest. Then he headed for his daughter's studio.

"Jenny, Elena's here."

The teenager looked up from the painting she was working on. "Neat. I thought we weren't going to see her till the wedding. Now she can help me with the perspective in this picture."

"She, uh, she's upset and she needs our help."

"Dad, what is it?" Jenny frowned.

"She and Stephen have had a misunderstanding." His brief explanation of the morning's events had a somewhat subduing effect on the teenager. Yet she still couldn't entirely suppress her natural curiosity.

"What are you going to do if you don't marry Stephen?" she asked a little later that afternoon. Bill and Jenny were sipping iced tea and eating cookies Mrs. Matthews had baked.

Elena had barely touched her tea, and she was positive the cookies would go down her throat as easily as clay. The big man shot his daughter a warning look, but Elena only shrugged. "I guess I'll get busy working on some more paintings—and find myself some more art students."

"You're a super teacher. I'll give you a good reference," Jenny volunteered.

"Thank you." Elena turned to Bill. "Speaking of selling paintings, do you mind if I give Miles Henderson a call?"

"Of course not. I told you to make yourself at home here, and I meant it. You know where the phone is."

Suddenly overwhelmed by Bill's kindness, Elena stood up abruptly and hurried into the house. It was several minutes before she felt sufficiently in control of her voice to call the art dealer.

Under other circumstances his enthusiastic response to her tentative greeting would have put her in good spirits. Instead she had to press her lips together to keep from breaking down again.

"Are you still there?" Henderson inquired.

"Yes. Sorry."

"I hope you're calling to say you can bring some pictures in."

"I am."

"Well, when can you come down?"

She glanced out the window at the car she shouldn't have driven by herself. "I have to arrange for a ride. Would tomorrow or the next day be all right?"

"Either one is fine.'"

After hanging up, Elena stood staring at the phone. She didn't really want to talk to Maggie or anyone else at Rancho Palo Colorado. But she should call and let the house-keeper know that she was all right.

Maggie picked up the receiver on the first ring, as though she had been sitting and waiting beside the phone. "Oh, thank God. I was so worried about you. I was going to call the police in a few minutes."

"Maggie, I'm sorry I troubled you like that. Truly. But I had to get away from the ranch."

"Are you all right?"

"*Sí.*"

"You sound like you're still upset."

Elena didn't deny the observation.

"Where are you?"

"Bill Delaney's house."

"You drove all that way? Oh, Elena, you could have had an accident."

"I'm fine."

"I could send Hal to pick you up," Maggie suggested hopefully.

"I'm not coming back. At least not for now."

"Elena, you can't mean that."

The young woman pressed her palm to her forehead, suddenly aware that her temples were pounding. "Maggie, I've got to sort things out for myself. I can't do it at the ranch."

"But what should I tell Stephen?"

"You can tell him where I am."

The housekeeper hesitated. "Do you want me to have him call you?"

"Maggie, please stop trying to manage things between us. He's a grown man. He can decide for himself what he wants to do."

There were a few moments of silence on the other end of the line. "I guess you're right," Maggie finally said.

When Elena returned to the patio and reported the outcome of her call to Miles Henderson, Bill volunteered to take her down to the gallery the next morning.

Mindful of the importance of the occasion, he dressed in a pair of gray slacks and a clean white shirt. After they'd gotten into the car, he turned to Elena and laid his large hand over her smaller one. "You look so sad and pale."

"I guess I should try to put on a smiling face for Señor Henderson."

"He'll probably be concentrating on your work so hard that he won't notice."

"I hope so."

Bill started the engine. "Did you sleep last night?"

"Not much."

"Listen, do you think it would help if I called Steve and talked to him?"

"No!"

"You don't have to take my head off."

"Bill, *disculpe*—forgive me." She sighed. "It's just that this is something the two of us have to work out for ourselves. If we can work it out," she added under her breath.

"No, you're right."

By the time they arrived at the gallery, Elena had manufactured a less gloomy disposition. And she couldn't help being genuinely pleased with Henderson's reaction to her work.

"These are marvelous. Better than I expected. Your style has matured since you did that portrait you brought in last month."

"Thank you."

"I can take six pictures. And when I sell one, we'll replace it with another."

The prices he set for the paintings were higher than Elena had anticipated.

"Do you really think I'm worth that much?" she asked incredulously.

"Every penny."

Bill beamed and gave her a quick hug. "See, I told you you were good."

As they left the gallery, Bill glanced at Elena. "You know, I just had an idea."

"What?"

"You could donate one or two of your pictures to the auction. It would be good publicity for you and tax-deductible."

Despite everything, Elena laughed. "That's what Mary Falconer told us to say when we went out looking for donations, remember?"

Bill looked embarrassed. "You're right. I guess I don't have to give you the spiel."

"I'd be honored to donate a painting. Truly. If you really think someone would want one of my pictures, instead of a trip to Acapulco."

"Believe me, there are people who will be a lot more interested in having an original Elena Castile." Bill opened the car door. "Where to now?"

"You should be at work. I can't keep asking you to drive me everywhere."

"If you feel that way, we can stop at the Motor Vehicle Department, so you can take the road test."

She'd been surprised to discover when she'd gotten her learner's permit that she didn't need an appointment for the driving test. "You wouldn't mind sparing the time?"

"I don't have to be at the store until this afternoon."

"Then I'll accept the offer. A few days ago I would have thought I needed more practice. After getting myself out to your house on the freeway, I believe I can tackle anything."

Elena easily passed the driving test. It was her second victory of the day, and it helped give her the feeling that she would be able to take care of herself, come what may. Of course, since that first scene in Stephen's office, she'd come to realize that supporting herself on the proceeds of her paintings wasn't going to be easy. But now she also had the option of giving art lessons, as well.

Several days passed, during which Elena didn't hear from Stephen. She tried to keep busy and not dampen the spirits of the rest of the household. But she found it difficult to keep up her end of a conversation. When she and Jenny weren't working together in the studio, she often flopped onto her bed and lay there, staring up at the ceiling.

What was Stephen doing now? she wondered. How was his leg? Was he having any more pain? The thought brought a mist of tears to her eyes. She glanced at the phone on the bedside table.

Why didn't he call her? Did he still feel the same way about the portraits? Or was he waiting for her to call *him* and apologize for painting them? Well, she knew one thing for certain. Even though she loved Esteban, she wasn't going to make that call. If the two of them got back together, the overture was going to have to come from him.

And what if she and Stephen didn't work out their differences? The thought brought a lump to her throat, and she swallowed convulsively. Sitting up, she rubbed her fingers against her throbbing temples, hardly able to deal with her own churning emotions.

Stephen hadn't called her. More than likely he never would. If they didn't marry, she knew one thing for sure; she was going to pay back all the money she owed him. There was the Camaro he had given her, for example. It would have to be returned. And the paints and art supplies. She would pay for what she had used. He could keep the rest.

The deal Stephen had made with her father was another matter entirely. He'd paid a large sum of money to have her sent here to be his bride. Now she felt honor bound to clear away that debt. For a moment she closed her eyes and clenched her fists. Even if by some slim chance they did marry, she would insist on returning the money to Stephen. It was a staggeringly large sum. Naturally she wouldn't be able to manage it all at once, but over the years she would make payments. Since she had come to this country, she had begun to view herself differently. At home she had almost been her father's property—like one of his prized horses. Here, whether she married or not, she felt a new sense of autonomy.

WEDNESDAY NIGHT Elena hardly slept. Finally she closed her eyes sometime in the small hours of the morning, only to awaken at the first light of dawn with a leaden feeling in her chest. She had been trying all week to hold herself together. But this was Thursday—the day she and Stephen were to have been married. Now she didn't know if she could pretend that she wasn't dying inside.

What kind of day was it? she wondered sadly, her gaze drifting toward the window. Gray fog had rolled in during the night, obscuring the bright colors of the bird of paradise flowers that grew along the wall. It was like her distorted vision of the fireweed picture, after Stephen had slammed out of the studio. Perhaps this was the way things would be for her from now on—drab and lifeless.

If she had been by herself, she probably wouldn't have been able to get out of bed at all. But she was a guest of Bill and Jenny, and that meant disrupting their household routine as little as possible. So she forced herself to get up and take a shower. Water as hot as she could stand it helped reassure her that she could still feel something, even if it was only discomfort. It also got her moving.

By the time she wandered into the kitchen, she was feeling more herself. Bill and Mrs. Matthews were talking in low tones. When the housekeeper glanced toward her, the conversation stopped abruptly.

"I didn't mean to interrupt," Elena began.

"You haven't really," her host assured her.

Automatically Elena went over to the coffee maker to pour herself a cup of the dark, steaming liquid.

Bill cleared his throat. "I was wondering if you could do me a favor today."

"Of course."

"I promised Jenny a visit to the natural history museum, but something has come up at the store that needs my personal attention."

"I'd love to take Jenny to the museum."

"I was hoping you'd be able to."

As she slid into her chair, Elena wondered whether Bill had manufactured the business problem as an excuse to keep her from moping around the house today. She knew he was just as aware of the date as she was herself. But whatever his reasons, she was glad she had something to occupy her time.

By late morning the fog had burned off, leaving the sky a brilliant, clear blue. A nice day, after all, Elena thought as she changed into a casual cotton skirt and jade-green top. In the driveway, Bill was helping Jenny into the front passenger seat of the Camaro and stowing the wheelchair in the trunk. They had already eaten an early lunch, so as to give themselves a long afternoon at the museum.

"Are you sure you're not going to have any trouble getting the chair set up again when you get there?" he wanted to know.

"Dad, *I know how to do it*," Jenny insisted. "I can show Elena."

Bill patted her on the shoulder. "Then I'll see you all later. Have a good time."

"We will," the teenager told him.

The museum was less than a ten-minute drive from the Delaney house. Like many other Santa Barbara public buildings, it was of white stucco, with a red tile roof and decorative ironwork over the windows. But in front was a most uncharacteristic sight—the huge skeleton of a blue whale that had washed up on shore several years before. As Elena wheeled Jenny toward the building, they stopped beside the massive creature's whitened bones, and the teenager reached out to run her hands gently along its rib cage.

"They have neat things here!" she exclaimed.

"I see." Despite her feeling of depression, Elena couldn't help being intrigued. For a moment her own fingers stroked the massive bones as she tried to picture a living creature of such enormous size.

Jenny cleared her throat. "You probably think it's stupid for someone as old as me to want to come to the museum."

"Of course not!"

"I don't usually. But I thought it would be a good way to get you out of the house."

"So it was your idea."

"Yes." Jenny looked uncomfortable. "Elena, can I tell you something?"

Elena knelt beside the wheelchair. "Of course."

"When Dad first brought you over to our house, I was angry, because I felt he was pushing me into something I didn't want to do."

"I understood that."

"You were real clever, pretending you just wanted to draw Dad's picture. I knew what you were doing, but I wanted to see if you were any good."

Elena smiled. "I'm glad we got to be friends."

"Me, too."

"So let's go enjoy ourselves."

Jenny looked relieved. "The thing I remember liking best is the rattlesnake, where you can press a button and make the tail shake. The sign says it's the only poisonous snake in California."

"Do you have the exhibits memorized?"

Jenny laughed as Elena pushed her into the shady entrance courtyard with its splashing fountain, camellias and tree ferns.

"Dad and I used to come here a lot when I was a little kid. And then sometimes I'd go with Carol."

Elena heard the wistful note in Jenny's voice again. She must miss Carol. The thought reminded her of Stephen, and she felt a sudden stab of pain in her heart. But she was determined not to spoil this outing.

"Where to first?" she asked in a voice that was only slightly unsteady.

"The rattlesnake."

"Do you want to see the mammals?" Elena asked, after they had made their pilgrimage to Jenny's favorite exhibit.

"Let's not go in there. I used to think the deer and the otters were cute when I was little, but now it makes me sad to think that they're dead."

"I suppose I feel the same way," Elena agreed.

"Then let's go see the wave machine. You can turn the crank."

They spent almost an hour among the deep-sea displays and in the hall of minerals, and had just entered the Indian exhibit when Elena felt Jenny's fingers dig into her arm.

Bending down, she looked anxiously at the teenager. "Is something wrong?"

"There's a man following us," she whispered. "I saw him in the doorway to the mineral room, and now he's here again."

"There are lots of people at the museum this morning. I'm sure he's just looking at the displays, like everyone else."

"No. He's following us, and he keeps staring at *you*." Elena started to turn, but Jenny kept whispering urgently. "I'm afraid of him. He's got a hat pulled down over his face. But one side is—"

Elena whirled around and looked up quickly. Standing several yards away, dressed in jeans and a gray flannel shirt was Stephen.

As Jenny had said, his face was partially shadowed by a floppy fisherman's hat. But there was no way it could hide the still-vivid scars on the left side—or his guarded expression. His hands were thrust into his pockets, but his stance was far from relaxed.

A giant fist seemed to squeeze Elena's heart, and she sucked in a sharp, painful breath. "Esteban." She wanted to rush to him, but her legs seemed to be rooted to the floor tiles. Swaying slightly, like a slender tree buffeted by the wind, she grabbed the edge of Jenny's chair to keep from falling.

Stephen clearly saw the reaction, and his expression changed to something Elena couldn't read.

The whole little scene had taken no more than a few heartbeats.

Jenny's head shot up, and she looked from the woman beside her to the man with the daunting appearance.

Elena had momentarily forgotten about the teenager. Her eyes were on Stephen as he began to walk slowly but determinedly forward. Elena could see that he still limped slightly, but he no longer needed his cane.

As he came to a halt in front of them, Elena pressed her suddenly ice-cold hands nervously to her sides. She felt disoriented, yet ingrained social skills came to her aid. She glanced from Stephen to Jenny.

"Jenny Delaney, this is Stephen Gallagher. Stephen, this is Jenny," she recited in a thin voice.

To her credit, the teenager recovered quickly from her initial reaction to seeing Stephen's face.

"I'm glad to meet you," she said as she offered her hand.

Gravely Stephen reached down and shook it.

"Elena told me a lot about you."

His eyebrows shot up, but he didn't take the bait.

"How . . . how did you know we were here?" Elena hesitantly inquired.

"Mrs. Matthews."

"Oh."

A well-dressed older couple had stopped at the entrance to the room to watch the interchange. Elena could see that Stephen was uncomfortable about drawing the attention of strangers, and was trying hard not to show it.

Determinedly he looked down at Jenny. "I'm sorry to interrupt your visit to the museum, but I needed to talk to Elena."

"That's okay."

"Do you think—?" Stephen began again.

"I don't mind if you take me home," Jenny finished the sentence for him. "Elena has been so down in the dumps all week. I was hoping you'd call her or something," she added in her characteristically direct manner.

Elena felt her cheeks redden as she stared at the teenager. But Jenny only shrugged.

Stephen studied the backs of his hands.

"What took you so long?" Jenny questioned.

"I—"

"This really isn't the place for a personal discussion," Elena said, coming to his rescue and her own.

He gave her a grateful look and suggested that he follow Elena and Jenny back to Bill's.

After Elena had started the Camaro's engine, Jenny turned to her. "Listen, I'm really sorry I said I was afraid of him. It's just that I didn't know who he was."

"That's all right. It's a shock when you first see his face."

"I know." The girl stole a sidelong glance at Elena. "I guess in a way I'm lucky I'm just in a wheelchair."

Elena swallowed the lump in her throat. "He doesn't like the way he looks, either. That's why he stays at the ranch almost all the time."

"So he must have really cared about you if he came to the museum, where he knew there'd be a lot of people."

Elena nodded, not trusting herself to speak.

"I like him." Jenny paused. "I guess I have a good idea what he's been through, too."

"Yes." The clipped syllable was about all that Elena could manage. On the way back to Bill's, she concentrated on her driving and on pulling herself back together.

At the Delaneys', Stephen helped Jenny out of the car and into her chair.

"You're almost as strong as my dad," she commented.

Stephen smiled. "I'll accept that as a compliment."

"Are you sure you don't mind if we leave you here?" Elena ventured.

"Are you kidding? I know the two of you want to be alone."

Over her head, Stephen's gaze met Elena's.

When the teenager had wheeled herself into the house, he thrust his hands into his pockets once more. "She's quite a kid. Very perceptive."

"Yes."

He looked down at the tips of his sneakers. "She's right. I shouldn't have waited so long to talk to you. Will you come for a ride with me?"

There was no way she could refuse the request. "Yes."

Stephen let out the breath he'd been holding.

CHAPTER THIRTEEN

STEPHEN DROVE out of town heading west along the coast. Although Elena glanced at him questioningly, he kept his eyes firmly on the road.

"Where are we going?" she finally asked.

"I thought you might like to walk along the beach."

"All right." She knew her voice registered her surprise. It was a nice day, and there would be more people down by the ocean than there had been at the museum.

Stephen turned off the highway at Refugio Beach. After paying the toll, he found a parking place shaded by a tall palm.

"Why don't we leave our shoes in the car?" he suggested, beginning to untie the laces of his right sneaker.

The state beach was crowded with families enjoying the fine summer weather. As Elena and Stephen made their way down to the firm strip of sand at the edge of the waves, she saw a number of people glance at Stephen's face and then quickly look away. He tugged his fisherman's hat farther down over his brow and walked silently on. The quick gesture and the set of his shoulders were the only indications he gave that he was aware of the attention.

The wind blowing off the water tossed Elena's dark hair in front of her eyes. As she swept it back over her shoulder, she stole a nervous look at Stephen. He had hardly spoken since they'd left Jenny's. And he hadn't touched her at all.

Before they reached the water, he paused and carefully rolled up the legs of his jeans. Elena suspected it was more from wanting something to do than from any worry about getting his pants wet. Leaving his side, she walked down to the edge of the surf and lifted her head, breathing in the salt tang of the air. A dozen yards offshore, a pelican skimmed along the surface of the whitecaps.

"Look." Elena pointed toward the graceful bird.

Stephen nodded and then started off down the beach. The relatively wide expanse of sand soon gave way to a narrow white strip, hemmed in by a line of tall cliffs. A few hardy plants clung to its sheer face. At the base was an uneven pile of rounded sandstone rocks that had been tossed onto the shore by the sea. Elena couldn't resist reaching down and picking up a small one. Water had hollowed out several intriguing-looking tunnels through the porous stone.

"I've never seen anything like this," she murmured, and slipped it into the pocket of her skirt.

"Mmm."

They walked on for a few minutes more without speaking again. Stephen had slowed down. Elena glanced at him, wondering if his leg hurt. But he didn't say anything about it.

Elena had always loved the beach, and on any other occasion this small stretch of California coastline would have been an unfolding panorama of natural delights. But this afternoon she was much more aware of the man who trudged quietly along beside her.

As they rounded a small point, he stopped for a minute and reached down to massage his calf. Then he glanced back over his shoulder. Most of the sunbathers and bodysurfers were now out of sight.

Elena licked her lips and felt the wind take the moisture away almost immediately. She was aware that Stephen's eyes had followed the tiny movement. "You said you wanted to talk," she ventured.

"I'm working up to it."

"Why did you wait so long to call me?" The question was more of an accusation than she had intended.

"I kept picturing the way you looked with paint smeared all over that hand-knit white sweater. I guess after I did that to you, I wasn't sure you wanted to have anything to do with me."

Whenever words failed her with Stephen, Elena always fell back on the most fundamental type of communication—showing him how she felt. Without even thinking about it, she found herself reaching out and grasping his hand.

There was no way she could have anticipated her own reaction to that simple touch of her flesh against his. After the deprivation of the past week, it was as though an electric circuit had suddenly been completed. The spark leaped from his hand to hers. Or perhaps it was the other way around. But it hardly mattered. Only the intensity of the contact was important.

Stephen stopped dead in his tracks. She heard him suck in a deep, agonizing breath. Then she was being pulled into his arms with a desperate strength that took her breath away. "Elena. Oh, God, Elena. Sweetheart."

His grasp tightened around her shoulders. Her own arms circled his waist. Suddenly it was impossible to get close enough.

Frantically her hands slid up and down his broad back. He was no less frenzied in his need to touch her, gather her to himself. His lips skimmed her face, her neck, her hair—anywhere that they could touch as she twisted against him, mirroring his actions.

"Mi amor."

"This was supposed to be our wedding day." His voice was rough.

They were both speaking at once, so that the words were jumbled together and carried off by the wind. But it didn't seem to matter.

"Yes. When I woke up this morning, I wanted to make the world go away."

"All I knew was that I had to talk to you. I didn't know what I was going to do, if it ended between us before it had really begun," he admitted.

"I wanted to call you so badly. But I couldn't. It had to be your decision."

"Yes. I figured that out."

They clung together for long moments. Finally he led her out of the wind into the sun-warmed shelter of the cliffs. She saw him brush one hand across his cheek. Perhaps the salt breeze had stung his eyes. Or perhaps they were brimming with the same moisture that blurred her vision.

"I shouldn't have tried to destroy your painting. I didn't have the right to do that." The admission was barely audible.

"Do you still feel the same way about them?" She held her breath, waiting for the answer.

"I wish . . . I wish I could lie to you."

She sighed heavily and looked away from him across the rolling swells of the waves. "Then you still don't see what I was trying to show."

His fingers tightened on her shoulders. "I thought about it for a long time—all week, actually. After I cooled down, I imagine I came to some kind of understanding of what you wanted to express."

"But you don't see it for yourself?"

"Elena, you've studied art. You know that two people don't necessarily see the same thing when they look at a painting or a piece of sculpture."

She nodded reluctantly, silently admitting that he was right. All week she had been telling herself that Stephen would have to meet certain conditions if she came back to him. Now that she was back in his arms, all her intellectualizing suddenly meant nothing. What did she really want from the man she loved? she asked herself now. A reassuring lie or honesty?

She looked up at him, and caught her breath sharply at the force of the emotions in the depths of his eyes. A few moments ago she had told him that the first move toward reconciliation could only have come from him. Now she realized with heart-wrenching clarity that *she* held their future in her hands.

"You'd risk—losing me, because you have to tell the truth?" she asked hesitantly.

For long moments he stared down at her. Then he crooked a finger under her chin and gently brought her face up to his, so that she could read the veracity of his answer in his eyes. "Yes."

Now it was her turn to be silent. There were so many things she wanted to say to him, but she didn't know whether the words would make any impression—whether they'd even mean the same thing to him that they did to her. She had thought her art was a deeper form of communication. That had failed her with Stephen. What if words did, too? So she simply stood there, her fingers clutching the fabric of his shirt.

"Will you come back to the ranch? Will you still marry me?" he finally asked.

She could feel the coiled tension in his body as he waited for her answer.

"Stephen, after what I've been through this week, I don't think I have any choice."

He nodded fractionally, relaxed fractionally.

She found she had to be as brutally honest as he. "Even if I thought it wasn't going to work out, I'd have to come back to you now."

A muscle twitched in his jaw. "Then you're afraid that the two of us don't really have a chance?"

"*¡Ay!* Stephen, I hope with all my heart that we do."

He drew in a shuddering breath and clasped her tightly against the muscular wall of his chest. "So do I, *querida*. So do I."

She pressed her face into his shirt, breathing in his familiar masculine scent and reveling in the warmth and strength of his body. It had been like this the first time he had held her, so long ago in her father's garden. Now in the safety of his arms it was impossible to believe that they wouldn't always be together. *Until death do us part,* she thought.

"Until death do us part."

Her eyes widened. "I was thinking those same words."

"That's a good sign."

It was late afternoon when they started back along the white sand, hand in hand. Stephen kept the pace slow, and Elena suspected that his leg hurt. But she wasn't going to bring up the subject, if he didn't want to.

"I envy you living so close to the beach," she said instead. "Did you come down here often when you were a boy?"

He fell in easily with the change of topic. "Mmm-hmm. I loved the water. My friends and I used to come down here to bodysurf." He paused and looked over the deepening blue of the ocean. "And Dad and I had a boat down at the marina."

"A sailboat?"

"No, a cabin cruiser. We'd go deep-sea fishing." He laughed.

She hadn't heard him do that in over a week, and it was impossible to disguise her pleasure. "What's so funny?"

"I was remembering Maggie's reaction when we'd come back with a fish. She hated the smell. But we loved the sport."

"And what else did you like?"

He pointed toward a line of irregular shapes along the horizon that were almost invisible against the blue of the sky. "We used to take the boat out to the Channel Islands and go camping. It's primitive out there—and the wind can really blow."

"Will you take me sometime?"

"Do you like boating?"

"I don't know. I've never had the chance. But I'd like to try it with you."

He clasped her hand tighter.

"Why did you want to come down here?" Elena asked.

"Partly because I wanted to see how it would make me feel."

"And how does it?"

"Exposed." He didn't make any attempt to disguise his reaction. "I guess I still don't like to be stared at." As he spoke the words, he kicked up a little cloud of dry sand with his foot.

"Stephen, you've come so far. I want you to be—"

"Normal."

She shot him a sidelong glance, alarmed by the vehemence in his voice. "I didn't say that."

Stephen pulled her to a stop, his expression fierce. "Elena, you have to understand that I'm not the same man you met before the accident. If you can't accept that..." He shrugged.

"I have accepted it."

"I hope so."

"Is it wrong for me to want the man I love to lead a normal life?"

He didn't answer but started off again, his strides lengthening so that he quickly left her behind. She stared at the set of his shoulders, suddenly feeling alone and uncertain. And then she was running after him, anxious to catch up.

"DO YOU SWEAR each for yourself that the foregoing information is true and correct to the best of your knowledge and belief?" the blond woman behind the counter asked.

"Yes." Stephen and Elena both answered at the same time. They were standing with their right hands raised in the Santa Barbara County Hall of Records, where they had gone to apply for a marriage license.

She stole a glance at her husband-to-be. It was the first time since their talk on the beach that she felt she really knew what was in his mind. She pressed her shoulder against his, but he didn't return the reassuring gesture. She knew he was on edge and that he hadn't liked the curious attention he'd received as they'd sat at the heavy oak table near the door, filling out the detailed application form.

But that wasn't anything new. She had felt his disquiet for the past few days. Was he afraid she was going to run away again? Elena wondered. Or was it something else? She wanted desperately to ask. But Stephen had made it clear that he didn't want to discuss his private anxieties. It was almost as though he still didn't trust her, despite the fact that she had come back to the ranch. She didn't know why. She only hoped desperately that things would change after they were married.

"You give the certificate to the person who performs the ceremony, and they mail it back in," the middle-aged clerk was saying.

"Yes. Thank you."

Stephen turned toward the door. Elena paused for a moment and looked around the room one more time, caught by the conviction that she should try to remember this place, with its decorative columns and massive chandelier, shaped like an eight-pointed star. She wanted to be able to fix in her mind everything connected with the beginning of her life with Stephen.

If he had felt at ease among the crowds of noonday shoppers in town, they might have stopped for lunch at one of the outdoor cafés along State Street or down by the beach. Instead they headed back to the car.

"There's another meeting tonight of the committee organizing the auction to benefit the rehabilitation center." She cleared her throat. "Bill asked me to go with him."

"It's good for you to make those kinds of contacts."

"You could come, too."

"I don't have any interest in that sort of thing."

"I thought you used to."

His head whipped around toward her. "Who told you that?"

"Uh, one of the gallery owners I met, when I was first taking my pictures around. A man named Tom Mitchell. He's on the committee."

"Him." Stephen's voice dripped with contempt. "He joins groups like that to make contacts, not to help anyone else."

"But you just said I could do the same thing."

"That's not your only reason." Stephen bent to unlock the car door. "I don't want to continue this discussion."

Once they'd climbed into the car, they sat in silence. Finally Elena reached over and laid her hand on his where it rested on the steering wheel. She felt his fingers tense. Aside from that, he didn't move. It had been that way since their walk on the beach, when he'd held her in his arms with such fierce possessiveness.

Because she'd desperately wanted more of that closeness and reassurance, she'd sought opportunities to be alone with him. But whenever she'd touched him or pressed her lips to his, he had become like a statue. It was as if his self-control had gone into overdrive. Instead of responding, he simply waited for her to withdraw.

She had tried to get him to discuss his feelings, to tell her what was bothering him. But he wouldn't do that, either. He had become a stranger to her—more withdrawn than during the first week she'd been at the ranch. What was she to expect from him when they were married? And what about their wedding night? When he'd kissed her and caressed her in the past, he'd always been so loving. Was he still going to be like that? She didn't know. And he had made it impossible to discuss her fears and doubts.

Sighing, she took back her hand. They had their marriage license now. And the wedding was set for Wednesday. It was too late to change her mind, even if she wanted to.

Stephen didn't make much attempt at conversation during the drive back to the ranch. But as they turned into the driveway, he cleared his throat. "I have a lot of work to do so we can get away for the week after the wedding."

"I understand." *Don't lock yourself away from me*. The plea went unspoken.

They weren't going out of town for their honeymoon. Stephen had suggested that they spend their first week together at one of the luxury rental houses in the area. Since she knew he didn't want to mingle with the crowds at a resort, Elena had readily agreed, though she was nervous about being alone with the silent man he had become.

"I'll probably be busy all evening."

Stephen, don't do this to us! she wanted to shout. "Then perhaps I'll have dinner with Bill and Jenny before the meeting," was what she said instead.

"That's a good idea."

I wish you didn't think so.

THAT EVENING Elena drove to Bill's and left her car at his house.

"So where do you want to go for dinner?" he asked his daughter.

Not so long ago she would have said "nowhere." Now she answered, "J. K. Frimple's."

Father and daughter grinned at each other knowingly. Elena gave them a questioning look.

"You'll just have to wait and see," Jenny told her.

The hostess showed them to a quiet corner, where Jenny's wheelchair wouldn't be in the way. From a plastic banquette Elena surveyed the decor, wondering why Jenny and Bill thought the place was so special. It was rather nondescript, except for the enormous fig tree that sprouted out of the glass-enclosed center court. But that certainly wasn't the main attraction for Jenny. After a hamburger and French fries for dinner, she ordered a Hot Fudge Frimple.

"If you can't beat 'em, join 'em," Bill said, smiling as he ordered one for himself.

Elena, who hadn't been particularly hungry in the first place, settled for a cup of coffee.

When the desserts arrived, they turned out to be cream puff shells, filled with vanilla ice cream and topped with hot fudge sauce.

"Now I see why you were so quick to agree to coming here," Elena told Bill. "You wanted one of those gooey things, too."

"I plead guilty. Try it. Maybe you'll like it." Bill handed Elena a spoonful of the concoction.

"Good," she admitted after a cautious taste.

"Shall we order you one, too?"

"I don't think I could finish one by myself." She did, however, let Bill get another spoon from the waitress, so she could have several more samples.

The Frimples had almost disappeared, when Elena glanced over and saw Jenny staring down at her plate. The teenager was swirling melted vanilla ice cream and fudge sauce with her spoon.

"Jenny?"

"I think I ate too much."

"Is that what's wrong?"

She didn't answer for a moment. Then she looked up at Elena. "Dad and me and Carol used to come here. We used to have a good time."

"I thought we were having a good time now," Bill put in quickly.

"Yes." Jenny's voice was low.

"What's wrong, honey?" her father coaxed.

Jenny took a deep breath. "Carol decided she didn't want to marry you because of me, didn't she? She didn't want to have me for a daughter."

"That's not true."

"Tell me the truth, Dad."

Bill pressed his lips together before starting to speak. "The truth is complicated. When you fell off those rocks, I felt as if it was my fault for taking you up there."

"I wanted to go."

"I'm the one who's supposed to have adult judgment."
He sighed. "Afterward, I kept trying to make it up to you.
And that meant I wasn't paying any attention to Carol."

"Oh." The teenager thought for a moment. "But in a way
that still has to do with me."

"Your dad is right," Elena interjected. "Things that
happen between adults are sometimes hard for kids to understand. My parents are divorced, and when my mother left
my father, I thought it might be my fault."

"You did."

"Yes. But later I realized it wasn't true. Things between
them were very complicated."

"Do you think the problems with my dad and Carol are
complicated?"

Elena glanced at Bill. His eyes said, *Help me out.*

"Not all that complicated. I think your dad realizes he
doesn't have to spend every minute with you now. In fact,
I'll bet he understands that you're happier when he
doesn't," Elena said.

"Mmm-hmm."

The waitress, who had been hovering in the background,
came over and put the check on the table. Bill looked at his
watch. "I didn't realize how late it was getting. Elena and I
need to head for our meeting."

"I'm glad we had time to go out to dinner."

"So do I," Bill and Elena both said at the same time.

Jenny laughed, and the adults joined in.

After returning Jenny to Mrs. Matthews's care, they
drove to Mary Falconer's, where the meeting was being held
again.

"Sorry. I wasn't expecting anything like that," Bill murmured.

"Don't apologize. I think you and Jenny said some important things to each other this evening."

"Yeah."

If only Stephen and I could, Elena thought. But she didn't want to get into that.

"Maybe you need to let Carol know how you're feeling about things now," she said instead.

"The problem is, I don't want to risk being rejected again." He paused. "I've never talked to you about Jenny's mother."

"No, you haven't."

"I spent a long time trying to get over her. She left me when Jenny was just a baby. She didn't even want custody of her daughter."

"Oh, Bill."

"I met her on a buying trip down in L.A. She was an actress. I thought she loved me. I thought that when we got married and she came up here to Santa Barbara, she'd given up the idea of pursuing her career. Maybe she thought that too, at first. But after she had Jenny, I could see it wasn't going to work out. She wasn't happy staying at home with a kid. And I didn't see how I could move my business to L.A."

"I'm sorry."

"It was over years ago."

"Would I recognize her?"

"Probably not. She does some TV work, but she never made it big."

"And you raised Jenny by yourself."

"Yeah. For a long time I thought I could be both father and mother to her. Then I met Carol, and I started thinking differently."

Elena nodded in the darkness.

"And then I messed that up, too."

"You didn't mess it up. It was just something that happened."

Elena had a better idea now of why Bill's daughter was so important to him, and why he had trouble with rejection. And she also understood what it had cost him to approach her that day in the art supply store. He'd only done it because he was desperate to help his daughter.

She had been good for Jenny, too. But Elena knew that Bill had done a lot for *her*. He was a good friend and a kind, sincere, caring person. He deserved to be happy. Was there some way she could help him now? she wondered.

When they arrived at the Falconers', the hostess greeted Elena like an old friend. "I'm so glad you could join us again."

"So am I."

A number of people she had met last time, including Sam Goldner, made a point of coming up to speak to her. After a few minutes of conversation, Elena excused herself and crossed the room to where Carol was standing.

"Hello. I'm Elena Castile," she said, introducing herself.

"Carol Davenport." The blonde's voice was guarded. Cocking her head to one side, she looked Elena over. "I saw you come in with Bill—and last time, too."

Well, no matter what she had told Bill, this woman did care, Elena thought.

"Yes. He's the one who suggested I join the group." She watched to see what effect that piece of information had on Carol, and wasn't surprised when the blonde's expression tightened. "My fiancé was at the rehabilitation hospital when Jenny was there," Elena added.

"Oh. Your fiancé."

"Stephen Gallagher."

Carol nodded. "I remember reading about his accident in the paper. It sounded pretty bad."

"He's doing much better. In fact, we're getting married this week."

Carol's smile warmed. "Well, congratulations."

"I, uh, wanted to ask you a favor."

"Sure, if it's something I can do."

"I'm new in town, and I don't really feel comfortable, going around asking for contributions to the auction. But I want to do my part. I was wondering if we might try it together some afternoon."

"That's not a bad idea. I wasn't exactly looking forward to it, either. When would you want to go?"

She was about to say, *Not till Stephen and I get back from our honeymoon.*

"I'm free Monday afternoon," Carol continued. "We could meet around one-thirty."

Why not? Elena thought. Maggie was taking care of most of the wedding details. Getting out of the house would give her something to keep her mind off Wednesday.

"That would be good for me, too."

Carol extracted a small silver case from her purse and pulled out a card, which she handed to Elena.

"You're the relocation director for Sunrise Realty," Elena said, glancing at the business card.

"Yes. I work with people who are moving to Santa Barbara from out of state. We're in a small adobe on Chaparral," Carol told her. "It's different from the newer buildings in the area, so you shouldn't have any problem finding us. And you can park in our lot."

They chatted for another few minutes until Mary called the meeting to order.

As people were leaving afterward, the hostess drew Elena aside. "You know Bill spoke to me about auctioning off one of your paintings."

"He did mention that."

"He told me I could see some of your work at La Paloma Gallery. So I took the liberty of stopping in there," she went on.

"Oh?"

"He kept telling me how talented you were. But frankly, I was skeptical that an artist so young could produce the kind of work that Bill described. Well, I was wrong. Your paintings are very mature and very charming."

"Thank you."

"In fact, I've decided to purchase one for myself."

"You're serious?"

"Perfectly serious. And I'm hoping you'll be willing to donate more than one to the auction."

"I'd be honored."

"I was thinking that we could feature you in the publicity, which should help compensate for your time."

"That . . . that isn't necessary."

"But we'd like to do it for you."

Elena became aware that Bill had been watching the conversation. He grinned and gave her a thumbs-up sign.

As they got into the car a few minutes later, he turned to her. "I saw you go over and start up a conversation with Carol."

Elena could hear a good deal of emotion in the simple statement of fact. "She's very nice."

"Yes."

"Uh, what were you talking about?"

"The auction. Santa Barbara."

Bill sighed. "You're not going to tell me anything else, are you?"

"There isn't anything to tell yet."

Elena didn't know Carol very well. The only thing she did know for sure was that both Bill and Carol still cared, but they were afraid to risk getting hurt again. Could she help them get back together? She didn't know yet, so there was no use getting his hopes up prematurely.

Elena picked up her own car at Bill's and drove back to the ranch. She was excited about the events of the evening and wanted to share them with Stephen. But although it was after eleven when she returned, the light was still on in his office and the door was closed. Probably Stephen was trying to finish up some important business before going to bed. Rather than bother him, she went straight to her room, hoping that she could catch him at breakfast.

She set her alarm so that she would wake up early, but Stephen was already in the gym when she came down to the kitchen.

"This is like the first week I was here," Elena couldn't stop herself from remarking to Maggie as she buttered one of the housekeeper's blueberry muffins.

"What do you mean?"

"Stephen's avoiding me."

"Oh, I don't think that's true." Maggie's reassurance came a little too quickly. "He's just working overtime, so the two of you can enjoy your honeymoon without any interruptions."

"Mmm."

"Everything's all right, now that you're back."

Elena took a bite of her muffin. She hoped Maggie was right. Perhaps she was just reacting to her own jittery nerves. Stephen had admitted to her once that he had been testing her—seeing if he could drive her away. Maybe he couldn't stop himself from doing that now, and he wasn't going to relent until they were man and wife. In a strange way, the explanation was comforting. At least it was better than anything else her troubled mind could conjure up.

CHAPTER FOURTEEN

ELENA WAS RIGHT about Monday. Meeting Carol gave her something else to focus on besides the wedding.

She was becoming more familiar with Santa Barbara, and had no trouble following Carol's directions to the real estate office. The reception area of the old adobe building gave her a strange feeling. The well-worn tile floor and thick interior walls reminded her of the older structures on her father's estate at home.

"What was this place originally?" she asked when the petite blonde came into the room.

"The office for a working ranch up north. It was built in the 1930s. Isn't it terrific?"

"It makes me think of home."

"I was so preoccupied the other evening that I never did ask where you were from."

"Venezuela."

"That's an awfully long way." They left the office and climbed into Carol's Buick. "I made an appointment with Phil Baker at San Simeon Decorators," she said.

"Fine."

"So how did you end up in Santa Barbara?" Carol asked as she pulled into the afternoon traffic.

"I came to marry Stephen."

"Even after you found out what a terrible accident he'd been in?"

"I didn't know about it."

Carol's face registered her surprise.

"My father didn't tell me. It's a pretty complicated story."

"Mmm." The blonde didn't press for details.

But Elena found herself starting to talk—a bit hesitantly at first. Perhaps she wanted to explain how the engagement had come about because of her own emotional turmoil. Somehow it was a way of feeling closer to Stephen when he'd shut her out.

Carol listened quietly while Elena described how she and Stephen had first met and fallen in love, and how her father had forbidden their marriage at first and finally changed his mind. The only thing she left out was the part about Stephen paying her father. "I guess he thought I might have backed out, if he'd told me about the accident," she finished.

Carol shot her an assessing look. "In this country, women make their own decisions."

"I did."

"You weren't railroaded into this marriage?"

"Railroaded?" Elena's brow wrinkled for a moment. "I think I understand. No. I love Stephen. I wanted to marry him."

"Even when things had changed so much?"

"My *feelings* hadn't changed. The difference was that Stephen needed me more."

Carol didn't reply as she pulled into the parking lot beside the decorator's premises. As if by mutual agreement, both women let the topic of love and marriage drop for the time being.

"Phil worked with me on a model home project. So let me do the talking," Carol suggested.

Elena grinned. "I think I'm going to be watching an expert salesperson in operation."

"He's not even going to know I'm selling him anything."

After they were introduced, Phil Baker invited Carol and Elena into his small but practically equipped office. Elena had always wondered how a professional decorator might furnish his private domain. Phil had created a trendy but restful environment. The upholstered pieces were covered in peach, the carpeting was mushroom, and the wood trim and wall of shelves and cabinets were in a dark wood.

During the low-key conversation, Elena discovered that Carol had sent Phil a number of well-paying clients in the past so he was already in her debt and prepared to listen to what she had to say. It didn't take too much effort to convince him that donating his services to some lucky auction participant would be a good advertisement for his business.

As they returned to the car, Elena looked at Carol and shook her head. "And you told me you weren't looking forward to this. The rest of the committee members should take lessons from you."

"Phil had already made up his mind. He just wanted me to flatter him a bit." Instead of heading back to the office, Carol drove to a small café near the beach. "Want to stop for something to drink?"

"I'd like that."

They sat on the patio at one of the umbrella tables, screened from the ocean by a glass partition. Carol ordered soda water with lime. Elena decided to try the same thing and found she liked it.

After the waiter had left, Carol stirred her drink with the straw. "I wish my personal life were as uncomplicated as that piece of salesmanship you just saw. Did Bill tell you about me—about us?"

"Some."

"Is that why you came up to talk to me at the meeting?"

"Partly. I've gotten to like Bill very much, so I wanted to meet you."

"You know we broke up after Jenny's accident?"

"Mmm-hmm."

"At first I tried to be supportive. But even when he wasn't up there at the hospital with Jenny, it was like he couldn't focus on anything I was saying. I'd try to get him to relax with a drink in the evening. But he'd just sit there, staring across the room." She paused. "And when I'd try to make love to him, he just stopped responding."

Elena nodded uncertainly. This wasn't the kind of conversation she was used to having with someone she hardly knew. But she suspected that Carol needed a sympathetic ear.

"The stress finally got to me. I had stomach cramps all the time. I couldn't eat. I'd lie there in bed at night, wondering what to do."

"I understand," Elena murmured.

"Didn't Stephen's injuries make any difference to the two of you?" Carol suddenly asked.

"Of course. He pushes himself. Sets goals. And when he doesn't meet them, he's...not in a very good mood. It's hard for him to be open with me." Elena took a sip of her soda. "Sometimes I don't understand him. But I've usually been able to make him talk to me about it." *Except this week,* she added silently.

"Maybe you handle things better than I do."

Elena ran her fingers up the sides of the cold glass, watching the trails in the condensation. Carol had been very candid with her. Now it was tempting to pour out all the doubts she was feeling. At least Carol and Bill had been lovers. She and Stephen didn't even have that bond. His injuries had made a big difference in their physical relation-

ship. But despite her feelings toward Carol, she still didn't
know her well enough to tell her about that. In fact, using
Carol to reassure herself wasn't the reason why she had
suggested getting together.

It was Carol who changed the subject again. "Did Bill tell
you about his marriage?"

"Yes."

"Then you know his wife left him when Jenny was just a
baby?"

Elena nodded.

"I know that must have been terrible for him. But one
thing I wondered about was whether he was putting so much
effort into establishing his business that he didn't have
enough time for his wife."

Elena stared across the table at the other woman. She
hadn't thought about that. But it was obvious that Carol
had given the subject of Bill Delaney a great deal of consideration.

"So how did you meet him, anyway?" Carol asked.

Elena described her first encounter with Bill and the way
he wouldn't take no for an answer when he'd asked her to
give Jenny art lessons.

"See. He's so single-minded. Most of the time he can't
even bother thinking about what he puts on in the morning."

"Is that what's important to you?"

"I wouldn't have considered marrying him if it were." She
laughed. "Or like most women, I maybe thought I could
change him—or at least keep him looking presentable." Her
expression sobered again. "But it didn't work out that way.
After Jenny was hurt, he just didn't have time for me anymore."

"I think he felt guilty about the accident," Elena said.
"He didn't know how else to deal with it except by focus-

ing on Jenny. But she's made a lot of progress, and Bill's come to realize it's better for her if he draws back a little. I think he's the kind of man who's capable of learning from his mistakes."

Carol listened intently. "Why are you telling me all this?"

"Maybe because Bill's done so much for me. And I want to do something for him. He misses you."

"I miss him."

"I could see that when the two of you met at Mary's. How would you react if he called you?"

"I'm not sure. A woman likes to think she's the most important thing in a man's life. I'd always know I didn't mean as much as Jenny."

"Carol, I don't think that's really true. I think he's done some hard thinking about his priorities. You're very important to him. But the only way you're going to find out is by giving him a chance to prove it."

"Or a chance to break my heart again."

Elena wanted to tell her that happiness was worth taking the risk. But she didn't feel she had the right to push Carol into anything.

The blonde glanced at her watch. "I have to be getting back to the office."

"I'm glad we could get together."

"I am too." She gave Elena a direct look. "I really would like to do it again. Why don't you call me when you and Stephen get back from your honeymoon? We could have lunch."

"I will."

THE WEDDING was scheduled for eleven in the morning on Wednesday and would be followed by lunch. Elena awoke with a feeling of apprehension that she struggled hard to banish as she bathed and slipped into a cotton shift. Her mother's wedding dress, which she had brought down from the attic at home and carefully packed in her luggage, was hanging on the closet door. But she wouldn't be putting that on until closer to the time for the ceremony.

After a breakfast she hardly tasted, she went to find Maggie, who was setting up the buffet table in the formal dining room.

"Is there anything I can do to help you get ready?" she asked.

"This is your wedding day. You shouldn't be doing any of the work."

"Believe me, it's better if I have something to keep myself occupied."

"Nervous?"

Elena swallowed and nodded. Now was her last chance to ask Maggie for some guidance about tonight. Somehow she couldn't get the words out. Instead she turned to the china cabinet and began to take out the champagne glasses. They rattled together in her hands.

"Every bride is a little bit on edge," Maggie said soothingly.

"And does every bride have trouble believing that her wedding day is really going to happen?"

"Yes. But don't worry. Everything is going to go perfectly," the housekeeper added quickly.

"I hope so."

The doorbell rang, and Elena jumped.

"Probably the florist. I'll be right back," Maggie said, and went to answer the summons.

Three hours later, Elena stood trembling at the bottom of the stairs, while Maggie arranged the train of the satin wedding dress behind her. Although most of the flowers had been professionally arranged, Elena had put together her own bridal bouquet. The background was of white rosebuds and baby's breath. Interspersed with the white flowers were small sprigs of pink fireweed from the hillside behind the house and lavender from the garden.

"That bouquet is charming," Maggie whispered.

"Thank you."

"I've never seen a lovelier bride," Bill added as he stood beside her.

"Thank you," Elena managed again. She had asked Bill to give her away. The solid feel of his arm was reassuring as they waited for the signal to enter the living room, where the nuptials were going to be held.

Bill squeezed Elena's hand. "I'm glad you and Stephen worked things out. That week you were at my house, I wasn't sure what was going to happen. You're making me wish that Carol and I had been able to . . ." His voice trailed off.

"Don't put your relationship in the past tense yet," Elena murmured. It was easier to reassure Bill than to deal with her own doubts. But she would never have voiced the uncertainty on her wedding day.

"You're one of the few people who could get me into a tuxedo," Bill joked.

Elena looked at him and smiled, knowing he was trying to help her relax. Before she had time to reply, Maggie whispered that the priest was ready to begin.

As Elena stepped through the broad doorway, she saw Stephen standing at the end of the room, watching her. He was also wearing a black tuxedo, but with a lot more panache than Bill could muster. Her heart gave a little lurch at the sight of him. He was so handsome. Even the scars gave him a dashing air that few other men could match.

She saw his eyes sweep over her and focus on the bouquet for a moment. "You look beautiful," he whispered as she took her place beside him. She smiled at him shyly behind her veil just before the priest began to speak.

They had requested a simple, double-ring ceremony. When she and Stephen turned to face the room again, they were surrounded by a small circle of smiling faces.

"That was so romantic," Jenny said with a sigh.

Elena watched Maggie unashamedly brush tears from her cheek. Even Bill and Hal were misty-eyed.

"Well," Maggie exclaimed, "now we can all go out to the dining room and have some refreshments!"

It was difficult for Elena to get through the next hour and a half. She knew Stephen hadn't been in a social situation like this since his accident. Although they were among a small group of close friends in his own home, she sensed his discomfort as he tried to make small talk. Even on his wedding day, he didn't like being the center of attention. But there wasn't much she could do to help him.

Neither ate more than a few polite bites of the buffet Maggie had worked so hard to prepare. When it was finally time to cut the small wedding cake, Elena knew that Stephen was glad the socializing was almost over.

As she grasped the cake knife and felt Stephen's strong fingers wrap themselves around hers, she couldn't stop herself from yearning wistfully for a photograph of the two of them together. How did they look standing here? she wondered. Other couples preserved the special moments of their wedding reception in pictures, so that they could look back on the event. She would have to rely on her memory, just as she had at the Hall of Records.

After everyone had been served a piece of the cake, Elena caught Maggie's eye. "Could you help me change out of my wedding dress?" she asked.

"Of course."

Elena knew Stephen's gaze was following her as she went up the stairs. But she couldn't turn and look at him.

Hal had already taken their luggage to the house where they would be staying. Elena had decided it was silly to put on a fancy outfit just to drive for forty-five minutes. So after hanging up the wedding dress, she changed into a simple silk blouse, flowered skirt and sandals.

"Every happiness," Maggie said as she hugged Elena goodbye beside the car.

"Thank you."

Stephen, who had put on dark slacks and an oxford-cloth shirt, didn't speak until the Porsche was at the end of the driveway. "I'm glad that's over."

"The wedding?"

"No, the reception."

"You know, your face doesn't look as bad as you think it does."

His head whipped around. "Who said anything about my face?"

"I . . . I thought that's why you were uncomfortable."

"Well, don't make assumptions about what I'm thinking."

"If you'd tell me, I wouldn't have to guess. You haven't exactly been very talkative lately."

He turned back toward the road, but she could see the tightness of his jaw.

Elena tried to swallow the lump that had formed in her throat. Once they got away from the reception, she had hoped things would be different. But the man sitting next to her was still a stranger. What was she going to do now?

As they drove silently into the hills, Elena pretended to look at the scenery—and sneaked sidelong glances at Stephen. She could tell he was making an effort to relax, yet he didn't seem inclined to talk.

The house Stephen had rented for the week was nestled in the hills overlooking Lake Cachuma. It was a very romantic setting, the untamed beauty of the mountain landscape contrasting sharply with the carefully tended gardens around the villa of wood and stone.

Elena got quickly out of the car and walked to the edge of the front patio, where she stood looking down at the jewell-like blue of the lake. She heard Stephen's footsteps crunching on the gravel of the driveway, and pressed her hands against her sides as he came up behind her.

"Elena." His voice was low.

"Yes."

"I'm sorry I snapped at you."

She nodded almost imperceptibly.

"Even after you agreed to come back, I kept thinking that somehow there wasn't going to be a wedding."

She drew in a sharp breath. The fears hadn't been unfounded. The idea of backing out had crossed her mind more than once.

"I guess I didn't dare to let myself be happy," he continued.

"Why didn't you tell me what you were feeling?"

"Because it's still hard to share my private doubts."

Still uncertain, she stood stiffly, her face turned away from him. He took a step forward, then reached to grasp her hand. For a few moments longer the two of them stood looking at the magnificent view. "Let's go see what the house is like inside," Stephen finally murmured.

"All right."

Elena waited nervously as her new husband opened the front door. Then she followed him slowly into the small foyer. Beyond was a living room with floor-to-ceiling windows overlooking the lake and the mountains. The furnishings were an opulent but comfortable mixture of fine antiques and modern upholstered pieces.

"I didn't know you could rent anything like this."

"Only if you know the right people. It belongs to the president of a company back East. He loves the Santa Barbara area, but only gets here a few times a year."

Elena nodded.

"The kitchen is stocked with everything we'll need for the week."

"Oh."

"Do you want to have a look at the bedroom?"

No. Not yet. Can't we get to know each other again first? Would he be angry if she asked that of him? Elena wondered. Without speaking, she followed him down the hall.

Her gaze bounced off the wide bed covered with a heavy burgundy comforter. Beyond it was another gleaming expanse of glass, looking out on the valley.

"Not much privacy," Elena blurted.

Stephen laughed. "There can't be anybody out there except an occasional helicopter pilot. Besides, I'm hoping that you'll be a lot more interested in what's going on in here than what's outside the window."

As he had done on the patio, he came up to stand behind her. This time he wrapped his arms around her waist and pulled her back against himself. She might have sprung out of his grasp, except that it was too firm. Quickly he turned her around.

"I've waited a long time for this," he murmured. Then his lips were descending to hers in a hungry kiss that spoke of pent-up needs and demands.

Always before Elena had melted under the heat of his kisses—but not today. When he felt her resistance, his head snapped up and she saw him look down at her assessingly. For a frozen moment neither of them spoke.

"So, sweetheart, when it finally comes down to it, you can't make love with someone who looks like me."

This wasn't the way she had dreamed of beginning her marriage. She licked her lips, knowing that she had to make him understand what she was feeling. "Stephen. I love you. Truly. But all this week, when you wouldn't let me close to you, when you turned into a stranger—I started worrying about what was going to happen between us tonight."

When he didn't speak, she forced herself to continue. "I feel so stupid. I don't know very much about what happens between men and women. It isn't something I could get Anna to talk about."

"*Querida*, I should have understood all that."

CHAPTER FIFTEEN

ELENA CLOSED HER EYES and pressed her face against Stephen's shoulder. "I want to please you, if you'll tell me how."

"You do please me, sweetheart—very much."

When she tried to protest, he smoothed gentle fingers against her lips. She had been so open, so passionate in her responses to him that he had let himself forget how very inexperienced she really was.

"Don't you want to...to make love to me?" Her voice was far from steady.

"Despite what I said a few minutes ago, I can wait." Threading his fingers through hers, he turned and led her back down the hall to the living room. "I think both of us need to relax."

"But—"

He ignored her protest. "I'd be more comfortable if I could stretch my leg out. Do you think we could put a quilt down in front of the couch, the way we used to in the evenings?"

"Your leg. Of course. Does it hurt?" Elena looked at him with concern and then began to scurry around, spreading a comforter on the thick carpet and gathering pillows.

Stephen lowered the puffy Austrian shades, dimming the light in the room. Then he disappeared into the kitchen. When he returned, he was carrying a bottle of champagne in an ice bucket and two glasses.

"This was in the refrigerator. I thought a glass would help us both unwind a little bit."

Elena nodded.

After popping the cork, Stephen settled himself on the blanket with his back against the pillows at the bottom of the sofa. When he stretched out his long legs, he sighed, hoping he had disguised the tension he was feeling.

"Do you want me to take off your shoes?"

"That would feel wonderful."

Elena knelt and eased off his loafers, her fingers lingering for just a moment on the strong curves of his arches. When he had come up behind her in the bedroom, she had been afraid. Now she could admit how much simple pleasure it gave her to touch him.

"Thank you." He held out his hand. She looked at him shyly, then gingerly settled into the pillows beside him.

Stephen poured them each a glass of the champagne. His eyes met Elena's as he handed one to her.

"To the beginning of our marriage."

"Yes." Elena touched her glass to his and then took a large gulp.

He laughed. "Easy. You need to stay coherent so we can...talk." Reaching out, he stroked her dark hair back from her face, feeling the fine sheen of moisture on her skin. Neither one of them spoke for a few minutes as they sipped the wine.

"This week you stopped trusting me, didn't you?" he questioned softly.

"I'm sorry."

"It wasn't your fault." His lips skimmed over hers in the lightest of kisses. He felt her tremble.

"*Querida*, I think the best thing is for the two of us to get comfortable with each other again."

Elena nodded.

"We won't do anything you're not ready for. Not now. And not tonight. Agreed?"

She nodded hesitantly.

He pulled her close, so that he could nuzzle his face against her hair. Then he turned his head, finding the sensitive places along her neck and chin.

Despite her lingering nervousness, Elena snuggled into the caress. This was the man she loved, not the stranger she had feared confronting tonight.

They talked in quiet tones about the way she'd felt that week, and about how he'd felt.

And while they talked, he continued to gentle her. It was a relief to feel the wariness seeping out of her. Yet he was burningly aware that his own tension was mounting.

"You said you liked it when I kissed you and touched you before. Can you tell me how it felt?" he asked.

The very words made a furnace of heat sweep over her. She wondered how she could tell him about such intimate feelings. "It's difficult to speak of these things."

"I understand that, sweetheart."

The acceptance and encouragement in his voice gave her the confidence to answer. "It made me feel good." His fingers pressed hers. "Tingly, I guess. Hot and shivery at the same time. When we were together like that, I didn't want it to stop," she finished in a rush.

He smiled. "That's the way it's supposed to be. That's how it is for me, too. It's the feeling of wanting to make love. The only difference is that men are ready faster."

"Oh."

"But when a man cares about a woman, he makes sure she's as ready as he is."

"What do you mean?"

"I'd like to show you."

He heard her catch her breath. "I'm not going to make any demands. All you have to do is enjoy the feeling of being kissed and touched again."

"Esteban, I don't understand. If we don't—I mean, how can you show me?"

Gravely he smoothed his thumb across her lips. "You have to trust me."

"I do. Truly."

He pulled her close and held her for several heartbeats, stroking his lips against her cheek. Then he lowered her to the quilt.

Reading the proof of her trust in her eyes, he smiled down reassuringly. But his insides were knotted with tension. He had said that he would demand nothing from her. But it was all he could do to keep his own hand from shaking as his finger gently outlined her jaw.

Lifting her hand, he folded her fingers and pressed them against his lips. At first he turned his head from side to side, simply enjoying the closeness. Then he opened his mouth and slowly began to press his teeth against her tender flesh.

"Mmm."

"Does that feel good?" he asked, adding the wet texture of his tongue to the caress.

"Very."

He watched Elena's face, seeing her eyelids flutter as his tongue stroked between her fingers. She had begun to move her hand against his mouth, clearly seeking on her own to increase the contact.

With his other hand he began to trace the curve of her lips, defining their shape. They parted on a breathy exclamation, and he gently slipped a finger inside, letting it glide along the sensitive inner surfaces. Her tongue and teeth found his fingertip, nibbling and stroking as he had done.

"I like that, *querida*."

Her eyes slowly opened. They were large and beautiful, the pupils already dilated with passion he could see. "I do, too. It makes me feel hot and shivery."

He wanted to strip off her clothes and cover her nakedness with his aching body. Instead he bent to brush his lips against hers. This time she didn't draw back. Her arms came up to clasp him around the shoulders as he once more moved his head from side to side. He savored her with controlled ardor, banking the fire of his own needs in order to satisfy hers. It was she who deepened the kiss, her tongue pressing forward to find his.

"Stephen."

He almost forgot himself then, almost devoured her mouth with the urgency he felt. But the memory of the vulnerability on her face as they'd stood by the window in the bedroom made him pursue the slow, seductive pace.

He wanted her hot and trembling in his arms. He wanted her to be as consumed with need as he was himself.

As his hands slid over the softness of her breasts, the fervor of her kiss increased. His breath caught in his throat as she began to twist against him, telling him silently that she wanted more.

The need to touch her was as elemental as the need to breathe. "Sweetheart."

"That's so good."

"You feel it here, too. Don't you?" He pressed the soft mound at the juncture of her legs.

"Yes." The admission as a choked whimper as she arched into his touch.

He murmured soft, sexy soothing words into her ear as he began to undress her. After unhooking the front closing of her bra, he captured one already aroused nipple with his mouth.

At the same time he let himself discover the delicate flesh of her inner thighs. She was so caught up by the sensations he was producing that there was no thought of fear or protest.

But he had to suppress his own groan of arousal as his fingers found the warm, moist, hidden core of her femininity.

"So sweet. So hot."

"Yes. I'm on fire!" she gasped as he continued to stoke her passion.

He was on fire, too. He might die from touching her like this. Yet he had committed himself to showing her just what pleasure she could expect when they finally made love.

She was shivering again—not with fear this time, but with the need for fulfillment.

He heard her ragged breathing.

"That's it, sweetheart. You're almost there."

Something in his voice make her eyes fly open. He had brought her into a world of white heat and blazing color. Now she fought the almost overwhelming pleasure of it so that she could look up and into his face. With the clarity she sometimes experienced when she was putting a likeness onto canvas, she suddenly understood what he was doing. He was thinking only of her. And in doing so, he was denying himself.

"Esteban, please." She caught his hand, pulling it away from her body.

"Anything, *querida*."

"It shouldn't be like this."

"This is for you."

"Don't you want to. . . to be inside me?"

A convulsive spasm of pure need racked his body. "Don't ask me that!"

"Stephen, let me please you." She reached out blindly, her hand finding the hard, hot shaft of his arousal where it strained against the fabric of his slacks.

"Sweetheart, for God's sake, don't!" he repeated. The strangled plea wedged in his throat. "You don't know what you're doing."

"Yes, I do." Her other hand began to fumble with the buttons of his shirt.

How much of this could he take? he wondered. With a muffled groan, he sat up and finished unbuttoning the shirt. It took him only a few more moments to shed the rest of his clothes. Then he turned back to Elena.

With a desperate urgency he pulled her against himself. The sudden reality of his hot flesh against hers made them both gasp.

But as he eased her down to the comforter again, he felt her tremble.

"*Mi amor.* You'll have to tell me what to do," she whispered.

"You're doing perfectly."

He began to kiss and caress her once more, until her whole body was trembling with the need for release.

Beyond her closed eyelids, a kaleidoscope of bright colors swirled and exploded. She felt them sizzle against her nerve endings like the maddeningly erotic touch of Stephen's fingers, the hot velvet of his mouth.

This was how he had wanted her—wild and shimmering in his arms. Eagerly he drank the broken little cries of joy from her lips.

Fighting to control his own aching desire, he began to stroke her with his body, barely entering her, then withdrawing, until her hips were wildly arching upward in supplication.

"*¡Esteban! ¡Ay Dios, Esteban!*"

"Soon, *querida*, soon."

He knew that the hot, moist friction of flesh against flesh would bring her what she craved. He also knew the urgency of his own need for release. He had wanted this for so long that once he became part of her, it was all going to be over rather quickly.

He bent to suck a taut nipple into his mouth. At that moment he felt the first tremors of gratification begin to ripple over her body. Still he waited, stroking her pleasure until she was shaking uncontrollably and sobbing his name.

The bright colors spun and burst around her, scattered over her flesh. Blinding white, as if the door of a blast furnace had suddenly been thrown open, they transmuted to red and orange and then slowly faded to purple.

Only as he felt her climax begin to ebb did he penetrate her fully, burying himself in the tight, flaming sheath of her femininity. The sweetness of finally joining himself with her was almost overwhelming. He wanted it to last forever, but in a few white-hot strokes of ecstasy it was over.

When he came back to himself, he felt her shoulders trembling violently. Where her face was pressed against his chest, his skin was wet. "*Querida*, I'm so sorry. I didn't want to hurt you."

She couldn't let him think that. Desperately she gathered shreds of coherence. "You . . . you didn't hurt me."

"Then what—?"

"Please. I can't talk."

His hands moved across her quivering shoulders. Shifting his weight, he cradled her protectively against the length of his body, holding her until she was ready to tell him what she was feeling.

Finally she brushed the back of her hand across her eyes. His lips marked her hair line. "How are you?"

"Overwhelmed."

He might have chosen the same word to describe his own feelings.

"I didn't know something physical could be that—" she struggled to find a word that would convey her deep emotions "—breathtaking."

"Oh, sweetheart." He gathered her closer, dusting her damp face with kisses.

"Why didn't you tell me?" she whispered.

"I didn't know."

Her eyes searched his.

"I thought I wanted you—needed you. But until a few minutes ago I didn't understand how much. Loving you makes the difference, *querida*."

"Yes. Loving you."

Neither one of them could speak for some time. Now that her skin was no longer heated by passion, Elena slowly became aware that the room was chilly.

"Are you cold?"

"A little."

"Perhaps we could continue this discussion under the covers, if you're not still nervous about getting in bed with me."

She caught the teasing note in his voice. "I think it's a little late for that."

As she sat up, Elena looked down at the end of the comforter and began to laugh.

Stephen followed the direction of her gaze. "What's so funny?"

"You're not wearing anything except your socks."

He grinned. "I guess I was in a hurry, after all."

"Not in too much of a hurry to take me with you."

Stephen helped Elena up. Then seeing that she had become conscious of her state of undress, he draped the quilt around her shoulders. Before they started down the hall to the bedroom, he pulled the bottle of champagne from the ice bucket and picked up the glasses.

He waited until she had settled herself under the covers, the sheet tucked up around the tops of her breasts. Under the circumstances, the modesty was beguiling.

After he had joined her in bed, Stephen refilled their glasses.

"To a memorable beginning," he said.

Elena smiled at him as she took a slow sip. "Yes."

Shoulder to shoulder they sipped the bubbly wine.

"This is good. Last time I couldn't even taste it," Elena admitted.

"Neither could I."

She looked at him questioningly.

"I was worried about getting you to trust me again."

"Stephen." She launched herself into his arms, spilling champagne onto her shoulders and down her front.

"Oh!"

"Not to worry." Grinning, he lifted the sheet away from her body before it could get wet and bent to lick the wine from her skin.

Her exclamation of surprise turned into a little gasp of pleasure as his tongue trailed down to the tops of her breasts.

"I'm sorry. I'd better behave myself."

"Why?"

"Because you're not used to making love, and you might need to, uh, recuperate."

"I might welcome the opportunity to get used to it." She leaned over and slid her breasts seductively against his chest.

He gasped. Then his mouth covered hers.

This time there was no shadow of uncertainty in her eyes as he began to arouse her. In fact, her hands and lips were as eager as his own.

Her need built inexorably. This time she knew what it was she wanted. "Stephen, I have to feel you inside me again."

There was no way he could resist that throaty invitation. Yet when he had entered her, he held himself very still. Bracing himself on his hands, he looked down into the dark passion of her eyes.

"I love you, *querida*. More than I can possibly tell you except with my body."

"I feel that way, too."

Soon she could only move against him, rocking her hips, reaching upward, trying to satisfy the runaway need.

He brought her slowly upward from one plateau to the next. She grasped for the summit, digging her nails into his shoulders. Still he held back, reveling in her pleasure and his own until it was impossible to continue the sweet torture of denying himself satisfaction.

Even as his own climax seized him, he felt her body convulse, heard her gasp his name.

Aftershocks of pleasure rippled through Elena as he kissed and stroked her. She closed her eyes and rubbed her cheek against his, feathered her fingers through his hair. The sweet intimacy of the moment was still almost too much for her.

To be with Stephen like this. Close and warm and free to show him how much she loved him. She hadn't known how desperately she'd longed for it.

"I like this," she whispered simply. "This is the way I wanted it to be with us."

He clasped her tighter. "So did I. For such a long time."

CHAPTER SIXTEEN

LIKE THE WEDDING, there were no photographs from their honeymoon. But there were scenes that would never be erased from Elena's memory. Each was unique. And each was very precious.

THEY WERE LYING on the quilt in front of the couch, her head resting comfortably against the cushion of hair on his chest. With a slender finger she gently traced the line of a scar that angled downward toward Stephen's abdomen. Now it was raised and pink. Not so long ago she knew it must have been an angry red. She felt him tense slightly, but he didn't capture her hand or brush it aside, the way he would have done once.

She smiled to herself. He had taught her many things about the physical relationship between men and women, and he had brought her great joy in the teaching. But there had been things she wanted him to understand, too. Just as he had longed to know her body, she longed to know his, as well. That meant letting her explore his imperfections, as well as his strengths.

"Was that one of the bad ones?"

"No. Not all that bad."

"I wish I could have been with you then."

"This is better."

She squeezed her eyes shut as a wave of emotion swept over her. "What was the worst?" she whispered.

He drew in a breath and held it. "Not anything physical. Not the pain, although God knows there was enough of that. I hadn't seen you in such a long time, but I was afraid I was going to die without having a chance to tell you how much I loved you."

"Mi amor."

His hand combed through the rich darkness of her hair, letting the strands drift through his fingers. He fanned them out across his chest, thinking how beautiful they looked.

"That was over a long time ago."

She smoothed her cheek against him, listening to the strong, regular beat of his heart. What if she had never experienced this intimacy with the man she loved so much? That would have been a tragedy.

"THIS IS, UH, VERY GOOD."

Stephen snorted. "You mean you like fried eggs hard enough to use as roofing shingles?"

"They're not that bad."

"I wanted to fix you breakfast in bed. Maybe I should have stuck with the frozen waffles."

"It's the thought that counts."

"We can't eat thoughts."

"Well, your coffee isn't half bad. And the waffles are fine."

He picked one up and took a bite. "Not much I could do to ruin them."

Elena slanted her husband a look. Clad only in a pair of faded jeans, he was propped comfortably against the pillows.

"I love you," she murmured.

"I never get tired of hearing that."

She munched a waffle, knowing she was simply buying time. "Can we talk about something important?"

"If you like."

"The money you sent my father."

His fingers tensed on the coffee mug he held, and for a moment she feared the handle would snap off. "What about it?"

"I want to pay you back."

"You can't be serious."

"How would you feel if the situation were reversed?"

"Don't be ridiculous."

She forced herself not to drop her gaze. "It makes me feel dishonored."

"It shouldn't. You had nothing to do with it."

"I can't help the way I feel. You, of all people, should understand that."

He nodded. "Why are you bringing this up now?"

She couldn't suppress a nervous little laugh. "I wanted to talk about it before the wedding. But I was afraid you'd get angry." She took a swallow of her coffee. "I guess I was afraid you might tell me you weren't going to marry me, after all."

"I wouldn't have wanted to talk about the money, but I never would have said that, *querida*."

"You did once, when I first arrived."

He winced at the memory. "That was my pride talking, not my heart."

She moved closer, so that she could lay her head on his muscular forearm. "I've felt so open with you these past few days. I thought that the two of us could speak to each other of anything."

He covered her hand with his. "That makes me very happy. It's the way I want it to be between the two of us."

"And what about the money?"

"It brought me the thing I wanted most in the world."

"That's true for me, too."

"Then why talk of reimbursement?"

"*My* pride. Perhaps it's as stubborn as yours."

"You have such clever ways of making me understand things."

"Then you won't mind if I start to pay you back a little at a time from the sale of my paintings. It could take years. But it will be a start."

"If it makes you feel better, I won't mind." *And I'll put it into a trust fund for our children,* he added silently.

"YOUR BACK is like satin."

"Stephen, please. Let me turn over."

"Not yet, sweetheart. Mmm. I love the way your shoulder blades taste."

She angled her face toward him, her eyes dark with passion. "I have to. Please. I have to touch you."

"No. Wait. Take a deep breath."

The only sound in the room was that of air—hissing in and out of her lungs—and in and out of his.

He continued to stroke her until his need for more was unendurable. "Now."

"Oh—" Her hands reached for him, slipping across the damp warmth of his skin.

"Yes. Like that, *querida.*"

"Yes, like that. Don't stop. Oh, God, don't stop."

IT WAS ONE of those rare days when the early-morning fog burned off almost at once. But the air was still chilled. Stephen came out onto the patio, tucking his flannel shirt into his jeans.

Elena, who had thrown his robe over her sheer gown, was clearly so absorbed in what she was drawing that she didn't hear him. For several minutes he stood watching her. She hadn't bothered to comb her hair. It was still mussed from his attentions the night before. She sat with her feet tucked up under her, only the toes peeking out from under the folds of the robe. Her chair was turned toward the mountains. Her face was a study in concentration.

When she sensed her husband's presence, she looked up. "Stephen. I thought you were sleeping."

"I was. You're barefoot."

"I didn't want to wake you up. But I just had to catch this light. It's so perfect."

"What are you drawing?"

"The mountains. I know it's our honeymoon. But do you mind if I work a little bit?"

"Of course not. I was enjoying watching your face."

"Why?"

"The look of absorption. It's as if your thoughts were focused on a single beam of light."

He went around to stand behind her, and she tilted her head inquiringly.

"Could you keep working? I'd like to watch."

"All right."

The soft pencil began to move smoothly over the paper again. Elena finished two sketches and started another.

"Nice," he murmured. "I like seeing the shapes of familiar things form from those quick strokes of yours. I like trying to figure out how you capture the branches of a a tree in just a few deft lines."

"I just do what seems right."

"For me it's like a magic trick." His fingers caressed her shoulder. "Would you do me a favor?"

"Anything."

"Do a painting of this same scene. I'd like to hang it in my office, with the other one you did before you came here."

"I was already planning the painting—to give to you."

"DOES LOUNGING IN BED at three in the afternoon make you feel wicked?" Elena asked.

"Uh-uh."

"Why not?"

"Because this is one of the few times in our lives when we don't have any responsibilities to anyone else. We can do absolutely anything we want to do. And I don't feel guilty about that at all." Leaning over, he punctuated the declaration with a series of random kisses that started on her face and ended in the sensitive hollow at the base of her neck.

Elena snuggled against him. "I guess you're right."

"One of the things I've liked best has been the chance to talk."

"Oh, really?"

"*One* of the things." He looked at her. "Do you remember the afternoon I knocked over the glass on the patio?"

"When you were still in the wheelchair?"

"Yes. Were you watching from the window?"

She wound her fingers into the edge of the sheet. "Why do you ask?"

"You were, weren't you?"

"Mmm-hmm."

"I think I felt you standing there in the shadows behind your shutters."

"When you got out of the chair, you looked so sexy in your bathing suit with your hands behind your back."

"That's why I was doing it, *querida*."

"You devil."

Stephen rolled over and propped himself on one elbow. "Tell me what you were thinking about."

"I'm embarrassed."

"With your husband? Still?"

"A little."

"I want to hear about it."

She raised her gaze to his. "I saw you sitting there almost naked, and I started thinking about that first time in my father's garden, when you kissed me."

"Mmm."

"Watching you and thinking about when we'd been together turned me on."

"There's an interesting idiom for your collection."

"I have the feeling you're going to make sure I know all the ones that have to do with making love."

"Mmm-hmm."

ELENA BENT DOWN and tossed a bell-shaped eucalyptus pod into the water. The current caught it, spun it around, and rushed it over the rocks that lined the streambed.

She and Stephen had walked down the path from the house, and were sitting on a boulder in the tree-shaded valley at the bottom of the hill.

"I wish we didn't have to go back to the real world tomorrow," she said with a sigh. "This week has been wonderful."

Stephen meshed his fingers with those of his wife, and she leaned back against the solid wall of his chest. "For me, too."

"And your leg is so much better."

She felt his rumble of laughter. "I think we've finally found a cure for what ails me. Do you think I should write an article about it for the rehab center's newsletter?"

"I hope you're not serious."

"Just teasing."

They sat watching the rushing water of the little stream and listening to the gurgle of the current over the stones.

"It's so peaceful here. I wish we could stay a little longer," Elena finally murmured.

He picked up her hand and pressed the palm against his lips. Then, unable to stop himself from increasing the intimacy, he slid his tongue against her soft flesh. "We'll make sure we get away like this again soon."

"I hope so."

"But I'm anxious to bring you back to the ranch, too." He gazed at her. "I never realized it before, but sharing your life with someone gives everything more meaning. It's not just *my* ranch anymore. It's ours."

She turned and looked at him, and he smoothed his thumb tenderly against her lips.

"Before the wedding, you must have felt as though you didn't quite belong there."

"Everyone was kind to me."

"But it wasn't like being *home*."

"That's true."

"Well, it is now."

She wrapped her arms around his neck and drew him close. "You've given me so much."

"It's the other way around, *querida*. I feel as if I'm finally coming home, too. Because you'll be living there with me as my wife."

The words sent a strong current of emotion through her soul. It was impossible to imagine being happier than this.

CHAPTER SEVENTEEN

WHEN THEY ARRIVED at the ranch early the next morning, Elena found herself folded warmly into Maggie's ample embrace. "I'm so glad to have you back."

"It's good to come home."

Stephen shot his new wife a warm look at her acknowledgment of the conversation they'd had the day before.

"Well, you two seem to have had a good time," Maggie observed.

Elena flushed. Stephen simply grinned and smoothly changed the subject. "And what did *you* do while we were away?"

"Caught up on some of the cleaning that never gets done. Baked some pies and put them into the freezer."

"That doesn't sound too exciting."

Maggie looked a bit sheepish. "Well, I did go up to Santa Ynez and play Indian bingo."

Stephen laughed. "Oh, I see. And did you win?"

"Don't ask. Let's just say I enjoyed myself."

Elena looked from Maggie to her husband. "And what exactly is Indian bingo?"

"It's just like regular bingo. Do you know the game?"

She nodded.

"Well, the Indian tribe up there runs a hot game. It's one of the area's big tourist attractions. The parking lot is always full of buses," Stephen explained.

The three of them talked amiably for a few more minutes, then Stephen and Elena excused themselves to take their bags upstairs. At the young woman's request, Maggie had moved Elena's things into the master bedroom at the end of the hall.

As she stood looking around the room, Stephen came up and put his arms around her. "Welcome home," he murmured, brushing his lips against her hair.

"It seems strange, finally to be here."

"No, it seems very right."

She turned and wove her arms around his neck. For a long moment they stood locked together—as though neither of them wanted to give up the special intimacy of the past week. With a sigh, Stephen gently disengaged himself.

"I'm afraid I have to go deal with the stack of messages that must have piled up while we were gone."

"I understand. Will I see you at lunch?"

"I hope so. I'll let you know."

One of the first things Elena did after settling in at the ranch was to get in touch with Carol Davenport.

"I was hoping you'd call. Do you want to come down one day next week and have lunch with me?"

"That would be wonderful."

They decided on Tuesday and agreed to meet at a small Japanese restaurant on upper State Street.

"Well, marriage certainly agrees with you," Carol remarked as Elena seated herself at the table.

"Yes."

"I was thinking the last time we met that maybe you were worried about how things were going to work out with you and Stephen."

Elena looked up in surprise. "I didn't know it showed."

"I didn't want to pry."

They opened their menus. "I've never had Japanese food. What's good?" Elena asked.

"Teriyaki anything. Why don't you try the combination plate?"

The meal started with a clear soup. As the two women ate, Elena sensed that Carol wanted to say something.

Finally she pushed aside her bowl. "I've been thinking a lot about you and Stephen—and me and Bill."

"Oh?"

"Going ahead with your marriage took courage."

"No—"

"It did, whether you realize that or not." Carol paused while the waitress cleared the soup bowls away. "What Bill and I had together before Jenny's accident was very, very good."

Elena nodded.

"The last time I saw you, I told you all the reasons why *he* messed up the relationship. But since then, I've been thinking about what *I* was doing. Maybe I didn't try hard enough. Maybe I was afraid to take on a kid in a wheelchair."

"It's a big responsibility."

"I'd hate to think I was a coward."

"What do you mean?"

"I mean, I think maybe I'm going to call Bill."

"I'm glad."

"It may not work out."

"But—"

"But I'll never know unless I give it a try."

DURING THE NEXT FEW WEEKS Elena and Stephen settled into married life. In many ways it was an ideal arrangement. And sometimes Elena wondered why she couldn't simply count her blessings.

Her own work was going very well—because her happiness was reflected in her paintings. Miles Henderson had sold several of her pictures and had asked for more.

In most things that counted, her life with Stephen was what she had dreamed of. She kept telling herself how lucky she was that her husband was home during the day, so that the two of them could lunch together and then perhaps steal an hour or two for a ride across the ranch—or some time alone in their bedroom. And the nights in each other's arms were their special joy.

But there was one aspect of their relationship that Elena didn't know how to cope with. She had thought that with the secure base of their marriage to fall back upon, Stephen would feel comfortable getting out among people. However, he resisted all her efforts to change the pattern he had set for himself. The knowledge that he still harbored self-doubts troubled her, and she didn't know what to do about it.

Two weeks after they arrived home from their honeymoon, an invitation came from Mary Falconer, the chairwoman of the auction committee.

"She's having everyone over to dinner on the fifteenth," Elena told her husband enthusiastically as they sat relaxing in front of the fire. Seeing the doubtful look that crossed his features, she hurried on. "They're a really interesting group of people. And they're all so warm and friendly. I'm sure you'd enjoy an evening out with them."

When Stephen continued to look uncertain, she added quickly, "Bill would be there. And Sam Goldner. You like both of them. And you'd get to meet Carol. I think she and Bill are going to start dating again."

Her husband stroked one finger along his jaw, and her eyes fastened on the achingly familiar gesture. "I do know some of the people on the committee already," he mused.

Elena held her breath, waiting for him to continue.

"But sweetheart, I don't think I'd fit into that crowd anymore."

"Stephen—"

Although he smiled at her, his expression was edged with tension. "Don't let me stop you from enjoying their company."

Elena looked into the dancing flames. She didn't want to go alone. She wanted to be with her husband. She was proud of his strength of character, his accomplishments, his ability to conquer adversity. She wanted her new friends to see those qualities as well. She wanted his old friends to see how well he was doing.

But he had pulled back into his shell. She realized he was sincere in his suggestion that she go to the dinner by herself. Just because he felt the need to isolate himself at Rancho Palo Colorado, he didn't want to hold his young wife captive, too. She didn't think the decision was a good one. He was cheating himself out of so much that life had to offer. And his reclusiveness affected her, as well. He was forcing her to compartmentalize herself in a way that she found disquieting. She could be warm and secure at the ranch with Stephen, or venture into the world on her own. But she couldn't integrate the two aspects of her life in any sort of normal way. The growing realization was disturbing.

He had been through much and come far. Should she tell him how she felt now? Or should she give him more time to be absolutely secure in their relationship? She glanced at Stephen, noting the rigid set of his shoulders and jaw. Her casual mention of the dinner invitation had disturbed the tranquillity of their evening. Perhaps the best thing to do was to think of another, more subtle, way to approach the subject.

A few days later, as they walked along one of the garden's sandstone block paths, he confirmed Elena's conviction that he was reluctant to leave the ranch for any reason. Stephen paused beside an orange trumpet vine, and she caught a brooding look on his face.

"What are you thinking about?" she asked.

"A company I'd planned to buy."

Having first assured himself that Elena wasn't bored by the details of his business, he had gotten into the habit of discussing them with her.

"Which one?"

"Lexco—the Denver manufacturing plant I told you about."

"Is there a problem?"

"An investment banker friend of mine has heard some rumors. Lexco may be hit with a patent infringement suit. He thinks I should look into them pretty thoroughly before I make any decisions."

"That sounds like a good idea."

"I've talked to their management team, and they've invited me to come out there."

"And?"

He had brought up the subject himself. She waited for him to continue. Instead he plucked one of the trumpet-shaped blossoms from the vine and tucked it into Elena's hair. Standing back to admire his handiwork, he smiled. "I like the effect."

Elena reached for his hand. He had said all he wanted to for now. Perhaps he would talk more about it later.

When he didn't return to the topic, she decided that maybe the thing to do would be to get him used to leaving the safety of the ranch in easy stages. Why not start with a short trip to town? They had talked about redecorating some of the rooms in the hacienda, and Stephen had listened with approval to Elena's ideas. So it wasn't too difficult to work the conversation around to asking if he'd like to come downtown and help her pick new wallpaper for the master bathroom.

"There are so many suitable patterns. It gets confusing when you're sitting there, looking at all those books of samples and wondering which one is really the best," Elena told him.

"You could take Carol with you. Or maybe that decorator—what's his name?—Phil Baker—could help you."

"I'd like *your* opinion."

"It's probably not as important to me as it is to you."

She wasn't willing to give up. "But you're going to be in there every morning, taking a shower and shaving."

"Then why don't you pick some patterns you like and bring the samples out here for me to look at?"

Elena knew when she'd been outmaneuvered and reluctantly agreed to his suggestion. After that she tried to stop herself from pressing the issue. But she found her own tension mounting as she struggled to say nothing. Even when she didn't bring up the subject with Stephen, plans for getting him to leave the ranch continued to form in her mind. She could feel the pressure to voice them building up inside herself; it was as if too much helium were stretching the fragile skin of a balloon. Sooner or later she knew the need to speak was going to burst through.

BILL DELANEY LOOKED at the familiar oak door and nervously straightened his tie. It was dark red with a subtle black stripe. Jenny had picked it out to go with his gray sport coat, black slacks and white shirt. She'd said he looked handsome. He felt like a department store dummy.

Taking a deep breath, he raised his hand and rang the doorbell.

"Just a minute."

Carol opened the door and smiled.

"You look beautiful."

"You look pretty good yourself."

He grinned self-consciously. "Jenny picked this outfit."

"She's got good taste." Carol stepped aside and ushered him into her apartment, while she got a sweater and her purse.

They were having dinner at the Palace Café, a New Orleans-style restaurant they'd enjoyed when they'd been seeing each other.

After the first burst of conversation, there was an awkwardness between them. Neither of them said much in the car on the way over.

"Well, how have you been?" Bill asked after they'd been seated and the waiter had taken their drink orders.

"Fine."

"I hope the blackened redfish is still good."

"And the fried chicken salad. I remember the first time you made me try that."

He shifted the positions of his knife and spoon. "Carol, it's damn hard for me to come right out and say it, but I've missed you a lot."

Her eyes met his. "I've missed you, too."

He let out the breath he'd been holding. "You know that first night I bumped into you at Mary Falconer's?"

"Mmm-hmm."

"I asked her to call and invite you to the meeting."

"I thought you might have. But I guess I was still afraid to... to let myself get close to you again."

Their drinks came, and Bill took a swallow of his whiskey sour. "I—"

She leaned forward slightly. "What?"

"I never was very good at being subtle. Honey, I know I let things go to hell between us after Jenny's accident."

"It wasn't all your fault. I didn't know how to cope with it, either."

"But I shouldn't have shut you out." His eyes searched hers. "I want to know what you think about trying again—the two of us, I mean."

"I wouldn't have called you if I weren't willing to do that."

"Oh, Carol. You don't know how good it is to hear you say that."

She reached across the table and pressed her palm over his hand.

"That night at Mary Falconer's. There was so much I wanted to say to you," he admitted. "It was all bottled up inside me, and I couldn't get it out."

"I felt the same way."

The waiter's arrival to take their dinner orders was only a brief interruption in their conversation.

"Bill, we have to talk about Jenny. I don't mean what we did or didn't do after the accident. I mean how we'd—"

"Cope."

"Do you think she could accept me again, after the way I disappeared from your lives?"

Bill turned up his hand so that he could fold his fingers around Carol's. "She misses you. She was worried that it was her fault you'd broken off with me."

"Oh, no. That poor kid."

"I told her that wasn't true."

"I'd like her to hear that from me."

ELENA HAD FINISHED an art lesson and come onto the patio to find Bill whistling as he shucked ears of corn into a paper bag.

"I never thought about doing that outside," she observed.

"Mrs. Matthews suggested it. Keeps the mess out of the kitchen."

"Jenny had some exciting news. She told me this afternoon that she's begun to get the feeling back in her legs."

Bill's eyes glowed. "Yes!"

"Do they think she's going to be able to walk?"

"They're very hopeful."

"I'm so glad for her."

"Not any gladder than I am." He cleared his throat. "I have something else to thank you for."

"Oh?"

"Carol and I went to the Palace Café for dinner last night. And then went back to her place and talked."

"And?"

"And it was good—more than good. We felt comfortable with each other."

"That's wonderful."

"I guess the most important thing I've learned recently is that people need to communicate with each other better."

"Yes," Elena agreed, thinking about herself and Stephen.

Bill crumpled the bag of corn husks. "Um, is everything all right with you?"

"Why do you ask?"

"You've been looking a little distracted."

"Sorry." Elena shifted her sketch pad between her hands.

"Don't apologize. Just tell me what's bothering you."

"I . . . I don't want to talk about it."

"Is it Stephen?"

Elena nodded reluctantly.

"Is he treating you all right?"

"Yes. Of course. We're very happy."

"Then what is it? Can I help?"

"Bill, you've done so much for me. But this is something that Stephen and I have to deal with ourselves."

He nodded.

Elena hadn't expected to see the Delaneys again until the next week. But Bill called several days later and asked if Elena wouldn't mind stopping by early with some blank canvases that Jenny needed. Something about the tone of his voice made her agree to come right over.

Bill was waiting at the top of the driveway, a proud expression on his face.

"What is it?"

He gestured toward the patio, and Elena almost dropped the canvases she was holding.

"Jenny!"

The teenager was standing up, supported by a set of crutches. She looked even more pleased than her father, and Elena was reminded of a similar scene on her own patio—the day she had first seen Stephen standing up.

"When did this happen?"

"I've been practicing with my physical therapist. It was hard to keep it a secret. I almost blabbed the last time you were here, but I wanted to surprise you."

There were tears in Elena's eyes. "This is wonderful."

"I can't really walk much yet. But I can stand up."

"Give yourself time." Elena gave Jenny a careful hug, mindful that she wasn't used to balancing on her feet.

"Enough for today," Bill told his daughter a few minutes later and helped her into one of the patio chairs.

"Can you stay and have some lemonade and cookies with us to celebrate?" Bill asked.

"I'd love to."

Elena was still smiling when she pulled into the driveway at the ranch. And Stephen was as pleased as she to hear the good news.

He was in such a mellow mood that she decided to introduce a topic she'd stayed away from for weeks. She waited until after dinner as they sat on chaise lounges beside the pool. Since the weather had been hot and dry for weeks, they had gotten into the habit of cooling off in the evening with a swim.

"You know, the auction is this Friday."

"You're not expecting me to go."

"No. But I was thinking about having some of the friends I've made on the committee out to dinner to celebrate— maybe at the end of the month," Elena ventured.

"Like Bill and Sam."

"Well, yes, Bill and Sam. And some of the other people I've gotten to know. Like Mary Falconer and Carol." When she had talked about Bill's newly reinstated relationship with his former fiancée, Stephen had seemed pleased. But perhaps that was only because he knew that Bill was no longer an unattached man who was spending a lot of time with Elena. She studied his face. He seemed to be giving the idea serious thought. Perhaps in his own home, where he felt secure, he wouldn't be so reluctant to entertain her friends.

"You could invite some of the other people in town you haven't seen for a while," she suggested.

"I don't think so. Listen, why don't you make it lunch instead?" he asked.

"Would you like that better?"

"I didn't mean with me."

"Stephen—"

"You can have anyone you like out here. But don't ask me to help with the entertaining." He hoisted himself out of the chair and strode toward the water, with only a remnant of the limp that had been with him since he'd put his crutches aside. "Are you coming in? It'll be too cold to swim in a little while."

"None of the people I'm thinking about is going to stare at your face." Once again, words had tumbled out of her mouth before her brain could censor them.

He whirled around to confront her. "Oh, so that's it. You're still obsessed with my face."

"No, you are."

"Drop it, will you," Stephen warned.

"I'm trying to help you."

"Then let me live my life the way I want to."

"But you're missing so much," she argued.

"You're not satisfied with the way I am."

"That's right."

His eyes blazed blue fire. "So you've finally admitted it."

"I meant I'm not happy about the way you've shut yourself away from everything. My God, what are you going to do when you need to get your teeth cleaned? Make the dentist come out here?"

He glared at her. "Don't be ridiculous."

"It would be ridiculous—if you hadn't dug yourself in here like a rabbit in a burrow."

Flinging the words at him, Elena turned and went back into the house. That night they lay rigidly in bed, not touching and not speaking. And over the next few days they were cool to each other,.

Stephen closeted himself in his office, the way he had during her first week in Santa Barbara and the week before their marriage. Elena spent more time in her studio. Yet now she found it hard to concentrate on her work. She felt restless and anxious—the way she sometimes did when her period was about due. She'd been so preoccupied with other things that she'd let the date slip away from her. But that could explain why she was so overwrought.

Putting down her paintbrush and cleaning her hands, she went downstairs to the desk in the den to check the calendar. To her surprise, she discovered that her period was overdue. In fact, she was more than a week late.

For a few moments she stood looking at the dates in the leather-bound book. Then, heart pounding, she counted the days again more carefully. Her first calculations had been correct. She was definitely late, which was unusual for her. Was there something wrong? Or was there a more logical explanation? She and Stephen had been making love with a great deal of enthusiasm for more than two months, without using any form of contraception. She might very well be pregnant. Was it too early to find out? She hoped not. Suddenly it seemed overwhelmingly important to know.

With hands that had started to tremble, she called the doctor's office.

"We could give you an appointment next week," the receptionist replied to her initial inquiry.

"I was wondering if I could come in sooner." It was hard to keep the disappointment out of her voice.

"Let me check the schedule for today. There may be a cancellation."

Elena stared out the window at the garden while she waited for the woman to come back onto the line.

"Mrs. Gallagher, there *is* a cancellation this morning. I can pencil you in, if you can be here by ten-thirty."

"Yes. I can make that."

Hurriedly Elena ran back upstairs to change out of her jeans and into a skirt and blouse. She brushed her hair and put on a bit of makeup.

"I have to go into town," she told Maggie breathlessly, almost colliding with the housekeeper in the front hall.

"Will you be back in time for lunch?"

"I don't know."

An hour and a half later, flushed with excitement, she stood in one of the ornate phone booths on State Street, dialing the ranch. It had been a simple matter—a quick and easy lab test—to confirm that she and Stephen were going to have a baby! Perhaps that would make a difference in his outlook on life.

CHAPTER EIGHTEEN

WHEN MAGGIE ANSWERED the phone, Elena asked to speak to her husband.

"Is something wrong? You sound strange," the housekeeper replied.

"Everything's fine. But I do need to talk to Stephen."

"I'll get him."

He kept her waiting for almost five minutes before coming onto the line. "Sorry, something's come up this morning that I've been scrambling to stay on top of. Do you remember that company in Denver I was telling you about? Lexco."

"Yes."

"They're pressuring me to make an offer."

"Oh."

"So why are you calling from town?"

Somehow she couldn't stop herself from issuing a challenge. "I'd like you to meet me down here for lunch."

"Sweetheart, this is pretty short notice. And I'm trying to stay with the Lexco situation. I'm expecting another call from Denver any minute."

"Would you do it if I'd given you a weeks' notice?"

Elena could hear him sigh over the phone lines. "Are you going to start that again?"

"No." She made an effort to keep her voice steady. "Stephen, this is important. I have to talk to you about something."

"Then come back to the ranch now. I may be tied up with this thing all afternoon."

Once again she couldn't stop herself. She threw the next angry words at him. "You wouldn't have met me down here, even if all you had to do this afternoon was ride Storm Dancer! Well, maybe this time I don't want to come back to the ranch."

Something in his voice seemed to go flat, lifeless. "That's up to you."

"Stephen, please."

"I'm sorry."

"You may be."

"Elena, you haven't picked a good day for a confrontation."

"Is there ever a good day?"

In the background, she heard his other phone ring.

"I'm sorry. I've got to take this call. We can talk about this when you're calmer." The line went dead. Elena clutched the receiver for several seconds before hanging up. She stood gazing out at the noontime traffic, her vision misted by tears that she struggled to hold in. A passerby stared curiously into the phone booth, and Elena turned her head away. She didn't want anyone to see her like this.

In one part of her mind she realized that she wasn't being quite rational. She didn't know why she had deliberately provoked a showdown with her husband. What had driven her to do it?

What if she stayed in town all afternoon? Would Stephen worry about her? Would he even notice?

She closed her eyes in a silent moment of self-reproach. Even in her present overwrought state, she could recognize that she was behaving childishly. But when she hadn't gotten the reaction from Stephen that she'd wanted, her usual self-control had just snapped.

She took a deep, steadying breath, trying to calm her pounding heart. Hadn't Stephen put her through enough? Didn't she deserve to have him do things her way just for once?

Although she wasn't sure where else she wanted to go, pride wouldn't let her drive back to the ranch just yet. She had left her car at the public lot across from the library. Now, instead of retrieving it, she wandered over to El Paseo and sat down at one of the umbrella tables in the center courtyard. But the salad she ordered might as well have been grass, for all she could taste of it.

After pushing away the practically untouched plate, she paid for her meal and crossed the street to De La Guerra Plaza, where a small band was putting on a noontime concert. The crowd of office workers and tourists that had gathered was obviously enjoying the lively music. But it didn't hold any interest for Elena.

Listlessly she fetched her car and drove down to East Beach. On another afternoon she might have stopped to admire the stunning dolphin statue in the traffic circle at the end of the pier. Now she simply trudged past it and across the stretch of grass that separated the ocean from the roadway.

She and Stephen had come to an important understanding down at the beach. She wanted him here with her now, even though this was a very different place from Refugio Beach, where the two of them had walked together before their wedding. Refugio was hemmed in by high cliffs that gave it a very private feeling. It was wild and unspoiled—its narrow strip of sand scattered with rocks tossed up by the waves.

East Beach was more like a manicured park, with a wide expanse of palm-dotted grass and a carefully tended white strand that stretched down to the blue ocean. Elena walked slowly past the children's pool and the concession stands, watching the gulls wheel in the sky and the waves rush back and forth at the water's edge. Although the morning had been overcast, the fog had burned off and the sun was hot. The air was clear and dry. The wind was brisk. Shaking back her hair, she shaded her eyes and looked out over the water.

She and Stephen had been honest with each other the last time they'd walked along the sand. For a moment she clutched that knowledge to her heart. And then it came to her with blinding clarity; she wasn't being honest with her husband now. Why hadn't she joyfully told him about the baby as soon as she had known herself? Was she trying to punish him? Or was she using the child as a way of getting him to do what she wanted?

Despite the warmth of the sun, the painful speculation into her own motives made a sudden ball of ice form in the pit of her stomach. My God, their baby wasn't even going to be born for almost eight months, and already she was using it, at worst as a weapon, at best as a pawn.

It was a tactic worthy of her own father, she realized. She found herself pressing her palm against her abdomen in a protective gesture.

Her father had tried to keep her mother from leaving him by telling her that if she left, she would never see her daughter again. And later he had not hesitated to arrange a marriage between Elena and Stephen to improve his own financial situation.

As she stood there facing the curling surf with unfocused eyes, a line of biblical text jumped into her head. "And the sins of the father will be visited upon the sons unto the third and fourth generation."

She had always thought the saying was strange. In fact, she had often wondered exactly what it meant. Now she knew. It applied to daughters as well as sons. Your father treated you in a certain way. Maybe he beat you. Or perhaps the abuse was psychological. But the experience marked you, and when you grew up, you did the same thing to your children, and they did the same to theirs—unless the cycle was somehow broken.

She had known that her father was a product of his own harsh upbringing. She had assured herself that she was very different. The realization that she was preparing to repeat his sins made the lump of ice in her stomach expand into a glacier that seemed to spread throughout her body.

Elena stood there in frozen silence, her heart pounding. Then she made a conscious effort to calm herself. Recognition was half the battle. It wasn't too late. She would not be like her father. She would not use her child for her own purposes.

She didn't know that tears were shimmering on her cheeks until she reached up to wipe them away. All at once she wanted desperately to talk to Stephen—the father of the child she carried—the man she loved. She could picture him in his office at the ranch. He had sounded harried. Was he still working, or had her angry words made it impossible for him to concentrate? He must have been puzzled by her call. He must be wondering when she was coming back. Then her hand flew to her mouth as she realized what she had actually said. She had told him that she might *not* be coming back.

The need to let him know that she hadn't meant it became an agonizing pressure inside her chest, making it hard to draw breath. Elena turned to scan the stretch of beach she had just crossed. To her profound relief she spotted a phone next to the concession stand. She could call the ranch right away.

Maggie answered on the second ring.

"I have to speak to Esteban," Elena said without preamble.

"Elena, where are you?"

"Down at East Beach. But I have to talk to Stephen," she repeated.

"I'm sorry. He's not here."

She stared incredulously at the receiver. "Not there? *¿Qué pasa? ¿Dónde está?*"

"He's gone to Denver."

Elena couldn't believe she'd heard right. "Denver?"

"Apparently something serious is going on at a company called Lexco."

"Yes. He told me about it. But—" She tried to take in this new information. "I didn't expect him to go out there. I mean, he never—"

"Leaves the ranch," Maggie finished the sentence for her.

"I—"

"Why don't you come home?" Maggie suggested gently.

"Yes."

She drove back toward Rancho Palo Colorado in a haze of unreality. For months she had been trying to crack Stephen's siege mentality. Now suddenly he had taken the initiative. Had he made the decision to go to Denver before or after they had talked? And why had he gone *now*?

Elena's fingers tightened on the steering wheel. Was a confrontation in another city less painful to Stephen than the one his wife had been trying to provoke?

Maggie was waiting at the front door when Elena pulled up in front of the hacienda.

"Did Stephen leave me a note?" were the first words from her mouth as she scrambled out of the car.

"I know you're upset. But come on into the kitchen and let me fix you a nice hot cup of tea."

Elena sighed. "I guess that means no."

Apparently Maggie wasn't going to say anything more in the driveway, so Elena followed her inside and obediently sat down at the kitchen table.

"What kind of tea do you want?" the housekeeper asked.

The doctor had told her not to drink anything with caffeine. "Herb tea. It doesn't matter what kind."

A few minutes later, the strong aroma of mint filled the kitchen. Elena stared down into the mug that Maggie set before her. "Did Stephen decide to go before or after I talked to him?"

"He was on the phone off and on all morning, conferring with the people in Denver. I know he was pretty worried about the situation out there."

"But he didn't tell you he was leaving until after I called," Elena clarified.

Maggie nodded. Then she seemed to make a decision. "I wasn't going to say anything until Stephen got back—but the doctor's office called just before you arrived."

Elena's chin jerked upward. "They didn't say there was anything wrong, did they?"

"No. Nothing's wrong," Maggie said comfortingly, seeing Elena's round eyes.

"Then what?" Elena inquired anxiously.

"You forgot your prescription for prenatal vitamins and iron."

"Oh."

"Did you just find out today?" Maggie asked softly.

"Yes. That's why I went into town to see the doctor."

"It's wonderful news. I know Stephen will be excited."

Elena fought back a sudden rush of tears and shook her head. "I was calling to ask him to meet me in town. I wanted to give him the news at lunch. Then I got angry when he wouldn't come."

"I see."

"I don't even understand why I was so hateful to him," Elena murmured.

"Pregnant women sometimes have funny mood swings. They react to things in strange ways. It's the hormones, I guess."

"You don't know how much I wish now that I had just told him about the baby over the phone."

"I have the name of the hotel where he'll be staying in Denver. You could leave a message and ask him to call you."

Elena considered the suggestion and rejected it. "He probably has a lot on his mind, if he was worried enough to go out there in the first place. I think it would be better to wait now."

"You may be right."

After drinking half the mug of tea, Elena stood up and rubbed a hand across her forehead.

Maggie looked at her consideringly. "What you need is a good rest. Why don't you go upstairs and lie down? I'll let you know if Stephen calls."

"All right." The emotional turmoil of the afternoon had exhausted her. It was an effort to simply climb the stairs. But once she had taken off her skirt and blouse and slipped under the covers, she acknowledged that she did need to relax.

Stephen didn't call that evening. Or the next day.

"Are you sure you don't want to leave a message for him?" Maggie asked.

Elena shook her head. "He'd call if he could." But even as she spoke the words, she wondered if they were true. The last night Stephen had been home, they'd lain in bed next to each other, stiff and uncommunicative. And when she'd phoned from downtown, she'd provoked a tense scene. Why should he want to talk to her now? If he called, he had every right to expect more of the same.

Elena was in her studio Friday morning, trying to work, when the phone rang.

"It's for you," Maggie called.

Heart pounding, Elena snatched up the receiver. "Hello. Stephen?

"Sorry—what?"

To her disappointment, the voice on the other end of the line did not belong to her husband.

It was Mary Falconer, head of the fund-raising committee. A cloud seemed to have eclipsed her eternally sunny disposition. "I'm glad I reached you," she said anxiously.

Despite her own depression, Elena responded to the distress in her friend's voice. "What's wrong?"

Mary sighed deeply. "I've been running back and forth between my office and the kitchen, looking up phone numbers and making calls. You remembered that we decided to save money by putting together the floral decorations at the auction ourselves. Well, Johnson's just delivered two thousand carnations, and the woman who was supposed to be in charge of arranging them fell and twisted her ankle. She's not going to be able to do it. I've got a whole crew of worker bees ready to help. But I need someone with artistic sensibilities to be in charge."

As her friend poured out the story, Elena realized that she'd forgotten all about the auction.

"I know it's short notice, but I was wondering if you'd be able to take over," Mary continued.

"Did you try Phil Baker?" Elena asked.

"I thought of him first. But he's tied up this afternoon. Please don't say no. There's so much riding on this evening, and the whole thing's going to be ruined, just ruined, if we don't have a festive atmosphere."

Elena knew Mary had to be exaggerating. She also knew the committee chairwoman had put in months of time and effort to make the auction a success. No wonder she was so upset by this last-minute crisis.

"Mary, I know how much this means to you, but I don't know if I could do the kind of job you're picturing."

"Elena, just say yes. I'll come down and work with you. And don't worry about going home to change before dinner. You can bring your clothes to my house. I'm having a hairdresser and a makeup person in. They can help you get ready."

There was no way Elena could refuse her friend's urgent entreaty. "All right. When do you want me to come?"

"Right away."

"I'll be there as soon as I can."

The dinner and auction were being held at the plush swim club, which was part of the Biltmore Hotel.

After packing what she'd need for the evening, Elena went downstairs to tell Maggie where she was going.

"I'm sorry Mary Falconer had an emergency. But I'm glad you're getting out of the house," the housekeeper informed her.

"If Stephen calls—"

"I'll give him the number," Maggie assured her.

Elena drove straight to the Biltmore. A Santa Barbara landmark since the early part of the century, the luxury hotel sat on spacious grounds overlooking the ocean.

After surrendering her car to one of the uniformed attendants, Elena hurried into the adjoining swim club. A dozen hotel staffers and committee members were hard at work in the large dining room. The round tables had already been covered with crisp white cloths and set with china and cutlery.

Mary was pacing back and forth on the bandstand in front of a gold-veined, mirrored wall. When she spotted Elena, she jumped down and rushed over. "Thank goodness you're here. I think the most important thing is to get the centerpieces done. Then we'll worry about the rest."

Elena took a moment to look around the room and check the florist's cartons. In addition to the carnations, they contained baby's breath and ferns. After determining how much there was of each, she began to arrange some in one of the small vases packed in another box.

"That's beautiful!" Mary enthused as Elena stepped back to view the results. "We'll just copy it for the other tables."

After several of the women had started to work on the centerpieces, Elena turned to the front of the room.

"The hotel probably has some latticework panels," she told Mary. "Why don't we flank the bandstand with them and weave some of the flowers through?"

Mary eagerly agreed and sent one of the hotel employees to get the required props.

It took only a little experimentation to work out an attractive red and white pattern. After Elena showed them what to do, three committee members began to help her with the job. By three in the afternoon the dining room was beautifully festooned, and Elena was exhausted.

"I can't thank you enough," the committee chairwoman gushed when she inspected the results of the day's work. After hugging Elena, she stood back and gave her a critical look. "But you're all done in."

"I'm fine."

"Nonsense. Let me take you back to my house, so my gals can pamper you."

Elena was too polite to protest. And she *was* curious about Mary's private health spa. But nothing could have prepared her for the degree of luxury she was about to experience.

The maid had set out a snack of fruit and pâté. After she and Mary had had a bite, Elena took a shower and a long soak in the whirlpool bath before flopping onto a padded table and letting the masseuse complete the relaxation process.

She had time for a nap after that. Yet she had a hard time falling asleep. She kept thinking about Stephen. Why had he really gone to Denver? And what was happening there? How was he dealing with the executives at Lexco? Was he able to handle their reaction to his appearance? Or had it been too much for him? Had he gone away somewhere by himself?

Suddenly she sat up in bed. Was that why he hadn't called her? Or was he angry at the way she'd ordered him into town?

Finally she did get a little bit of sleep. Mary woke her at five-thirty, so that she could have her hair washed and set in an elegant upsweep.

While her nails were being manicured, Elena made a decision. There was nothing she could do about Stephen right now. And she had been looking forward to this evening for months. It would be ridiculous not to try to have a good time.

By seven-thirty that evening, Elena hardly recognized herself. Turning before the mirror, she inspected the lines of her white silk gown, noting the way the long darts emphasized her figure. Her waist hadn't changed yet, but her breasts were already a bit fuller. Reaching up, she touched her hair. Masses of dark waves crowned her head, with a few tendrils of hair cunningly arranged at her cheeks and neck. Subtle shadow set off her dark eyes. And she had never seen her lashes look so thick. She couldn't help enjoying the picture she made. Then she fought to suppress a stab of pain. She wished that Stephen could see her looking like this. She wished he was going to be with her tonight.

When she and Mary arrived at the hotel a little after eight, the cocktail reception was already in full swing.

"I've got to go over a few last-minute details. Do you mind if I leave you on your own?" Mary asked.

"No, that's fine."

Elena located one of the bars and ordered herself a Perrier with lime. Turning, she surveyed the crowd. The men were in tuxedos, the women in a rainbow assortment of long gowns. They might have been dressed for a night at the opera in Paris or Rome.

Carol joined her. "You look spectacular," she said.

Elena's eyes swept over the petite blonde. She was wearing a warm pink evening dress that made her skin glow. Or perhaps it was just reflecting her inner radiance. "So do you."

"Bill and I saved you a place at our table. I hope you'll be able to have dinner with us."

"I'd love it."

"I hear you're the one who did the flowers this afternoon."

"I had a lot of help."

"Don't be modest," Carol admonished. "This place is beautiful, and you get the credit."

Apparently the women who had worked with Elena that afternoon had been generous in their praise. As she wandered through the displays of items to be auctioned off, people went out of their way to compliment her on the way the room looked.

The two paintings she'd donated were near the front of the room. Elena couldn't help going over to see them.

"They're quite good. I wish you'd brought your stuff to my gallery," said a voice behind her. She turned, to find herself confronting Tom Mitchell.

Elena flushed and wondered how to respond.

"But you didn't really give me a chance. Why not?"

"I think I feel more comfortable with Miles Henderson."

"Yes. I understand he's put a pretty stiff price on your pictures. I'm not sure they're worth as much as he's asking."

"He's sold a number of them."

"Well, if I can get one of these at a good price, I may just see if I can undercut him."

"As you wish," Elena answered stiffly and turned away in search of better company.

When she saw Bill motion to her across the room, she threaded her way through the crowd in his direction. He had asked a number of old friends to share his table, including Sam Goldner and Phil Baker.

But even though Elena enjoyed the company and the conversation, she couldn't help thinking nervously about the upcoming auction. Tom Mitchell had made her worry about her paintings. Would they fetch a good price? Or would they turn out to be the bargains of the evening?

After the dessert plates and coffee cups had been cleared away, a drumroll ushered Chip Hayden to the bandstand. A portly, white-haired character actor who was now semiretired and living in Santa Barbara, he'd agreed to serve as auctioneer.

"Are any of you old enough to remember that I played this part in *Winner Take All*?" he asked the audience.

Several white-haired members of the group clapped and cheered.

"Then I'm among friends."

The role came back to Hayden easily. And he put a lot of energy into his performance. After only a few minutes, he had drawn several members of the audience into a lively bidding war for the cruise to Mexico.

Next up were the catered dinner party and the professional consultation with Phil Baker. Elena watched him out of the corner of her eye as Hayden described his talents. She could tell the decorator was nervous, apparently for the same reason she was.

But he needn't have worried. The well-dressed matron who finally secured his services paid far more than she would have, if she'd simply gone into his shop and made an appointment.

"I'm glad that's over," Phil whispered to Elena when the spotlight had shifted away from him.

She nodded.

The weekend at Sam Goldner's resort also went for a good price. It was half an hour later before the first of Elena's paintings was brought to the front of the room. Since she'd wanted to donate something special, she'd made another version of the painting she'd begun on her honeymoon. The original was in Stephen's office. This one showed the mountains from a slightly different angle. But she knew it captured the same warmth and serenity that the setting had made her feel.

She held her breath as Hayden opened the bidding at $150. Apparently several people had decided they wanted the picture. There was an immediate raise to $175, then to $200.

As he'd threatened, Tom Mitchell was one of the bidders. Elena didn't want him to have the picture. But when he raised the price to $700, the woman who had made the last bid dropped out.

Mitchell's face bore a look of smug satisfaction. Hayden raised his gavel. "I have $700. Going once. Going twice. Going—"

"Seven hundred and fifty dollars," came a decisive male voice from the back of the crowd.

Elena's heart slammed against her ribs. She and everyone else in the room turned to look at the bidder who had just entered the auction.

It was her husband.

CHAPTER NINETEEN

ALL EYES FOCUSED on Stephen. Like the rest of the men in the room, he was wearing a tuxedo. But there was no way he could blend invisibly into the crowd. Elena was aware of a variety of reactions as the assemblage took in the scars that still slashed the left side of his face from temple to jaw.

More than one person gasped. Others leaned over to whisper to their neighbors.

But Stephen didn't flinch or turn away. As though the scrutiny of three hundred pairs of eyes were the most natural thing in the world to him, he slipped his left hand casually into the pocket of his formal trousers and leaned back against the wall.

She knew he had deliberately called attention to himself. Had he realized how he'd feel? Would he be able to handle it?

Her pulse pounded in her ears as she watched him standing there impassively. The rest of the crowd might assume he was relaxed. Only she understood what the display of indifference was costing him. She saw his tension in the tautness of his neck and in the way he held his lips together.

His eyes sought hers, and their gazes locked. To keep her own hands from trembling, she clasped them in her lap. She wanted to get up and stand at his side, but knew this was something he had to do alone. Instead she tried to put everything she felt for him into her smile. Although he didn't smile back, he nodded in acknowledgment.

Chip Hayden's voice broke into the wordless exchange. "Seven hundred and fifty dollars. Do I hear $800?"

Elena's chest tightened. She could feel the tension in the room. The crowd sensed a battle in the making.

Mitchell made an affirmative motion with his hand.

"I have $800. Do I hear $850?" The auctioneer looked pointedly at Stephen, who nodded. "I have $850."

People looked from Stephen to Tom Mitchell as if they were watching a tennis match. Elena's fingers clenched together more tightly.

Without waiting for the auctioneer, Mitchell called out sharply, "$1,000 for the painting."

"One thousand three hundred," Stephen countered.

There was absolute silence in the room. Mitchell glared at Stephen, hesitated, and bid again.

"One thousand five hundred," Stephen answered promptly.

When Chip Hayden looked at Mitchell again and raised questioning eyebrows, the man scowled and shook his head. Elena saw him muttering something she was glad she couldn't hear.

"Fifteen hundred dollars going once, going twice, going three times," the auctioneer sang out, then paused dramatically.

Elena suspected that she wasn't the only person in the room holding her breath.

"Sold for $1,500!"

The tension broke and a spontaneous burst of applause rose from the crowd. "Well done!" someone shouted. Another man whistled loudly.

Stephen waited quietly until the clamor subsided. Although his eyes scanned the group, they kept returning to Elena. "Since I already have a picture in my office very similar to the one I've just purchased, I'd like to donate this one to the rehabilitation hospital."

There was another round of clapping. Both Elena and Tom Mitchell got out of their seats. Mitchell headed for the exit. Elena made her way across the room to Stephen. They looked at each other for a moment. Then he silently threaded his arm around her waist and pulled her against his side.

"After all that excitement, I think I could use a break," Chip Hayden announced from the bandstand. "We'll resume the auction in twenty minutes."

Elena moved closer to Stephen. It was difficult to take it all in, but she knew something important had just happened. And it didn't really have much to do with donating an oil painting to the hospital.

"*Querida*, I've never seen you look more beautiful," he whispered.

"And I've never seen you look more handsome."

He searched her face, but there was no more time for private conversation.

"Steve. Glad you could make it for the big bash."

Elena looked up, to find herself staring at a grinning Sam Goldner.

"So am I," Stephen answered as he accepted Sam's outstretched hand.

"I already know your charming wife," Sam continued. "From the committee meetings."

Stephen nodded. "Elena's told me about them. Sorry I couldn't join you this year."

"You had a good excuse." Sam shook his head. "I was thinking about bidding against Mitchell myself."

"I was thinking about letting him have the painting for $1,400, since that was double what he thought he was going to get it for originally," Stephen admitted.

Both men laughed.

More people had come to gather around Stephen, and Sam relinquished his place. Some, like Goldner, were old friends who wanted to welcome him back. Elena could see that others were just curious. After all, this was Stephen Gallagher's first public appearance in almost a year.

A middle-aged couple Elena didn't know joined the group, and Stephen introduced them as the Standishes.

"We heard about your accident. You're looking exceptionally fit for a man who wasn't supposed to walk again," Ted Standish remarked.

"Thank you," Stephen answered easily, but Elena could feel the tension in the arm that circled her waist. She had to stop herself from jumping in with a quick remark that would change the subject. Stephen had made a decision about tonight, and she wasn't going to spoil it for him.

He continued to talk affably with the men and women who came up to him, but Elena kept wishing that Chip Hayden would resume the auction. Finally he did.

As people returned to their seats, Stephen dipped his head so that his mouth was close to Elena's ear. "Do you think it would be impolite if we slipped out of here?"

"I was wondering the same thing. Let me get my evening bag."

He waited while she returned to the table to retrieve it.

"Leaving?" Bill asked. He and Carol were sitting rather close, she noted.

"Yes."

"He was fantastic, you know," Carol told Elena.

She grinned. "Yes. I know."

"Call me."

"I will."

Chip Hayden had begun to describe the next item to be auctioned off—a private lesson from one of the world's most famous cooking instructors, who happened to live in Santa Barbara. A number of women were anxious to pay for the privilege.

Elena and Stephen were able to slip out of the room without attracting any more attention. Hand in hand they crossed the expanse of manicured lawn in front of the hotel. But before they reached the parking lot, he stopped in the shadow of a date palm and swept her into an embrace that all but took the breath from her lungs. Then his lips descended to claim hers.

They were starving for the taste of each other. When he finally lifted his head, he drew in a steadying breath. "Now I know a good reason for going away occasionally. So I can come back to you. *Querida*, I've been wanting to be alone with you ever since I saw you in there."

Elena pressed her face into the starched whiteness of his shirt, breathing in his familiar scent. She wanted to ask him about the trip, talk about what had just happened at the auction. But those things were pushed into the background by the need to show him just how much she loved him. "It's going to be a long ride home."

She felt a rumble of laughter in his chest. "That's what I was thinking."

He grabbed her hand again. She assumed he was leading her to the parking lot. Instead he took a path that wound through a complex of cottages behind the hotel. Stopping in front of one, he pulled a key from his pocket.

"We have a room at the inn, my dear," he said with a chuckle.

Before she could blink, they were inside the cottage.

The laughter died as his mouth came down again onto hers. Her hands dug desperately into his shoulders, her body molded itself to his. All at once she discovered that she had never been more frantic to get close to him. And she knew he felt the same. His lips found her cheeks, the hollow above her chin, the curve of her brow, and then came back to her mouth. Her hands ranged over his back and shoulders, as though she couldn't quite assure herself that he was real and solid and in her arms.

His hands came up to close hungrily around her breasts. "Oh!"

"God, I'm sorry. I didn't mean to hurt you."

"It's not your fault. I'm just a little tender."

"You aren't having your period?"

She shook her head. "No. It's not that." When he tried to say something else, she reached up and pulled his mouth down to hers, driving away whatever question had been in his mind.

His fingers fumbled at the back of her dress, but didn't find a zipper. "How the hell do you get out of this damn thing?" he muttered.

"Like this." She moved slightly and tugged at the side zipper. Then she drew the fragile silk dress over her head and let it fall to the floor.

Stephen took the opportunity to tear off his own clothes. Urgently he pulled her back against his hard length. The friction of their naked bodies brushing against each other drove them rapidly beyond the limits of endurance.

He lifted her, the hard, pulsing shaft of his manhood probing against her softness.

"Stephen, what about your leg? Are you all right?" she inquired, even as she clung to him.

"Better than all right."

Then he was inside her, and she could think about nothing else but the joy of being one with him. The shattering climax came quickly. Afterward they clung to each other, kissing and trying to catch their breath.

"I love you." They spoke at the same time.

He continued to hold her. But now that the tension had been dispelled, she sensed his fatigue. "When did you sleep last?" she asked softly.

"I don't remember."

"Then why are we standing here?"

They crossed to the bedroom, and he waited while she turned down the sheets on the king-size bed. When they had slipped under the covers, he pulled her close. "Damn bed's too big."

"Mmm."

A few moments later he was asleep. And she couldn't keep her eyes open, either.

Sometime before dawn she was awakened by the delicious sensation of his lips nibbling at her neck. Turning, she melted against him. This time they made love slowly, savoring the precious luxury of being together again.

"I've been worried about something," she told him playfully afterward.

"What?"

"Going home this morning in a crumpled evening dress."

"We're not going home this morning. We're going to stay here."

"And do what?"

He grinned at her wolfishly.

"I see."

"I had Maggie pack you a suitcase," he added. "It's in the dressing room."

"You thought of everything."

"It was a long flight home."

"Did you have anything last night besides airplane food?"

"Not even that. I was too keyed up." He reached over and grabbed the room service menu. "What do you want for breakfast?"

The question made Elena realize that she was starving. Apparently morning sickness wasn't going to be one of her problems. "The works."

"Hotcakes, eggs, bacon, toast?"

"And fresh-squeezed orange juice."

Before the waiter came with the order, Elena slipped into a dressing gown, and Stephen pulled on a pair of faded jeans. Until now, when anyone besides herself might see him, he had always put on a shirt to cover the scars on his chest. The realization that he no longer felt the need to do that made her heart swell. But she suspected that if they were going to talk about it, she would have to start the conversation.

They rolled out the breakfast cart to a small, private terrace bright with flowers and foliage.

"I was shocked to see you at the auction," Elena began.

"I can imagine."

"You were wonderful."

"I didn't like the idea of Mitchell getting that painting."

"That's not exactly what I meant," Elena clarified. "I'm talking about the way you forced everyone to look at you."

He laughed. "I guess I decided to get it over with all at once. Or maybe after I got past the reaction of the airplane passengers and the management team in Denver, I figured what did three hundred or so more people matter?"

She reached across the table for his hand.

His large fingers enveloped her smaller ones. "The things you were trying to tell me finally got through to me. But I had to do it my own way. I realize that now."

"I shouldn't have pushed you," she whispered.

"I needed the push. And I needed to know that whatever happened, you'd be there, loving me."

"Oh, Stephen—and I—"

"No. I knew you were trying to make me see what I was doing to myself because you *did* love me. But sweetheart, you have to understand something. I can't promise that I'm suddenly going to behave just the way I did before the accident. I think I've probably had enough of crowds for a while."

Elena nodded wordlessly.

"You saw the way some of the people reacted to me last night. Some were shocked. Some were curious. Some were probably grossed out."

She opened her mouth to object, but he hurried on. "I was prepared for that. I came to the auction to prove something to myself. That's why I went to Denver, too."

They sat with their hands clasped across the table, not speaking for several moments. "And what about Denver?" Elena finally asked.

"Well, after they got over the shock of seeing me, the Lexco top management held me captive for two days, trying to persuade me to go ahead with buying the company."

"It doesn't sound like much fun."

"It wasn't—for them or me. Despite their best efforts to convince me otherwise, I'm not going to make a decision until I have my own people's opinion on the patent infringement problem."

"I kept hoping you'd call me."

"I couldn't say what I wanted to over the phone."

"Oh, Stephen. When I called you from town the other day, I never should have—"

"You sounded so upset. I would have come and met you, but I'd already committed myself to the Denver trip."

"I'm glad."

He cocked a questioning eyebrow. "What do you mean?"

"I mean, I thought you'd decided you'd rather face the people in Denver than me."

"Never." He looked at her gravely. "What was it you wanted to talk about? Something bad?"

"No. Something good. But I'd worked myself up into some kind of terrible emotional state, and I guess I was making your meeting me in town some kind of test."

He waited, letting her tell him about it in her own good time.

"I guess my only excuse is that pregnant women sometimes do crazy things."

"Pregnant women?" He started to smile.

"Mmm."

"Oh, *querida*." He pushed back his chair, came around the table, and pulled her to him, his arms making a protective circle around her shoulders. "When did you find out?"

"Just before I called you."

"And then you came back and found that I had left."

She nodded against his chest.

His fingers caressed her back. Then he crooked a finger under her chin and turned her face up to his. "So that's why you ordered that big breakfast."

"Which is going to get cold, by the way."

Breakfast was only the beginning of their lazy day of warmth and closeness.

"I'm glad we're here—just the two of us," Elena told Stephen.

"Yes."

"I...I've been thinking about my father. I guess because of the baby. I'm going to write and tell him."

"You haven't written to him since you came here, have you?"

"No, but I've been writing to Anna, my duenna. So I know everything's been going as well as can be expected for him."

Stephen nodded. "I was thinking you'd be happier if you sorted things out with him. But I didn't want to push you."

"So you were worried about me, too."

"Yes."

"I think I feel secure enough not to be angry at him anymore."

"I'm glad."

There were so many things to talk about. Stephen confided that he'd been thinking about Hal's idea for a stud farm. "I'm going to go ahead with it," he told Elena. "If you approve."

"I'd like that."

"If it's successful, I'm going to drop some of my other business interests. That way I can concentrate more on the ranch."

As he elaborated on the plans, Elena snuggled against him. Later that morning, while Stephen was taking a shower, she got out the sketch pad and pencils that Maggie had thoughtfully packed in her suitcase. Settling herself comfortably in bed, she began to draw a picture. It showed Stephen—scars and all—dressed in the tuxedo he'd worn the night before. He was standing in the center of the auction crowd, looking handsome, a bit wary, but determined and forceful.

He came back just as she was finishing.

She held her breath while he picked up the picture and inspected it. The mattress shifted as he sat down beside her on the bed. "Do I really look this way to you?"

She searched his face. "You understand what I intended?"

"Yes."

Elena was so choked with emotion that she could hardly speak. "It's not just me," she finally managed to say. "That's the way a lot of people saw you, too."

"You mean after they got over that first shock of seeing the scars?"

"The scars aren't what matter."

"Elena." He gathered her closer. "I needed you to help me understand that."

She tipped up her face and smiled at him, the way she had smiled across the room full of people.

With the end of one finger, he touched the tear glistening at the corner of her eye. "*Querida*. Where did you acquire all your wisdom?" he asked softly.

"From loving you—and realizing what was important to me," she murmured, just before his lips captured hers.

Especially for you,
Christmas from
HARLEQUIN HISTORICALS

An enchanting collection of three Christmas
stories by some of your favorite authors captures
the spirit of the season in the 1800s

TUMBLEWEED CHRISTMAS by Kristin James

A "Bah, humbug" Texas rancher meets his match in his
new housekeeper, a woman determined to bring the spirit
of a Tumbleweed Christmas into his life—and love into
his heart.

A CINDERELLA CHRISTMAS by Lucy Elliot

The perfect granddaughter, sister and aunt, Mary Hillyer
seemed destined for spinsterhood until Jack Gates arrived
to discover a woman with dreams and passions that were
meant to be shared during a Cinderella Christmas.

HOME FOR CHRISTMAS
by Heather Graham Pozzessere

The magic of the season brings peace Home For
Christmas when a Yankee captain and a Southern heiress
fall in love during the Civil War.

Look for HARLEQUIN HISTORICALS CHRISTMAS
STORIES wherever Harlequin books are sold.

HIST-XMAS-1R

Harlequin
Superromance.

COMING NEXT MONTH

#386 NORTH OF EDEN • Sandra James
If mountain guide Randy Pierce didn't agree to help
Zach Corbett track an escaped killer through Oregon's
treacherous Cascades, the headstrong U.S. marshall
would set out alone. Randy had already lost one man to
the deadly peaks, and her greatest fear was that the
mountains would claim another....

#387 JULIANNE'S SONG • Kit Bakker
To professional storyteller Julianne Blanchet, home was
south Mississippi. And yet for every Cajun, home was
also Acadia. To Julianne, coming to Nova Scotia, the
land of her ancestors, meant far more than a search for
a lost family fortune. It meant meeting Ian, the man her
heart had always longed for....

#388 INTERLUDE • Jenny Loring
Birch and Julia Cheney had just celebrated a blissful
five years of marriage when Birch was blackmailed by
his father into promising something that betrayed
everything he and his wife believed in. Suddenly,
frustrations and secrets sprung up in the Cheney
marriage. Each prayed it was an interlude and that
they would be celebrating the joys of their relationship
once more....

#389 CONNECTIONS • Vicki Lewis Thompson
Sociologist Emily Johnson liked doing fieldwork, and if
that meant slinging beer in a Tucson bar... well,
sometimes there were compensations. Like Ned Tucker.
This gravel-voiced construction worker was almost more
compensation than Emily could handle—especially
when she began to fear for his life....

Wonderful, luxurious gifts can be yours with proofs-of-purchase from any specially marked "Indulge A Little" Harlequin or Silhouette book with the Offer Certificate properly completed, plus a check or money order (do not send cash) to cover postage and handling payable to Harlequin/Silhouette "Indulge A Little, Give A Lot" Offer. We will send you the specified gift.

Mail-in-Offer

OFFER CERTIFICATE

Item	A Collector's Doll	B. Soaps in a Basket	C Potpourri Sachet	D Scented Hangers
# of Proofs-of -Purchase	18	12	6	4
Postage & Handling	$3.25	$2.75	$2.25	$2.00
Check One				

Name _____

Address _____ Apt # _____

City _____ State _____ Zip _____

ONE PROOF OF PURCHASE

To collect your free gift by mail you must include the necessary number of proofs-of-purchase plus postage and handling with offer certificate.

HS-3

Harlequin®/Silhouette®

Mail this certificate, designated number of proofs-of-purchase and check or money order for postage and handling to:

INDULGE A LITTLE
P.O. Box 9055
Buffalo, N.Y. 14269-9055